The Last Time
I Saw Paris

The Last Time I Saw Paris

Elizabeth Adler

St. Martin's Press

New York

www.stmartins.com

Map courtesy of the author

Library of Congress Cataloging-in-Publication Data

Adler, Elizabeth (Elizabeth A.).
    The last time I saw Paris / Elizabeth Adler.—1st ed.
        p. cm.
    ISBN 0-312-26982-X
    1. Americans—France—Fiction. 2. Middle-aged women—Fiction. 3. Paris (France)—Fiction. 4. Married women—Fiction. I. Title.

PR6051.D56 L3 2001
823'.914—dc21   2001020252

First Edition: July 2001

10 9 8 7 6 5 4 3 2 1

For all those women who would like to take Lara's journey

And for the man who lived through it—
and who saved the receipts

And with special thanks to Dexter Rosen, golden retriever,
who still carries his blue blankie everywhere

Lara's Journey

Chapter One

Lara Lewis looked around the spacious master bedroom of her beautiful San Francisco home. Early morning sun slanted off the tall Venetian mirror, half blinding her, and she quickly closed her eyes again, wondering why she had woken with that sinking feeling in the pit of her stomach. And then she remembered. Today was her forty-fifth birthday.

Eyes still firmly closed, she reviewed the mental picture. She was married to an eminent surgeon, mother of two grown-up children. The perfect doctor's wife, she had devoted her life to helping her husband and family and today, suddenly, she was middle-aged.

Whenever she looked in that antique Venetian mirror, she saw herself only too clearly; she was too plump, too curvy, dark curly hair pulled back revealing those telltale lines on her forehead. Lara sighed; she needed more than a shot of Botox to help her now.

There was no Lara Lewis Ph.D.; no Lara Lewis famous journalist; no Lara Lewis who had rafted down whitewater rapids;

no Lara who'd flown a plane, or climbed mountains in Nepal—all those women she had once meant to become. All she was, was Dr. Lewis's wife.

Yet, twenty-five years ago, when she married Bill, she had been young, slender, vital, ambitious, and, so Bill had told her, beautiful. It was strange, she thought with a pang, that beneath that prim doctor's-wife, forty-five-year-old too-curvy exterior still beat the heart of that pretty young woman, eager for all life had to offer.

She turned to look for Bill but the expensive linen pillow had only a slight dent where his head had lain. She could hear the shower running. Bill did not sing in the shower. Not now. He never listened to music anymore either. At least, not with her.

Bill Lewis had dazzled her when she first met him and he still had that effect on her now. It was as though he had mesmerized her, fascinated her, captivated her. *Dominated* her, her friends had warned.

Bill was still a good-looking man, lean and in great shape. His dark hair was streaked handsomely with silver, exactly the way it was supposed to at fifty-three, making him look even more distinguished. He always wore hand-tailored suits, expensive English shirts complete with gold cuff links and a heavy gold Rolex that was a permanent fixture on his wrist. Lara wondered vaguely if he even took it off when he operated. She guessed he must.

She sighed again. Bill was not the kind of man anyone said no to. People catered to him, admired him, went out of their way to please him. He was an internationally famous cardiac surgeon, known for his pioneering work on transplants, especially with children. Didn't actors say you should never work with children? You just couldn't win. Well, she guessed in her case it was true. She was definitely low on Bill's priority list.

Today—her birthday—Bill was flying to Beijing, and on the team he was taking with him was Melissa Kenney. Tall, slender, smart, and blond. *And* in her early thirties. *And* a pediatric specialist.

Lara's heart dropped even lower as she thought about Melissa. Instinct told her Bill was having an affair with her. Why else those "emergency" runs to the hospital at midnight? Why else those extended weekends away "at a conference"? Why else that abstracted look, the impatient glance at his watch, the not hearing her, not listening to her? Not *noticing* her anymore.

Loneliness clung to her heart and she turned her face into the pillow. She felt vulnerable in her new middle age. Bill had been the only man in her life, her only lover. The thought of losing him terrified her. She wouldn't know how to cope with anyone else, in her life, in her bed. And who would want her anyway, the plump, rejected, lonely ex-wife?

Panic sent her leaping out of bed, as though standing on her own two feet would somehow help her face things, just as Bill walked into the bedroom.

Lara tugged self-consciously at her pink cotton nightshirt. She smoothed her sleep-snarled hair, wishing she had woken earlier and was all perfumed and pretty for him, though she seemed to remember a time when Bill would turn to her in bed, telling her she smelled delicious, of sleep and of last night's fading perfume and female scents that turned him on.

Bill was already dressed for travel in a dark suit, the gold cuff links and gold watch in place.

Caught with sudden longing, Lara said wistfully, "I want to

come with you." She was already mentally throwing a few things into a case, she could be ready in a flash, five minutes, even; she could wear sweats, put on her face on the way to the airport. . . .

"I already told you, Lara, Beijing is not for you." Bill's deep voice had an exaggerated note of patience as though he was controlling his irritation. "Not comfortable enough," he added. "Food's not your style; you'd be bored and complaining in two days."

"Since when do I ever complain?" she retorted indignantly. "And I heard the food's okay in Beijing, there's even a Starbucks there now." She knew from the look he threw her that once again she had said the wrong thing.

"Don't be silly." Bill adjusted the knot in his blue silk tie in the mirror.

A new tie, Lara noted, recognizing it was from a fashionable designer. She wondered who had bought it for him. Hoping to make amends, she said hopefully, "At least when you get back, there's France."

Bill smoothed back his hair, adjusted the new tie again approvingly. "France?"

He seemed not to know what she was talking about. Lara's heart dropped; he *couldn't* have forgotten. "Our Second Honeymoon. I told you I'd planned it all exactly the way it was the first time. We're staying in exactly the same room at the Ritz in Paris, we're driving south to the Mediterranean, just the way we did before, the same little auberges, the same restaurants and cafes."

She clasped her hands anxiously together; she was betting their future on this Second Honeymoon, betting on it getting

Bill away from Melissa, betting on it returning life to the way it used to be, when they were young and in love.

"Oh. Sure, it'll be great." Bill hardly seemed to remember their plans, let alone care.

The doorbell rang, making Lara jump.

"There's the limo." Bill picked up the bag she had packed for him last night. He turned to look at her, finally. "Oh, I almost forgot. Happy birthday." He took a narrow, ribboned package from his pocket, gave it to her as he headed for the door. Then he remembered, turned, dropped a hasty kiss on her hair, and walked quickly from the room.

"Call me when you get there." Lara's voice echoed in the empty room.

She heard his footsteps on the stairs, then the slam of the front door. She ran to the window. The driver was smiling good morning, holding open the car door, and Lara caught a glimpse of long, silken legs in elegant high-heeled sandals. Her heart did a somersault. *She knew those legs.*

She stood holding back the curtain until long after the limo had disappeared from sight.

Slumping onto the bed, she opened her birthday gift. Bill usually gave her the latest novel or sometimes flowers, bought, she had no doubt, by his secretary. But this was different.

Her eyes widened and she stared, stunned, at the necklace, a narrow, glinting strip of diamonds centered with a lover's knot. Small, discreet, and in perfect taste.

For a wild moment she wondered if Bill had given her the wrong gift, if this had been meant for Melissa of the long, silken legs. Yet, didn't a lover's knot symbolize the tie that binds? Perhaps Bill had meant it as an apology, as a symbol of their future. She pushed her long, tangled hair out of the way, fastened the slender, glittering trophy around her neck, turned to see how it looked.

That treacherous Venetian mirror reflected the sparkling necklace, and her forty-five-year-old naked morning face above it. Her golden-brown eyes under straight black brows looked back at her, only now there were little lines around them. The curve of the cheek and chin were the same as always—or were those curves lower now? Her wide, vulnerable mouth was tense with worry and there was even a white hair this morning among those once-glossy dark curls.

She searched that face in the mirror, seeking her old self and not finding it. A tear rolled down her cheek and she tasted the bitter salt as she whispered, "Oh, Lara, Lara Lewis. Where did you go? Where are all your dreams? Your plans? Your hopes? *Where are you?*"

Somewhere along the road of life, she had lost her.

Was she alone in feeling like this? she wondered. Or were there hundreds, maybe thousands of women out there, just like her?

The lost ones.

Chapter Two

Sitting at a cafe table, Lara gazed at the smiling faces of her best girlfriends as they sang "Happy Birthday," blushing as the waiter placed a tiny chocolate cake covered with fresh violets and lit with a single candle on the table in front of her. She felt uncomfortable, out of touch, not quite of today, hair pulled back in her prim doctor's-wife Saks suit, the skirt a bit too long, heels too low.

"At forty-five, you'd think you would have gotten over that girlish blush," Susie teased.

"After all, it's not like your first kiss," Vannessa said.

"From that high school hunk and hero, Flabby Moxon," Delia added, grinning.

"Oh, my God, remember Flabby Moxon?" they wailed in unison.

Lara nodded. "I remember. Behind the bicycle sheds. I was just unlocking my speedracer—hot pink with silver stars on it—when he sneaked up behind me." She shuddered. "I just wanted to die right there and then. . . ."

"Because guess who was right behind you . . ."

"Buzz Johnson." Lara laughed. "The John Travolta of Madison High and the love of my life. Or so I thought then. *And* Buzz saw the kiss. But even worse were Flabby Moxon's soggy lips . . . ugghhh . . ." She shuddered again, remembering.

"So with those soggy lips, why else would he have been called Flabby?" Vannie asked.

"Because he had"—Delia glanced over her shoulder to make sure no one was listening—*"breasts,"* she whispered loudly, and they all burst out laughing.

"I hardly think Congressman John W. Moxon, Republican, of California, would be happy to have his voters know such a personal thing about him now," Susie said. "Besides, only his wife knows for sure."

They were still laughing as Lara blew out her candle. She cut the little cake into four equal pieces and handed it around.

"Maybe Flabby's had liposuction," Delia mused. "Men do these days, you know. Male breast reduction, they call it."

"Jeez, Delia, I'm eating my cake." Susie was disgusted. "Anyhow, what kind of guy would do something like that?"

"A guy with tits," Vannie said and choked on her cake. They yelped with laughter as Delia thumped her energetically on the back.

But Lara's tears of laughter threatened to become real tears as she looked at the faces of her girlfriends. She had known them forever. Of course they were no longer girls, but somehow "women friends" didn't have the same nostalgic ring about it. It couldn't express the length and breadth of their friendship, spanning so many years, so many experiences.

They were the same age, born within months of one another. Their families had known each other, they had played together in preschool and started "real" school on the same day, clinging together like a single, many-limbed creature clutching four Snoopy lunch pails, climbing onto the little yellow bus, refusing to let their mothers accompany them.

They had shared sleepovers and double dates, birthday parties and graduations, proms and failed romances. They had shared secrets and sexual encounters, college and jobs, weddings and babies. Their lives were as intertwined as liana vines in a jungle, and sometimes it was hard to know where one stopped and another began.

Two were blond, two dark. Susie had started out mouse brown and graduated to honey-colored streaks that set off her golden-tan skin. She had always been the outdoors girl, the tennis player, the ace swimmer, and now the golfer. She was still skinny, still lithe, still always on the move, though she had been married to an architect for twenty years and had a clutch of teenagers running in and out of the house.

Vannie was the natural beauty, golden blond, with huge green eyes, long legs, and a slender but voluptuously rounded figure. She had driven the guys wild right through high school, but she had been the last to marry and when she did, she had surprised them. Vannie had married her college English professor, a small, discreet balding man who wore tweed jackets and glasses and who, she said, loved her for her intellect rather than her body. The Girlfriends said they hoped she meant *as well as* her body, but the truth was, beautiful Vannie was the demure one, the lady, in pearls and a cashmere sweater, pleated skirt and loafers. Vannie had been a radiant bride as she walked down the aisle with her three best friends trailing her in perfumed wafts of crackling taffeta and tuberoses. It had turned out to be a solid marriage, though, sadly, Vannie had been unable to have children. Instead, she and her husband had adopted two Vietnamese babies, who were now approaching college age and on whom they doted. She still looked like Grace Kelly.

Delia was dark-haired and olive-skinned with flashing brown eyes and an Italian temperament inherited from her Sicilian mother. "I'm the only foreigner in Masonville, California," she had complained as a girl, but she was always laughing. Nothing kept Delia down, not even the breast cancer scare that, two years earlier, had left her bald and wounded and in terrible pain, sustained only by the strength and compassion of her friends and her large extended family. Delia was in remission now, with no signs of the "big monster," as she called it mockingly. But with her new short hair, she was living like a new woman, savoring every moment.

Lara had been the shy one, the introvert. The one who felt things too deeply, the collector of stray kittens and damaged birds. The others said Lara had so many wounds to her heart when she was a teenager, it was a wonder she didn't expire right there and then.

"Love" was something Lara was always searching for, and with her soft, pretty looks—smudgy amber eyes under winging Audrey Hepburn brows, flowing Pre-Raphaelite dark, curly hair—and shy manner, she'd had boys in love with her all the time. But Lara had always loved the one she could not have, the one who loved another. Until, at age twenty, she had met and married Bill Lewis.

Now, she stared around at her dearest friends. She hadn't meant to tell, but somehow, she just blurted it out. "I think Bill is having an affair."

Three pairs of eyes rounded in horror.

"Oh . . . my . . . God," Susie whispered.

"It can't be true." Delia shook her head in disbelief.

"Not *Bill*," Vannie said firmly.

"It's Melissa Kenney," Lara said. "The new pediatrician at St. Mark's."

Delia had met her. Her own husband was an orthopedic surgeon at the same hospital. Melissa Kenney was blond and cute. Not only that, somehow, Melissa's lipstick was always in place at the end of a long day and her white doctor's coat fitted her like a glove and never seemed to crease. "What makes you think it's true, Lar? Has someone said something?"

Lara lifted her shoulders in a helpless shrug. "How does any woman know? All those long unexplained hours away, those late-night 'emergencies.' Bill's restlessness, always pacing the bedroom floor glancing at his watch, staring out the window as though he couldn't wait to be somewhere else. Looking at me and not even *seeing* me anymore . . ."

"Honey, all guys get like that at times." Vannie patted Lara's hand reassuringly. "After all, you've been married for twenty-five years. Practically since you were kids."

"Besides, Bill didn't forget your birthday," Delia added. "And that's the *first* thing guys having affairs forget."

Lara touched the necklace, remembering how Bill had handed it to her as a sort of afterthought. It felt cold under her fingers. "Perhaps it's a farewell gift," she said doubtfully, "like the token retirement gold watch."

"Lar, that's not true," Vannie said quickly. "Bill would never do that to you."

But Susie's shrewd eyes met hers across the table. "So why didn't you tell us about this earlier? I thought we always told each other everything. Wasn't that the pact?"

Their childhood vow had been sealed in blood scratched from

their wrists with a tiny gold safety pin. Lara could remember Susie howling with the pain. Now Susie's eyes were filled with a different pain for her friend.

"Why didn't I say something?" She shrugged again, defeated. "I was ashamed, I guess."

"*Ashamed?* Is *that* what women are supposed to feel when our husbands run around on us? We should be *ashamed?*" Delia was outraged. "You should know better, Lara."

"Oh, God, it's so hard, it's just so hard." Lara hung her head, letting her hair shield her tears from them.

The Girlfriends looked at one another, stunned. For once no one knew what to say. Lara was the most unselfish woman they knew. She gave one hundred percent of herself. Everything she had would be yours if you were in need. She had always been there for her children, *and* for that selfish bastard Bill, who had taken advantage of her goodness, her niceness. She wasn't a saint, just good-hearted. Now, they felt for her. Of all the women to be dumped, Lara was the most defenseless.

"I woke up this morning," Lara whispered. "I was suddenly forty-five years old. And somewhere along the road of life I knew I had lost myself. I felt like nobody. Nothing."

"You are who you always were." Vannie flung a loving arm around her. "You're no different. It's . . ." She stopped, afraid to voice what she was thinking: that it was Bill Lewis who was different now. Success and dedication to his work had changed him. While Lara had brought up the children, kept the home fires burning, Bill had been forging ahead in his career. "What you need, honey, is a marriage counselor," she decided firmly. "Bring Bill to his senses."

"Or else a shrink," Susie suggested.

"The hell with it. What you need is a good day's shopping."

Delia slammed her fist angrily on the table, sending glasses crashing. "Screw Bill. Go out and spend all his money. If he's really in Beijing with Melissa Kenney, he deserves it. Go. Buy Gucci and Armani. Buy shoes and sexy lingerie. Make the bastard feel the pain in his pocket. I'll bet when he sees you decked out in Italy's best black labels and with the *La Perla* underneath, that bitch Melissa won't stand a chance."

Despite her pain, Lara was laughing. But shopping was not her game. She just wasn't a dress-up kind of woman. She shook her head, her tearful brown eyes warm with affection. "Whatever would I do without you," she said.

It was a statement, not a question, and instinctively each woman reached out her left hand to the center of the table, clasping the others' tightly. "All for one and one for All," they intoned, using the words they had snitched from Alexander Dumas's *The Three Musketeers* when they were just seven years old and had sealed their pact in blood.

Lara signaled the waiter and ordered four more margaritas, adding guiltily, "I'd like straight tequila but I thought it might look bad."

She was so serious that they laughed. "Oh, Lara, what do we care how things look anymore?" Delia asked. "I thought we had finally reached the age where we could just be ourselves."

And so did I, Lara thought sadly, as she sipped the frosty margarita. Oh, Bill, so did I.

Driving back to her empty house in smart Pacific Heights, Lara spotted the red bathing suit in a store window. High-cut legs, low-cut top, slinky. Sexy. Impulsively, she raced into the store, snatched it from the rack, and marched into the dressing room. She sighed as she looked at her reflection. She was too curvy for it, too plump. Maybe too old. But it was exactly right for a forty-five-year-old who needed some encouragement. Recklessly, she bought it—a present for herself.

Cheered, she drove back home. Dexter, the old golden retriever, met her at the door with his blue baby blanket. He had carried it everywhere with him since he was a pup, and nothing she could do could break him of the habit. He offered it to her now, and she patted him, ruffling his soft fur, making a fuss over him.

"You're a good old boy, Dex, aren't you?" At least with Dex there, the house didn't have that awful echoing emptiness.

The dog followed her into the kitchen, where she filled his bowl with Alpo, then fixed some coffee. She leaned against the cold granite counter, arms crossed over her chest, waiting for it to brew. Ten empty days stretched ahead of her. She had her volunteer work two mornings a week at the local seniors' home, where she organized entertainment and lunches and get-togethers for the mostly over-eighty residents. Then she had the fund-raising committee on Wednesday afternoons, and her tennis games with Susie at the club. And that was it.

The phone shrilled suddenly. It was her son. Josh was twenty-three and at medical school in Boston. He was an exact replica of Bill when she had first met him, with the same idealistic approach to his chosen profession. Josh wanted to be a healer like his father and she had no doubt he would succeed.

"Just wanted to say happy birthday, Mom," he said, and she thanked him for his card and his gift, a pretty scarf that she guessed a girlfriend had helped him pick out.

They chatted for a while about how busy he was, how tough the courses were, how rotten the Boston weather, and then he asked what she was going to do that evening.

Lara's heart sank as she thought about it stretching in front of her, an empty series of long, lonely hours. "I know what, I'll take Dex and go out to the beach house," she decided. "I always feel better there." *Less lonely* was what she really meant.

"Have fun. I miss you, Mom. Love you. Talk to you soon," Josh said. And then he was gone.

Minnie's call came two minutes later and Lara wondered if Josh had called to remind his sister that it was her birthday. Minnie was just twenty-one, pretty and bubbly, living in L.A. and hoping to become a movie star.

"Happy birthday, dear Mommy," she caroled over the phone. "I'm not going to ask how old you are because I know it's rude when a woman reaches 'a certain age.' I guess by now you would rather people forgot, anyway."

She was laughing as she said it and Lara smiled. "You know perfectly well how old I am, because I was twenty-four when I had you."

"Sorry I forgot the card and present, Mommy," Minnie said repentently. "I'm dashing out this very second to buy you something gorgeous and sexy."

Lara thought that was the second time today someone had suggested she needed something sexy.

"What did Dad get you?"

Lara told her about the diamond necklace, holding the phone away from her ear as Minnie's astonished whistle shrieked down the line.

"Wow, Mom, I'm impressed. Usually it's a bunch of roses and the latest novel. What's he got, a guilty conscience or something?"

Lara's heart skipped a beat, then she heard her daughter laughing. Of course Minnie didn't know. How could she . . .?

"When are you coming home for a visit?" she asked, wishing she didn't sound so wistful.

"Soon as I can shake free, Mom. I'll try, I promise."

They said good-bye and Lara put down the phone. She switched off the coffee machine and poured out the coffee, which she no longer fancied. She stared out the kitchen window at the surprisingly blue San Francisco afternoon. Of course Minnie wouldn't be coming home any time soon. Both her children were out of the nest. Josh was inundated with work and Minnie was wallowing in sunshine and glamour. She wished the best for both of them.

Dexter nudged her hand and she glanced down at him. Unconditional love shone in his golden eyes and she bent and kissed his soft head. "You know what we'll do, you and I, Dex?" she said. "We'll go to the beach house. I'll take you for long walks every day and in the evenings we'll just snooze by the fire and listen to the ocean." He gave a couple of excited barks and she laughed. There was no doubt *beach* and *walk* were in Dexter's vocabulary.

She raced up the stairs with the dog at her heels, flung a few things into a bag, grabbed some supplies from the refrigerator and put them in a box in the trunk of her white convertible. Dexter was already in the passenger seat and she climbed in beside him, ramming a Forty-Niners cap on her head.

Her heart seemed to lighten as they drove south out of the city toward Carmel and Big Sur with the radio blasting old Beach Boys and the wind blowing her hair. She would feel better out at the beach. She always did.

Chapter Three

The house stood on a rocky promontory overlooking the
Pacific and was their private haven. They had seen it, a
cheap tumbling wreck of a place, fallen in love with it, and
bought it in the space of a weekend twenty years ago when they
certainly could not afford it. Over the years they had fixed it up
and now they liked to think it had been the biggest bargain of
their lives. It had given their children long summers of pleasure,
been Bill's escape from his all-consuming work, and had been
Lara's refuge in times of trouble and loneliness. Like now.

It was a small gray-shingle Cape Cod with white shutters, a
rough little garden, and a large wooden deck with steps leading
down to the beach. Everything about it was simple and easy.
"Beach style," Lara called it, meaning "low maintenance."
Squishy old sofas with cream linen slipcovers; big cushions in
shades of blue; seagrass rugs on the pale wood floors; a gen-
erous fireplace with a bleached-pine antique mantel taken from
a genuine Nantucket sea captain's house, and wooden planta-
tion shutters instead of curtains. The kitchen was airy and spa-

cious and up to date, and the master bedroom had sloping ceilings, a fireplace, and a balcony overlooking the rocky ocean. The bed was covered in a simple white matelassé spread, and a comfortable old chaise was placed near the window. It was easy and comforting and fitted Lara like an old glove. She was more at home here than at the big house in Pacific Heights.

And so was Dex. He was out of the car and over the gate at the side of the house, racing across the deck and down the steps to the beach before Lara had even opened the car door. She was laughing as she carried the bags into the house.

The sun was just going down. She opened a bottle of Duboeuf Morgon and put it on a tray along with a glass and the French Vignotte cheese and crusty baguette she had bought in Carmel, then carried the tray out onto the deck. Dex came bounding back up the steps, shaking seawater all over her from his dip in the ocean. He sat, panting, beside her as she sipped the red wine and ate her bread and cheese watching the sunset. It reminded her of picnics with Bill, driving through the French countryside on their honeymoon—twenty-five years ago, when she was just a girl. How happy they had been then, and how wonderful every day had seemed in France, that magical country . . .

Sighing, she carried the tray back into the kitchen, stoppered the wine, rinsed out the glass, and put the plate in the dishwasher. A cold wind gusted in at the windows, so she closed them, then crumpled newspapers in the grate, piled on some kindling and a couple of logs, and put a match to them. She kneeled, warming her hands in front of the blaze, listening to the logs crackling and the booming of the surf along the shoreline. Dexter finished his dinner and trotted in from the kitchen. He dropped his blankie on the rug, kneaded it carefully with his big paws until he reached some obscure point of doggy satisfaction, then slid lazily down and closed his eyes.

Lara curled up on the sofa, her legs tucked underneath her. She wrapped the soft blue chenille throw around her shoulders and lay back against the cushions. Silence settled around her and in minutes she too was asleep.

When she awoke, the fire had burned out and the house felt cold. She had no idea how long she had slept and was astonished when she checked her watch and found it was 2:30 A.M. Now she was wide awake but there was nothing to do but go to bed. She would get up early, do some chores. There were always things to be taken care of in a beach house: fresh paint, minor repairs, leaking faucets, stuff like that.

She let Dexter out for a quick prowl, waited for him to come in, then trailed wearily up the narrow cottage stairs with him at her heels.

Peeling off her clothes, she took a quick shower to warm herself up, then put on sweat socks and an old gray T-shirt and climbed into the canopied four-poster that, because the stairs were too narrow to accommodate its gargantuan size, had had to be hauled up over the balcony and through the French windows.

Turning out the light, she huddled under the blankets and lay waiting for her eyes to adjust to the dark. She could hear Dex shuffling and the whoosh of the central heating system as it sent out welcome warm shafts of air and, as always, the roar of the ocean. Usually it was a lullaby, but tonight it did not send her to sleep.

The light of the half-moon fell onto the smooth, untouched pillow beside her where Bill's head should have lain. She stared at it for a long moment, wondering where he was sleeping. And if he was with Melissa. Her heart was a leaden lump in her chest, and she buried her forty-five-year-old face in her own mono-grammed Italian cotton pillow that was smooth as silk and twice as expensive. She thought angrily that women should be told about monogrammed linens. Like cigarettes, they should come with a warning label: *Caution: This may not last forever.*

When she and Bill were young marrieds, their cheap plaid flannel sheets, soft from many washes at the Fluff & Fold, had kept them warm when the cranky heating system in their old two-room walk-up had gone on the blink yet again.

Bill had been a resident at Chicago's tough Cook County Hospital then, and Lara was struggling with a boring job. They had been so poor, and so happy. A pang of nostalgia swept over her as she recalled the smell of mildew that had greeted them each time they opened the door of their walk-up apartment, and the eternal odor of spaghetti bolognaise; that was all she had known how to cook. She remembered how Bill's chilled naked body had felt, slipping into the narrow bed beside her. She so warm under the flannel, he still freezing from his drive back through the snowy streets after night duty at the hospital. And how she would burrow like a rabbit into his arms, snuffling the intoxicating smell of his skin, a mixture of soap and hospital antiseptic and the cit-rusy cologne he always wore, and the familiar musky, sexy male-ness of him. They never spoke. He didn't want to wake her and she wanted him to catch a few precious hours before the gruel-ing life of a hospital intern took him over again. That is, unless they made love, which is what usually happened. And then they did not need to speak. Their close-wrapped bodies, their cling-ing arms and searching lips had said it all. Hadn't they? Some-times Lara thought her memories seemed more like dreams.

Lying sleepless in the moonlit room with only the sound of Dexter's breathing for company, Lara felt suddenly overwhelmed by what was happening in her life. She had always thought of herself as a young woman, but now a younger one had taken her place. She was bewildered by the fact that she was getting older and afraid to face the lurking possibility that she might have to get older without Bill.

Throwing on her old robe, she walked to the window and stood looking at the powerful moonlit ocean, steel gray under silver gauze, doing the same thing it always did: surging in then flowing gently back out. Endlessly, infinitely. As it had long before she was born, and would long after she was gone. Somehow, there was no comfort in the sound of the ocean tonight.

She thought of the first time she had met Bill. He was tall, lean, dark, and very attractive. He was already in medical school, and he lived next door. She had been a plump, frizzy-haired teenager, too shy even to speak, except for a brief "Hi" in passing. Anyhow, she considered him an older man, out of her league and out of her life.

He was sitting on the porch steps outside his house and tears were rolling down his face. Lara had heard the news that his mother had just died. Bursting with compassion, she went to sit next to him. She took his hand and held it tightly. After a while he wiped away his tears. He looked into her eyes for a long moment, then he dropped a light kiss on her cheek. And was gone.

They did not meet again until she was seventeen and going off to college at Northwestern and Bill was already an intern at Cook County. For Lara, it was love at second sight. They had dated, courted, almost made out in the back of her mother's new Buick Riviera, but she had been too scared and he was a gentleman. They were married a week after she graduated.

For years after that she had played the role of helpmate, working all day in a gloomy local newspaper office to pay the rent, staying up nights to help him study. She had cooked endless pots of spaghetti bolognaise, taken care of the bills, fended off the creditors, been there for him. And after that, she had played the role of mother to their two children, as well as the father role since Bill was away so much. But her life had been so full, so busy, so crammed with kids and traumas and being a couple at social events that she had not anticipated any changes.

She stared at the silver ocean, thinking of Bill in Beijing with pretty, blond Melissa. She guessed proximity and a shared passion for their medical work had drawn them together, shutting her out of their charmed, clever, busy lives. How could she compete? What did she have to offer? Only a too-familiar body, a lifeline of memories, a lost world.

Putting a hand to her throat, she touched the tiny diamond lover's knot. Didn't they say it represented the tie that binds? Is that what Bill had meant when he gave it to her? Sighing, she hoped so. Anyhow, she would not take it off until he got back home. She would wear it like a talisman, hoping it would bring him back to her.

Dawn was breaking and she went downstairs and made herself a cup of Earl Grey tea—decaffeinated, though since she was already sleepless she didn't know why she bothered. She carried the steaming mug of tea out onto the deck and leaned on the rail, watching the tide coming in with the dawn.

She wondered what time it was in Beijing. Call the minute you arrive, she had told Bill, filled with that sudden anxiety about the flimsiness of airplanes, the vagaries of foreign weather, the reliability of air traffic control. Things she never even considered when she took a flight herself. Now, she wondered if he would remember.

Her thoughts turned to the trip they had planned. She had suggested it months ago and she'd thought Bill had seemed pleased.

Her honeymoon had been the most idyllic three weeks of her life, when innocence had been a state of mind, youth taken for granted, and every experience was fresh and new. They had flown to Paris, where they had stayed at the Ritz, a wedding gift from her mother. From Paris they had driven to visit the châteaux of the Loire, then down through the middle of France to the Dordogne. They had crisscrossed the country, ending up in Avignon, then plunged south to the blue Mediterranean and endless sunshine.

She remembered clearly the cities and villages they had visited, the hotels and auberges where they stayed, the restaurants they had dined in, even the places they had picnicked. Everything had gone like clockwork: perfect locations, perfect weather. Perfect lovemaking. And Bill was her first and only lover.

They had flown home from Nice three weeks later, sated with love, gorged on fine foods and wines, their eyes dazzled with vistas of châteaux and ruins and rivers and the bluest sea she had ever seen. It had been the most perfect time in their lives.

Now, she could not recall when they had last managed to spend three days together, let alone three weeks. But soon they were to retrace their honeymoon path through France, and she was counting on this trip to bring the old Bill, the one she used to know, back to her.

Chapter Four

When the cold morning fog finally began to unravel, leaving only scarves of lavender mist, Lara called Dex and they went for a long walk along the narrow strip of beach left uncovered by the tide. By the time they got back the sun was burning its way through and the day promised heat. She showered and changed into baggy white linen shorts and a black T-shirt, thrust her bare feet into Keds, hustled Dex into the car, and drove to Carmel in search of a newspaper, a cup of coffee, and a lemon poppyseed muffin.

Carmel's pretty tree-shaded Ocean Avenue was already filled with slowly drifting tourists and Lara ambled along at their same slow pace, gazing in the windows of antique shops and gift shops, clothing boutiques and art galleries, ending up at a cafe where she drank a double cappuccino and fed most of the muffin to Dex, who sat drooling at her feet. She knew it wasn't good for him, but thought, what the hell, every life had to have some forbidden little treat. Even a dog's.

Afterward, she bought a *USA Today* so she would have the

TV listings, then browsed the Pilgrims Way bookstore, where she picked up a copy of the latest Michelin guide to France as well as a biography she had been meaning to read, and a copy of Noel Coward's *Diaries.* Reading other people's diaries seemed like peeking into their lives, and she asked herself if she had become a voyeur now instead of a participant in life. Angry at the thought, she marched out of the bookstore and into the grocery, where, defiantly, she purchased Wonder Bread, brown sugar, bananas, a packet of Oreos, and a quart of milk. Then she returned to the car and drove slowly back along the highway.

The house was filled with sunlight and the sound of the sea, and she ran upstairs to put on the new red bathing suit. She rubbed a 15 sunscreen into her pale skin and tied her long curly hair up in a ponytail, then stared critically at her reflection, seeing how she truly looked in the bathing suit in the harsh light of day instead of in the store's flattering mirror that she could swear had taken five pounds off her. She saw soft pale skin in need of sunshine and free weights, round breasts spilling out of the top, high-cut legs that left more of her exposed than she had thought. She shrugged. What the hell, there was no one to see her. Grabbing a towel and the *Diaries,* she headed out onto the deck.

She was dragging the teak chaise into the sun when the wooden deck gave an ominous creak. There was a sharp, splintering sound and she watched astonished as the chair's back wheels sank into the hole that suddenly appeared. Dex jumped back, barking as though it were alive, making her laugh. But it was dangerous; the whole deck might be rotten. She tried to think when it had last been repaired but it was buried so long in the past she couldn't even recall.

Sighing, she went back inside, leafed through the Yellow Pages, and called a couple of decking specialists. Neither of them could make it out for at least a week, maybe two. "You're better off calling a contractor," the second one told her. "Try Dan Holland; he's reliable and he might be able to help you out."

Dan Holland was not there but a pleasant voice announced that if she left a message he would get back to her. She did that, then went back out and found a corner of the deck that felt secure under her testing bounce, dragged over another chaise, spread her towel, and breathed a sigh of relief as she lay down. Finally.

She put the phone and a can of Diet Coke and the *Diaries* on the small table beside her, pulled a shady straw hat over her ponytail, and stared out to sea. She wondered when Bill would call. *If* Bill would call. If he was thinking about her . . .

The long day drifted slowly toward evening. She and Dex walked the beach. The dog swam and she threw an old green tennis ball for him. She walked so far her calves began to ache and they turned back, ambling wearily home.

Tracking sand into the house, she went into the kitchen, gave the dog a bowl of water, and rubbed him off with an old towel. He rolled appreciatively on his back, then padded after her onto the deck, carefully avoiding the splintery hole.

It was almost five o'clock. A squadron of pelicans drifted overhead, riding the wind, immobile as a piece of sculpture, and the shrieks of gray-and-white gulls pierced the stillness. She leaned on the deck rail with the wind tugging at her hair, listening to the roar of the ocean and watching the spray bursting over the rocks. Waiting for the phone to ring.

But it was the doorbell that rang.

When she answered it, Lara gazed, stunned, at the young

man smiling at her. He was tall and lean, his skin was tanned the color of light maple syrup, and a shock of smooth, sun-streaked, light brown hair fell into his deep-blue eyes. She could see the line of the veins on his strong neck and the tiny pulse beating at the base of his throat, where fine golden hairs curled above the neck of his white T-shirt.

A breathless silence hung between them. Lara was suddenly aware of the too-small red bathing suit and those too-amply-displayed curves and the incongruous diamond necklace, and she wanted to run back inside, throw a big shirt over her pale nakedness. Then he said, "Hi, I'm Dan Holland. You called about your deck. I was out this way so I thought I might as well drop in, see if there's anything I can do."

"Oh. The deck. Of course." Lara collected her suddenly scattered wits, asked him in, and showed him the hole in the deck. While he looked at it, she ran upstairs and put on a shirt. When she came back down, Dan Holland was kneeling by the hole, jabbing at the wood with a screwdriver. He walked around, bouncing on the boards, testing their springiness.

"I'll have to check underneath, if that's okay," he said politely.

Lara watched as he ran down the wooden beach steps. She liked the way he moved, his easy stride. He was a man comfortable in his body; there was an air of solid confidence about him. She could tell he knew what he was doing and felt instinctively that she could trust him to do a good job.

He came back up the steps and said regretfully, in his slow drawl. "I'm sorry to tell you this, Ms. Lewis, but quite a number of the timbers are rotten. My guess is it's been a few years since they were touched. A couple of the big support beams underneath will have to be replaced, plus there's patches of dry rot.

It doesn't seem to have spread around the side yet, maybe because it's more sheltered around there, out of the spray and wind. Anyhow, ma'am, that's the bad news, I'm afraid."

He smiled as he said it, crinkling his blue eyes, and Lara thought how white his teeth looked against his outdoorsman-tanned skin.

"I guessed it would be bad news," she said with a sigh. "Can I offer you a cold drink, Mr. Holland? A Coke, a beer?"

"Thank you for the offer, ma'am, Ms. Lewis, but I have to be on my way." Unhurriedly, he tucked his screwdriver back into the tool belt at his hip.

Of course he would have to leave, Lara thought with a pang. A young man like that must have a busy life. . . .

"So tell me what the damage is." She was brisk, all business as he explained what needed to be done and promised to work up the costs.

"Thanks for stopping by. I appreciate it," she called after him, watching as he climbed into the bright-red, dust-covered Ford pickup, with *Daniel Holland Building Contractor* written on the side. A black Lab crouched in the back, tongue lolling, panting in the heat. Dan Holland waved once, then in a swirl of dust and exhaust, he was gone.

Lara wondered how old he was. Young enough to call her *ma'am,* anyhow. And she wondered about his wife, because a good-looking guy like that must surely have one. Probably kids too . . .

The insistently ringing phone jolted her back to reality.

"Hi. I thought you'd be out at the beach."

It was Bill. He had called her after all. "You arrived safely," she said foolishly, because obviously he had.

"The trip was okay," he was saying. "We had a bit of turbulence but that's the way it goes these days. Yeah, Beijing is something else, like nowhere you've ever seem. . . ."

And now I never will, she thought sadly.

He was telling her how busy he was going to be, how the president of China himself was coming out for the opening of the new hospital, that the cardiovascular wing was to be named after him. . . .

"About the French trip," he said, sounding hesitant. "We're going to have to postpone it."

Lara's heart stuck in her throat. She couldn't think straight, couldn't find the right words to express her shock. "But, Bill," she stammered finally, "we're leaving in three weeks; the tickets are in your desk drawer. I've made all the hotel reservations, I rented a car, even the restaurants are booked."

Oh, God, please let him say it's okay, she prayed silently. Let him say he can make it. I'm counting on this trip to get him away from Melissa, to get our lives back on track.

"It's important I stay here," he said, sounding suddenly very firm.

More important than I am, Lara thought, devastated, as he explained the many reasons he was needed there, and that he would be going to India on his way back to check on the new children's hospital in Delhi and offer his help. She couldn't object without sounding selfish. After all, he was saving children's lives.

"I'll call you again soon," he finished briskly. "Everything all right there? Kids okay?"

"Yes," she whispered. "Everything's okay."

"Good." There was a long pause, then he added, "I'm sorry, Lara. We'll do it some other time."

Lara put down the phone and walked numbly back out onto the crumbling deck. The bottom had just fallen out of her life.

What sort of a woman am I, anyhow? she silently asked herself, leaning on the deck rail, gazing at the darkening ocean, now I'm no longer the wife and helpmate? No longer the mother? No longer the lover? Who *is* Lara Lewis?

All she knew was that somewhere along the way, in the midst of all that daily living, she had lost her.

Chapter Five

Daniel Holland considered himself an ordinary man. A man who worked with his head as well as his hands, running his small contracting business efficiently. He unfurled the American flag on the Fourth of July and Labor Day, put Santa driving his sleigh in lights on his shingle roof at Christmas, and carved pumpkins for his front porch every Halloween.

Born in the small coastal town of Carmel, where he still lived, he was the eldest son of a building contractor. When his parents had died too young, Dan, as the oldest, had raised his younger brother and sister. Troy was now in medical school, intent on moving up in the world, and his pretty young sister, Hallie, was putting herself through college on scholarships and by winning local beauty contests, and in summers working alongside her brothers, sometimes even manning the jackhammer, but usually hauling stuff in the pickup, or sawing, hammering, and drilling.

As the eldest, Dan had been the first one on the college list, but he had turned down that opportunity. "I guess I'm gonna be the family failure, Dad," he had said. "But the truth is, working with you is what I really want to do." So instead he had attended a polytech, gotten himself a grounding in building and design, and now could build a house from scratch. He was proud of that and proud of his accomplishments, and he loved what he did. He even liked the small jobs, usually undertaken as a favor for one of the guys in the trade, like the one today for Ms. Lewis. It kept the handyman/contractor fraternity going.

He swung the Ford pickup into the narrow unpaved lane that led to the small fifties beach house he called home and parked in front of it. He sat for a moment, thinking of Ms. Lewis and how she had looked in that sexy red bathing suit that might have been a size too small for her. And the crazy diamond necklace she had worn with it. She'd had sand on her bare feet and red polish on her toenails and her legs were long and pale and slender. Her hair had been windblown and the sun had caught her brown eyes, making them gleam like topaz.

He grinned as he swung himself out of the truck, whistling for the dog, who was racing down the lane, running off energy. He'd surely noticed a lot about Ms. Lewis in the short time he had been there. She was different from the kind of women he usually met, which meant the local people he had grown up with, and the weekenders who came out from the city, bringing their high-priced wines and their high-pitched voices and urban sophistication with them to the beach. This woman wasn't like that. She was sort of shy and nervous, not quite sure of herself. Idly, he wondered why, and what could have happened to make her so vulnerable.

He strode into the little weather-bleached wooden A-frame where he lived alone, unless Hallie or Troy happened to be home on a school break. Then he fed the dog, put on Bob

Dylan singing "'Til I Fell in Love With You," stripped off his clothes, and turned on the shower.

Dan never thought about his good looks, just the fact that he looked like his dad. Rugged, fit, an outdoorsman. He scrubbed his hard, lean body vigorously, thinking about his life, which had not been easy after his mother and father had died, leaving him with the responsibility of his younger siblings. He grinned as he thought about them. For him, they made life worthwhile.

Before he went out, he sat down and drew up a list of the work needed on Ms. Lewis's deck with an estimate of the cost. He would drop it off first thing in the morning. It wasn't a major job, though it certainly could become one if she didn't take care of it now. It would take several days, and he would have to fit it in between his other work.

He was still thinking about Ms. Lewis as he drove into San Francisco to meet his girlfriend, wondering what she was doing out at the beach house alone. And whether there was a husband. Ms. Lewis certainly had stuck in his mind. There was just something about her in that red bathing suit. . . .

Chapter Six

She wasn't wearing the red bathing suit when he knocked on her door early the next morning, though. She was just out of bed and in an old pink terry-cloth bathrobe. Her hair was uncombed and she was clutching a steaming mug of coffee. Dan thought she looked tired.

"I hope you slept well," he said politely when she asked him in. "The sea air around here is supposed to put people out like lights right after supper."

Lara shrugged wearily. "Not me. I guess I'm too used to it." She took another mug from the cupboard. "Coffee?"

"Thanks, I'd like that." He put the work estimate on the table between them. "Here's what I think, Ms. Lewis. I reckon three or four days' work will do it, but I've already got a big job on further up the coast, and I'm afraid I could only work for you in the evenings. It would take longer, but at least it would get done."

"That's okay." She studied the estimate in between sips of coffee. "Seems fair to me, Mr. Holland."

"People always call me Dan."

She smiled at him then, showing the prettiest small white teeth. He thought her whole face changed when she smiled and realized that before she had seemed a sad person.

"I suppose you must know everyone around here." She poured more coffee and passed him the sugar.

"Born and bred in Carmel, ma'am."

Amusement made her eyes dance with topaz lights again. "Oh, please, if I am to call you Dan, the least you could manage is to call me Mrs. Lewis—or Lara, if you're going to be out here on my deck for hours at a time. Anyhow, I'd rather not be 'ma'am,' if you don't mind."

"You got it." He grinned back at her. "Lara. Nice name, Ms. Lewis. Like in *Doctor Zhivago*."

She shrugged. "Actually, I predate the movie. It was the name of my godmother."

"You have kids?" He spooned two sugars into his coffee and stirred it.

"A girl, twenty-one, an aspiring movie star out in L.A. And a boy, twenty-three, in med school in Boston."

"So's my kid brother. Only Troy's at Emory." He took a sip of his coffee, watching her.

"Are you married?" She blushed as she said it. She hadn't meant to ask such a personal question, it just popped out.

"No, I'm not married."

"Not yet," she added quickly.

"Not yet," he agreed with a smile. "My sister's a junior at USC. Both kids live with me, though, whenever they get home, that is." He saw her look of surprise and added, "Mom and Dad died ten years ago. I was the eldest and kinda had to look after them. Make sure they went to school, stayed off drugs, help put them through college." He shrugged. "I'm thirty-two—not much older than they are, but somehow I feel more like their father than their elder brother. I guess my life experience has been different from theirs." His blue eyes smiled at her over the rim of his coffee mug. "At their age I was already building houses."

Then he thanked her for the coffee and said he'd better be on his way. "I'll be here, say, between four-thirty and five this evening, then, Ms. Lewis," he said politely. "I'll pick up the timber on my lunch break."

"See you then," she called, watching as he climbed into the cab of the red pickup. "Cute dog," she added as the black Lab gave her a token bark.

"That's Milton. He was a stray, landed on my doorstep a couple of years ago. I called him Milton because I figured when he found a home he'd found the Paradise he thought he'd Lost. Home is where the heart is, hey, Milt?"

Lara waited until she saw the pickup turn into the road. As she closed the door, she realized that for the first time in days, she had not been thinking of Bill, and that she was quite looking forward to four-thirty and the handsome Dan Holland's return. At least it's someone to talk to, she explained to herself.

On the long walk on the beach in the cool gray early morning, her thoughts returned to reality and the canceled Second Honeymoon. Bill hadn't even sounded interested, let alone remorseful. *We'll do it some other time,* he had said so casually. Didn't he realize how much it meant to *her*? How much it *should mean* to him? Didn't he know how carefully she had planned it all, how long it had taken her?

She thought of the tickets sitting in the top-left-hand drawer of his desk. Bleakly, she guessed she had better call Delta and cancel them, *and* all those hotels and auberges. It had taken her endless research just to find them again after twenty-five years, tracing their route from the old scrapbook, where she had pasted every receipt from every cafe and restaurant, as well as menus and little cocktail napkins with the names of bars on them. She had saved postcards of villages and small hotels and had even made little maps of their routes. It had all been so glamorous and different—so *wonderful.*

"Oh, Bill, you *bastard,*" she wailed. "Why are you doing this to me? To *us? Why?*"

Her only answer was the scream of the gulls floating in the misty gray sky and the everlasting boom of the surf hitting the shore.

She picked up the phone. She needed to talk to Delia.

"I guessed you must be out at the beach," Delia said. "I called you at home last night. When there was no reply, we figured that's where you were. We decided not to disturb you."

Despite her worries, Lara smiled. Delia's upbeat, bouncy voice always gave her a lift. "Thanks, but I could use a little disturbing. The only person I've spoken to, apart from the gulls, is the local building contractor who's going to fix my deck. And Bill."

"He called, then?" Delia's voice slipped into neutral as she asked the loaded question.

"He called. He said he couldn't make the French trip. He's too busy."

"He canceled the Second Honeymoon?" Delia's voice trembled with outrage. "But you've been planning it for almost a year; he should bloody well make the time."

"I guess the truth is, he doesn't want to." Shoving her long, wind-blown hair out of her eyes, Lara said tearfully, "Oh, Delia, what am I to do?"

"Is Melissa still with him? I mean, you're *sure* about that, Lar?"

"I know she's there now. And he told me that he has to go on to India, to Delhi, to look at some new children's facility." Her voice shook as she added, "I don't know whether he's going alone."

There was a long silence while Delia thought about it, then she said, "Are you going to fight this, Lar? Or are you just going to walk away from it and let her have him? Is that your plan?"

"I don't have any plan. I'm still just trying to deal with it. I mean, what can I do, Delia? If he wants her that bad, he'll leave me anyway." Anger kicked in suddenly. "And goddammit, I don't know if I want a guy who's lusting after another woman."

Delia's laugh floated over the line. " 'Atta girl, Lara. A little anger is what's needed here. Blast the bastard when he gets home. Lay him on the line and stomp all over him. See what happens then."

Lara was laughing as they said good-bye. Delia was right; a change of attitude was what was needed. And the first thing she would do was pluck up her courage and plunge into that icy ocean.

She put on an old black bathing suit and with Dex at her heels ran down the steps to the beach. Shrieking, half in delight, half in shock, she plunged deep into the icy waves. She swam for a while then staggered back out, shaking seawater from her hair.

"What's needed here, Dex," she gasped, "is a breath of fresh air to clear the cobwebs from my befogged brain." The dog shook himself vigorously, spattering ice-cold drops over her, and she shrieked again, laughing. "Race you to the house," she yelled, pounding up the steep sandy slope.

Dex got there first and Lara was puffing and panting, dripping seawater as she climbed the wooden steps to the deck. And looked directly into Dan Holland's deep-blue eyes.

"Sorry if I startled you, Ms. Lewis," he apologized. "I just came by to drop off the lumber. When no one answered the bell, I guessed you were out and came in by the side gate. I hope you don't mind."

No man had looked into her eyes like that in years. For ever. Certainly not Bill. It took her breath away. She glanced at the pile of lumber stacked neatly on the deck. "Oh, no. No, of course not. Any time I'm not here, please feel free."

"Great, thanks. I'll be back around four-thirty, then." Lara was still standing on the top step as he turned away.

He paused with his hand on the wooden gate at the side of the deck. "Mind if I ask you something?"

She shook her head.

"Do you always wear a diamond necklace when you go swimming?"

There was a bemused look on his face and Lara laughed. "Always," she replied demurely, touching her hand to the lover's knot.

She could hear Dan Holland laughing too as he closed the gate and went on his way.

Chapter Seven

He let himself in by the side gate at 4:52 precisely. Lara didn't bother to check the seconds on her old watch but she knew to the minute what the time was. Of course, she told herself she hadn't really been waiting for him, and to prove it, she whistled to Dexter and took off immediately for a walk along the beach. To her astonishment Dan's black Lab appeared out of nowhere, loping along beside her.

"Sorry about that," Dan yelled from the deck. Shading her eyes with her hand, she looked up at him. "You whistle, he'll come," he shouted. "I guess he's anybody's when there's a walk going."

"Is it okay if he comes along?"

"Yeah, if you're sure you don't mind."

"I don't and Dex certainly doesn't." The two dogs were rapidly disappearing into the distance. She sprinted down the sand yelling for Dex but the dog took no notice, he was having too good a time. Lucky Dex, make the most of it, she thought. Happiness is fleeting, even in dogland.

The sun was low in the sky when she returned and half the boards on her deck were gone.

"You'll have to be careful until I get them replaced," Dan warned. "Keep an eye on the dog too; we don't want him to break a leg."

"I'll be careful." He had taken off his shirt while he worked and beads of sweat trickled down his chest. His body was so lean and hard Lara could have counted his ribs, had she cared to. Feeling suddenly pale and plump, she said quickly, "Can I get you a cold drink? A beer, maybe?"

"Beer would be great." He wiped his neck with a dusty cloth and began shifting the lumber closer to the area where he would begin to replace the boards the next day.

Aware of his eyes on her and wishing her butt looked smaller in the white linen shorts, Lara hurried into the house. Foolish woman, she silently chided herself, what do you care anyhow?

I care, someone inside her cried. *I care. I want to be thirty again, I want to be slender and beautiful with long blond hair and an uncreased white doctor's coat, nobly saving the lives of small children. . . .*

Dan took the beer from her with a polite smile. "I left a corner where you can still sit," he said. "I'll finish it up as soon as I can, I promise."

"No problem." She sank into the chaise and put her feet up. "Sit down, why don't you. And tell me about yourself."

He took a seat. "What would you like to know?" Throwing back his head, he gulped down the beer.

Lara stared, fascinated, at his smooth, strong, rippling throat. "Oh, I don't know," she said, gathering her wits. "I guess just who you are. What you are. What your life is like."

He rolled his eyes. "That's a pretty tall order, Ms. Lewis. And

I think your last question is the easiest to answer. At least without the help of a shrink." He laughed as she blushed. "I thought blushing had gone out of style. But, anyhow, I didn't mean to embarrass you."

"I'm sorry. Forget I asked." She tugged self-consciously at her shorts, which were creeping up around her crotch. They must have shrunk.

He said, "I have this little house at the beach. Nothing as grand as this, of course." His eyes took in the crisp gray shingles and the spare but stylish decor. "Just kind of a fifties A-frame that I'm gradually redoing."

"Whenever you can spare the time from doing other folks' work after hours." Lara wondered if she was imagining it, or did the air seem to tremble between them as their eyes met? Surely not. Dan Holland was only here because he was doing a job for her, not because he craved her company.

"Milt and I live there alone, except during school breaks, and then suddenly the place feels like it's bursting at the seams with the kids and their friends. A man can get used to living alone," he added thoughtfully. "The silence, only having to think of yourself. Usually, I put on some music and because I'm alone I can play it as loud as I want. Loud enough so it pours out into the night. I like to sit out there in the dark and let it wash over me in waves of sound, hearing it blend with the roar of the ocean. There's something elemental about it." He shrugged. "Anyhow, it just gets to me. Kinda sweeps through my soul."

"I don't think you need a shrink, Mr. Holland," Lara said, impressed. "I think you know exactly what you are and who you are and what you like."

His laugh boomed across the darkening shore. "The name's Dan. And I wish it were that easy. I'm a simple guy. I like what

I do and that's part of what I am. Right now, I'm putting up a taco stand in Monterey but I'm also working with a local architect on a new ranch we're building out in the hills behind Carmel. I'm making money. Not a lot, but enough to keep me happy, pay for my house, a couple of fishing trips to Mexico, the occasional ski weekend in Big Bear." He shrugged. "That's about it."

"What about your girlfriend?"

He raised a quizzical eyebrow, smiling at her. "Her name's Britt. I thought for a while there that maybe she was the one. Now," he lifted his shoulder, "I'm not so sure. I've been seeing her for ten months. She's a student at Berkeley."

Lara told herself she might have known. "I'll bet she's beautiful."

"Yes, she's beautiful. And ambitious. Not in the meaning of wanting a career. That's not Britt's style. She's ambitious for material things. Sometimes I get the feeling she's on the lookout for a better financial prospect than me." He laughed lazily. "I can't say I blame her."

"Then why stay with her?"

"She's kind of a challenge, I guess." He didn't add that she was also wild in bed because he knew he would make Ms. Lewis blush again. The thought crossed his mind for a split second about how wild Ms. Lewis might be in bed. It was intriguing and totally out of place.

"I'm not sure what I'm looking for in life," he added thoughtfully. "All I know is I haven't found it yet." His eyes held hers in that deep gaze. "How about you?"

"Oh, I'm a very ordinary woman. A mother . . . you know how it is."

"So what do you do with your days?"

"My husband is a specialist in cardiovascular surgery. He works with children a lot. Right now, he's in Beijing, then he's going on to India."

"That's him. What about you?"

She shrugged, baffled. "I look after the house, work with seniors, play tennis with my girlfriends. That sort of thing."

"The sort of things rich women do to pass their time."

"I'm not rich." She was on the defensive. "I mean . . . oh, hell, you know what I mean." She glared at him.

"I think I do, Ms. Lewis." He put the beer bottle down on the deck and stood up. "It's getting late. I'd better go."

He whistled and his dog came racing back up the steps from the beach. "See you tomorrow around the same time," he called as the gate clanged shut behind him.

Lara shivered as she drained the last of her wine. With the sunset it had turned cold again. She went inside and closed the windows. She set the fire in the grate and put a match to it, waiting until it caught before she went upstairs to shower.

"Serves me right for asking, hey, Dex?" she said with a shaky little laugh.

She fixed herself a childish comfort sandwich of bananas mashed with brown sugar on a slice of Wonder Bread, then, in her old pink robe, settled down in front of the fire with the Noel Coward *Diaries* to help her live vicariously. She thought maybe Dan Holland had got it right. Alone, you could eat what you pleased when you pleased. You could do what you liked. Be whomever you liked.

But it was awfully lonely, she thought sadly, when all you had to look forward to were Oreos and a glass of milk. She wondered if Dan was seeing the beautiful young student again tonight.

Chapter Eight

Lara wore the red bathing suit the next afternoon when Dan came by, just to prove to herself that it meant nothing. She needn't have bothered; he barely looked at her.

She sat under the big green umbrella at one side of the deck pretending to read her book, while he busied himself at the other side, whistling softly as he worked. He had taken off his T-shirt and was wearing only a pair of old gray shorts. Lara wondered what the Girlfriends would say if they saw him. There was no doubt that Dan Holland was a hunk. A *young* hunk, she reminded herself. And she was a woman in her middle forties who was in the process of being ditched by her husband for a younger version. Maybe she should introduce Melissa to Dan and they would be irresistibly drawn to each other, beauty to beauty, sort of like looking in a mirror. She would get her husband back and resolve Dan Holland's love life.

Except she didn't want to do that. She didn't want to introduce Dan to anyone, not even the Girlfriends. He was her secret and she wanted to keep him right here on her deck and just watch him. His thick straight hair, bleached by the sun, fell over his eyes; his body had that golden, outdoor, California look about it, and his muscles rippled from more than a decade of hard work. He stretched lazily, and he was so male it took her breath away.

He turned to smile at her. "Got to cool off," he said, running past her, down the steps to the beach. He dived into the waves with that wonderful confidence of the young and well-coordinated that his body could do anything he asked of it, and she watched him swim effortlessly into the red-gold path of the setting sun, at one with his watery world.

She had a beer waiting when he came back. His wet shorts clung to him, sleek as a second skin. "I'll get you a towel," she said, quickly averting her gaze. "There's an old pair of Bill's shorts too, if you would like to change."

He picked up the bottle of beer and drank deeply. "Thanks, Ms. Lewis, but don't trouble. I'll dry off in a couple of minutes in this heat, then I'll be on my way."

She sank into the chaise, staring out over the ocean, wishing he would stay longer. "How was Britt last night?"

"Britt was . . . I guess she was just Britt." He was leaning back against the deck rail, arms folded over his chest. "I've forgotten what I told you about her."

"That she was young and beautiful and expensive, and maybe in search of a richer guy."

He lifted the beer bottle in acknowledgment. "That's Britt in a nutshell." His eyes linked with hers. "And what did you do last night?"

"I put on my robe, ate a banana sandwich on white bread, and read about somebody else's life," she said honestly.

"It was probably more fun than my evening." He put down

the empty bottle and started gathering his equipment. "I'd better get going, Ms. Lewis. Tomorrow at the same time okay with you?"

"Oh, sure. Any time you want. The gate is always open if I'm not here." She was already promising herself that she would not be there when he came by tomorrow. Definitely not. Nor the next day either.

Silence settled over her as she sat on the half-torn-up deck. Twilight turned to darkness. There were no stars tonight. Stroking Dex's head absently, she thought about Bill and what she was going to do. Perhaps she was wrong and Bill was really going to India alone. His work had always come first, and after all, it was lives he was helping to save. *Children's* lives. Wasn't it she who was the selfish one, wanting him to come to France with her?

But her stomach churned as she imagined Bill with Melissa. She felt locked out, abandoned, a part of his past. She could bear it no longer. She had to know the truth.

Grabbing the phone, she dialed the hospital and asked for the pediatric department. The nurse on duty told her that Dr. Melissa Kenney was in China. Yes, she had been due back next week, but now there had been a delay. She was returning via India and would not be back for several weeks.

Lara dropped the phone and huddled into the sofa, staring at the empty fire grate without seeing it. Pain was a lead weight on her heart, dragging her into an abyss. Her life was being stolen from her and there was nothing she could do about it.

She had no sense of time passing, no idea of how long she had been sitting there until she became aware of Dex whining and realized that she was freezing. Her watch said eight-thirty. She let the dog out and stared wearily around the empty house.

It was so goddamn quiet. So lonely. Unable to bear the silence any longer, she ran upstairs, flung on a sweater and skirt, jammed her feet into flat leather sandals, grabbed the car keys, and headed for the door.

She remembered she had not even looked in a mirror, swung around, raced back upstairs again, dragged a brush through her hair and applied lipstick carefully. Melissa Kenney might have stolen her husband, but she was darned if she was going to let the bitch steal her pride too. She ran to the door, then back again to the dressing table for a spritz of Ceylon, a gift from Delia and now her favorite perfume.

She drove into Carmel and walked aimlessly around with Dex happily sniffing on his leash, until some time later she found herself outside a small bar. Tying the dog to a convenient ficus tree, she walked in and took a seat. She had never been into a bar alone before, and, self-conscious, she stared straight ahead, not looking at the other customers.

"What can I get ya, ma'am?"

The bartender had spiky red hair and she thought he looked all of twenty-two years old. She wondered wearily if there was a youth conspiracy and she was the only one born in the wrong era. Daringly, she ordered tequila on the rocks.

She took a big gulp, coughing as the tequila hit her throat like fire. At least this time she had gotten up the nerve to order it.

She caught the eye of a gray-haired man at the other end of the bar. He raised his glass to her and she looked hastily away. She drained the tequila and ordered another. The bartender put the glass in front of her and pushed the bowl of peanuts closer. Lara sipped her drink this time, staring vacantly into the mirror over the bar, wondering what to do with her new freedom. Because she had no doubt now that Bill was gone for good.

Walking down the street, Dan noticed the dog first, tied to the tree outside the bar. "Dexter?" he said inquiringly.

Dex gave a delighted woof and Dan bent to pat him and then he saw Lara Lewis sitting alone at the bar. She looked pale but pretty in a blue sweater with her dark hair curling softly around her face. His first instinct was to go in and say hello, but there was something in the droop of her shoulders, her unseeing gaze into the mirror that made him hold back. She looked like a woman who wanted to be left alone. Giving Dex a final pat, he went on his way.

Back home later, with music soaring to the rafters, Dan prowled the deck wondering about Ms. Lewis. She wasn't the kind of woman he'd expected to see drinking alone in a bar, but, then, she was a mass of contradictions. Shy enough to blush, yet opinionated too. She had told him almost nothing about herself. It was as though she had something to hide, yet she was transparently honest. He thought she was a very interesting woman. And he couldn't get the image of her in that red bathing suit out of his head.

You look different," Dan said to her the next afternoon.

Lara knew it. She had looked in the mirror earlier, seen the truth: the shadows under her eyes, the puffiness, the little lines. She wore no makeup, her face was naked, and her feelings were there in her eyes for him to see. She had nothing to hide from this stranger.

"I didn't sleep," she said curtly.

He nodded, "Seems to me you don't ever get much sleep. Perhaps you should see someone about that."

Lara gave a short, sharp bark of laughter. "A doctor, you mean. Thanks, but I have my own diagnosis. And I don't need any help."

Turning away, he went quietly about his work. Lara sighed. She hadn't meant to be rude, but rejection made a woman bitchy. She lay back in the chaise, not even pretending to read, watching him.

An hour passed in silence. He never even looked at her. When she could bear it no longer, she called softly, "I'm sorry I was rude."

He was sawing through a plank of wood. He finished what he was doing then glanced up at her. "That's okay, Ms. Lewis."

Her sigh was big and genuine. "When are you going to call me Lara? After all, I call you Dan."

"Okay. Lara."

He went back to his work and she sighed again. Another hour passed and the sun began its slow descent. She offered him a glass of wine but he said he would prefer a beer and not to get up, he would get it from the kitchen himself.

He came back with the opened beer and walked across the deck to where she was sitting.

Lara thought how unhurried and easy he was. There was none of the urgency about him that Bill had. None of the tension, the pacing, the furrowed brow, the ringing phone that Bill always jumped to answer. It was as though this man had all the time in the world for her.

He sat back in his chair, one leg hitched comfortably over the other, completely at home, completely relaxed. A smile lurked behind his eyes.

She folded her arms across her chest, uncomfortable under his gaze. "What are you looking at?"

He lifted a shoulder. "You."

"Not much to look at, really." She flipped back her long hair like a self-conscious teenager.

"Really?"

Now he was laughing at her. She got up, put on a Bob Dylan CD, a voice from her youth.

"My favorite," he said, turning up the volume.

Dylan's gravelly voice sighed out into the dusk and Lara was amazed how powerful the music sounded outdoors, lifting over the ocean. "I've never listened to it like this," she said.

"It's the only way. And you have the advantage of no near neighbors to complain."

"I like my solitude."

"Is that why you were alone in the bar last night?" He heard her sharp intake of breath and he laughed. "Lady, if you want to go to a bar alone, don't leave your dog outside. It's a dead giveaway."

Despite herself, Lara laughed. "I'd had some bad news," she explained.

"The doc's not coming back for a while, huh?"

She glared haughtily at him. "What are you, clairvoyant? I told you he was in Beijing. Now he has to go on to Delhi. He's an important man in his field."

He nodded. "Sure. I understand. My brother's planning on being a neurosurgeon. It's all he thinks about."

"Pity his poor wife." Lara's face was a mask, but he caught the tone of bitterness. He took a sip of the beer. "Troy's not planning marriage just yet."

"Are you going to marry Britt?"

"No."

"Why not?" She was standing with her back to him, gazing at the incoming tide.

"Because I don't love her."

"Oh?" She swung around. "And how do you know what love is?"

"Lara, I don't know. I'm just hoping one day I'll be lucky enough to find out."

The sun had set and a mist was rolling in. She was wearing only old gray sweatpants and a T-shirt, and she rubbed her arms, chilled.

"Time to go," he said, not looking at his watch.

"Yes. Of course. You must have things to do. . . . It's late."

"I hadn't noticed."

He was still sitting, still smiling that knowing little smile. There was something in his eyes, an expression she couldn't fathom.

"Did anyone ever tell you you're a beautiful woman, Ms. Lewis?"

Lara stared at him. Confused, she took a step back, ran her hands nervously over the baggy sweatpants. "I . . . no . . . well . . ." She felt the heat of the blush sting her cheeks.

He looked at her for a long minute, then he turned and made his way into her kitchen. He put the empty beer bottle on the counter.

"Then they should," he called over his shoulder. She heard him whistle for his dog, and they were gone.

Stunned, she dropped into a chair. *Fool,* she told herself angrily. *A man pays you a compliment and you go into shock. That's how pathetic you've become.*

"Fuck you, Bill." She pounded a fist on the arm of the chair.

"I'll go to Paris without you. I'll spend all your money on expensive French clothes and champagne. I'll have myself a ball."

She took a deep, shaky breath. For once she had made a decision about her own life. She was not just the mother, not just the good friend. Not just Melissa Kenney's rival for her husband's affections.

She was Lara Lewis, forty-five years old, a woman in her own right and on her way to Paris.

Her heart sank at the thought.

Chapter Nine

Vannie called an hour later and when Lara told her of her decision, she said worriedly, "I'll have to discuss this with the other girls. I mean, Lara — you . . . alone . . . in Paris. Somehow it just doesn't seem right."

"It's better than me alone in Carmel," Lara retorted, sounding more confident than she felt. "And it's also better than sitting and waiting to see if Dr. Melissa Kenney is going to allow me to have my husband back. Which, anyhow, I somehow doubt."

"Wouldn't you want him back?"

Vannie sounded wistful, as though she were already contemplating the loss of the first of the Girlfriends' husbands. Lara knew exactly how she felt. They had always been a gang, a team, and now it was beginning to break up, threatening their security. She said, "I don't know, Vannie. Right now, I'm just so" — she sought for the right word — "so *wounded*. Bill lied to me. He sacrificed us, our plans, our life, for Melissa. What can I say?" She shrugged her shoulders wearily.

The next call was from Susie. "If you insist on doing this

darn trip, then at least let one of us come with you," she said firmly, but Lara was stubborn.

"What does Delia think?" she asked.

"Delia thinks you should go, but as you can see, she's in the minority."

Lara laughed. "My count makes it even. Two against two."

"So who gets the deciding vote? Your kids?"

Lara thought if her heart could have gotten any heavier, it would have sunk. She was so selfish, only thinking of herself and her own pain, she hadn't given any thought to how a breakup might affect Josh and Minnie.

Delia was the next to call. "So, okay, when do we leave?"

"We?"

"Nous. Les deux femmes seules. Out on the town together in Paris. I hope you speak better French than I do, though."

Lara laughed. "Sorry to disappoint you, madame, but I'm making this trip on my own."

"Wouldn't it be more fun with the two of us?"

"It's not fun I'm looking for, Delia." Lara suddenly realized what it was she needed. "It's myself." She thought about it for a moment. "I don't quite know how to explain this, but this will be a . . . voyage of self-discovery. And I need to do it alone."

Delia understood immediately. She said, "When do you leave?"

"In a couple of weeks. Not long now."

"Of course I'll see you before you go. And I hope it works out for you, Lar," she added softly.

Chapter Ten

Dan Holland had never met a woman quite like Lara Lewis. She was so self-contained, giving nothing away—except what was revealed in her expressive face and her huge, sad eyes. There was an air of innocence about her that was missing in the young women he knew, a tenderness, a vulnerability, as though she had never grown that diamond-hard outer layer women these days thought necessary. The young women he met had a fuck-you attitude, as though life owed them and they were going to take it. He was drawn by Lara's gentleness, and he liked her self-consciousness, and he admired her intelligence.

Each evening after he had finished work on her deck, he would linger over a beer, talking about nothing in particular. About Carmel, his life, her kids. And sometimes there were long silences that said more than words.

Another week passed. Dan was working at the opposite end of the deck from where Lara was sitting reading a book, and even though he was concentrating on what he was doing, his peripheral vision kept her in view. He liked the way she looked in that red bathing suit with her breasts spilling over the top, and he liked her long legs and rounded hips. She lay back, eyes closed, the book resting on her stomach. Her skin had a faint sheen of sweat, and the coconut scent of Hawaiian Tropic drifted his way. He wanted to touch her. . . .

He worked until the sun went down and then, as usual, Lara asked him to stay for a beer. They sat opposite each other in the twilight, watching the sliver of moon begin its climb. She had changed into a flowing white skirt and shirt, thrown a soft blue cardigan around her shoulders, slipped her long, narrow feet into gold thong sandals. Gold hoops gleamed in her ears and he could smell her perfume, gentle and faintly spicy.

"A couple more days and I'll be through," he said quietly.

Lara nodded, telling herself it was better that way. She would miss him, though. Oh, yes, she would miss him. There was something real about Dan that she wanted desperately to cling to.

"Would you like to stay for supper?" She tried to sound casual, as though it were a spur-of-the-moment thing, but the truth was that morning she had driven into Carmel and bought food especially, knowing she would ask him. "It's just some stuff I bought in town: turkey, coleslaw, mashed potatoes, gravy . . ."

"Good home cooking."

He was laughing at her and she said huffily, "You don't have to stay."

"No. But I want to. And thank you for the invitation. I like turkey and mashed potatoes. And I like the company."

She smiled shyly. "It gets lonesome out here."

"It beats going to a bar alone too, I guess," he said, laughing as she glared at him.

Back in the house, Lara lit perfumed votive candles, which gave off the scent of rosemary and thyme, reminding her of Provence all those years ago, thanking God that Dan would never know how long she had agonized about this night. About what to wear and whether they should eat in the dining room or the kitchen, finally deciding on the kitchen because it would look less like a setup; about the bottle of wine she thought he would like and food he might enjoy.

Why am I doing this? she'd asked herself with a little illicit thrill. What am I thinking of? It's dangerous. . . .

She put on a CD, *Bill Evans with Symphony Orchestra,* soft, rippling piano and strings that sounded like the sea. When she turned Dan was standing in the doorway looking at her.

Tension zigzagged between them and the air seemed to tremble in the long silence.

"This is beautiful," Dan said quietly.

Nervous, she invited him to take a seat, served him some food, asked him to pour the wine. They talked about their "children"; about books and art and music; about anything but what was happening between them. And then he surprised her by telling her that once he had been a man with a dream.

He laughed at himself as he said, "I thought I could be a sculptor. You know, a modern-day Michelangelo, traveling to Carrara to choose my precious piece of marble from the great quarry, hacking away at it in my freezing garret studio."

"Then why didn't you pursue it?"

He shrugged. "Fate dealt me another hand. There was no time left for dreams. Now, it's just a hobby and I guess I'll never get to Carrara to pick out that marble. But as they say, that's life." He smiled at her. "And I'm a happy man."

"I envy you."

He looked steadily at her. "There's no need for you to envy anyone."

Avoiding his eyes, she began busily to remove the dishes. He took her hand, stopped her. "We'll do that later," he said. "Come, let's go for a walk along the beach."

It was cool out and Lara buttoned her sweater as they strolled barefoot along the shoreline, with just a slender moon and the glimmering phosphorescence in the waves to light their way. She was so aware of Dan's shadowy bulk next to her, so aware of his scent, his nearness, that when he caught her hand in his, an electric trembling hit the pit of her belly and she could not look at him.

He turned her gently to face him, put his hand beneath the soft hair at the nape of her neck, pulling her closer. She heard her blood pounding through her veins as she succumbed to the lure of that other world where all that mattered was the way he made her feel. Sensual. Alive. *Female.*

He was running his hands down her smooth back under the blue cardigan. "I can't get you out of my mind. I leave you here and I go home and think about you, wondering who you are, *what* you are. . . ."

This was so wrong, so against everything she was, she must be crazy. . . . She pulled abruptly away from him. "There's nothing to know."

Dan put his hand on her shoulder, turned her back to him. "There you go again," he said, exasperated. "*Why,* Lara? What's wrong? What happened to you?"

"I don't know. . . . No, that's not true, I do know." Suddenly, she was telling him about Bill and Melissa, about how her life was falling apart. That for years she had been all these women for Bill: the young lover, the wife and helpmate, the mother. Now it had all been taken away from her. And she was reduced to nothing. To no one.

Dan pulled her closer, stroked her back soothingly. "Bill made you feel worthless. He doesn't see you the way any other man would see you. The way *I* see you. How beautiful you are, *what* you are." His hands were on her shoulders; he felt her trembling. He crushed her to him, her breasts pressed against his chest, their bellies touching.

Then there was nothing else in Lara's head but the way she felt at that moment. The heat of her, the need, the *urgency* to draw even closer. She wanted to breathe him, touch him, taste him. . . .

And she was boneless, floating in space somewhere as they sank together onto the cool sand. She felt the hardness of his workman's hand as he smoothed the contour of her cheek, ran a finger tenderly along the length of the bone, touched her brow softly. His mouth was on hers again, drinking her in, catching her every breath.

He was in control, unbuttoning, lifting her arms out of her shirt, laying her half naked against the pillowing sand. Moonlight pearlized her skin, tipped her breasts with lilac, silvered her parted lips, glimmered from her half-closed eyes. She was weightless in his arms, her inhibitions gone.

He slipped easily out of his clothes and he was as beautiful as she had imagined. Narrow-hipped, lithe, hard. Golden hair dappled his chest, and as he bent over her he smelled of sunshine and the sea wind.

He kissed her breasts, tasted her nipples, inhaled the scent of her, and Lara wrapped closer, twining her arms around his strong young neck as if afraid he might run away before she had had enough of him.

"Lovely woman," Dan breathed in her ear. "Lovely sweet woman, do you have any idea how beautiful you are? How sexy you smell, how hot you feel?"

Passion throbbed in her belly. His hands were stroking her so gently: the curve of her hips, the tangle of dark hair, the scented moistness of her. Then his tongue explored her, tasting her essence greedily. Rocketing her to the other side of paradise.

When she could bear it no longer, he lay over her, holding himself just inches away, looking into her eyes. "I want you so bad," he whispered. "Tell me what you want, Lara. . . ." He sleeked his tongue in her ear.

Lara groaned, a heartfelt, honest-to-God from-the-gut groan. And she was lost. She was trapped by the odd limitations of erotic language. How else could she say, *Touch me here,* what other words were there for *Love me,* for *Give me your hand, your lips, hold me, kiss my mouth, oh, please, please. . . .* The poetry was in their bodies, not in their words, in what he was doing to her, and what, astonishingly, she was doing to him. She asked herself who was this woman. Could it really be her? Her cries were small and soft, inhibited by their newness to her. She was lost in the responses her body had never known it could make.

She reached down to touch him, felt him pulsate and the hardness that meant he wanted her as much as she wanted him. Boldly, she guided him into her, unwilling to wait a moment longer. But her cry was muted, as though she were afraid someone might hear, or that she herself might hear. She had never wanted to cry out before. Now, she wanted to yell, to dig her nails in, to grab and clutch, as the great breakers sent the beach trembling beneath her.

Afterward, he lay on top of her, still trembling. Her outflung hands were captured in his; her body, slick with sweat, was crushed beneath his, but she did not want to move. She wanted this moment to last forever. Because even if it never happened again between them, she knew she would never be the same.

As they emerged slowly into reality, the night air felt suddenly chilly. Dan sat her up and pushed her arms into the sleeves of her cardigan as though she were a little girl, fumbling with the tiny pearl buttons until she had to help him. He smoothed back her tumbled sandy hair then held her face in his two hands. "I'm not sure what love is," he said softly, "but somehow I think I've found it."

A shaft of pure happiness seemed to come from somewhere deep inside Lara as she bent her head, leaned into him. "I don't know what love is either," she whispered. "All I know is I want what I have with you tonight."

He pulled her to her feet, held her close, kissed her again. They were laughing as they shook sand out of their clothes. He helped her with her skirt, and she insisted on buttoning his jeans, running her hand over the gentle bulge that she now knew and for this moment called her own. She bent to kiss him through his jeans and he groaned. "Sweetheart, my love, don't or we'll never get back. And look, the tide is coming in."

The ocean was racing toward them along with the barking dogs. He grabbed her hand and they ran, slipping and stumbling along the ever-narrowing stretch of beach, scrambling, disheveled and sandy and wet and smelling of sex and love and seaspray, up the wooden steps to the deck and into the house.

The phone was ringing.

Lara froze. She knew it was Bill.

Dan stared, astonished at her as it shrilled on into the silence.

The wild, uninhibited sexy siren of the beach had disappeared. The color had drained from her face, and she seemed numb with fear. After a few more rings, it stopped, but the sound still echoed in the newly tense silence.

Lara turned to him, her eyes dark with panic. "What shall I do? What am I doing?" She ran toward the stairs, away from him, but he caught her arm.

"Why are you running from me?" he yelled, angry because she was afraid of what they had done. "Dammit, Lara, you only did what you wanted to do. Just the way your selfish, unfaithful husband did."

"Oh, what do *you* know," she cried, furious. "How can you *possibly* know what is between people who have been married for twenty-five years? How can you possibly *know* how I feel?"

She snatched herself away from him, eyes sparking anger. He stared at her, stunned into silence, betrayed by her guilt. Then he said quietly, "You're right."

He picked up his sandy shoes and walked toward the door. "I'm sorry, Lara," he said coldly. "But this is your call, not mine."

Then he opened the door and, without looking back at her, he walked out of her life. And like a fool, she just stood there and let him go.

Chapter Eleven

D an did not show up for work the next afternoon and Lara
paced the house, exhausted from a sleepless night, torn
with guilt about what she had done—and remembering every
detail of it.

Confused, she took Dex for a walk on the beach. When she
reached the place where she and Dan had made love she looked
for their imprint in the sand, but the tide had washed it away.
The moment was gone forever.

When she returned it was already dark. There was no sign
that Dan had been there, no note slipped under the door. She
couldn't blame him. She had destroyed something beautiful and
she would never see him again.

The phone rang and this time she leapt to answer it.

"I called last night but I guess you were out." Bill sounded
as though he was at the other end of the world, which, of
course, he was. Crackle on the line hid the tremor in Lara's voice
as she lied and said that she had gone to bed early with a headache and turned off the phone.

"How's it going?" Nervous, she twisted a strand of hair around her finger then let it unravel, waiting to hear him say he was never coming back.

He said, "It's going well." There was silence, then he said, "Lara."

"Yes?"

"When I get back there's something we have to talk about."

His voice was low, kind of subdued, and Lara wondered if Melissa was standing next to him, urging him on.

"About Melissa Kenney?" She was astonished by how calm she sounded.

There was a stunned pause, then Bill said, "I didn't realize you knew."

Don't you know, you fool, that after twenty-five years of being married to you, I know everything about you? Every thought, every move. I could be you, I know you so well.

She said, "I'm going on that trip to France alone."

"Lara, I don't think you should do this. Not the French thing, not—"

"Not our Second Honeymoon?"

"Take a vacation, by all means. But go somewhere else. A cruise . . . Take one of the Girlfriends with you."

A cruise, she thought bitterly. *The divorcée's reward.*

"I'm going alone, Bill," she said coldly. "And I'm going to Paris. I'll talk to you when I get back." And she hung up on him.

She slumped into a chair, trembling. Tears stung her eyes. The phone rang again a few seconds later. She willed herself not to answer. After a minute or two, it stopped.

That lonely silence that Lara knew so well settled over the house. Last night's ashes were dead in the grate, the candles had burned down, the flowers drooped. She leapt to her feet, ran upstairs, and quickly packed her bag. Her crumpled white skirt and shirt lay on the floor of the closet. She picked up the shirt and held it to her face, seeking his scent, but there was nothing. She flung it into the laundry basket, grabbed her bag, called Dex, locked up the house, and put the top up on the white convertible.

She drove back to San Francisco, speeding along the darkened roads, hardly thinking about what she was doing. Only that she had to get away from here.

The big house in Pacific Heights where she had lived with Bill for so many years, where they had brought up their children, had a life together, seemed cold, alien, hostile as she wandered listlessly through it. What use was a family room with no family? No kids bickering and threatening each other with extinction; no mayhem, no tears, no laughter. No TV with loud cartoons, no boom box blasting, no teenagers devouring pizza and Cokes.

When the children had left, she had lost her job. And now Bill was gone. And so was her lover. In the space of a week, her life had been turned upside down.

Chapter Twelve

From this point on it can only get better," Susie said firmly. The Girlfriends were sitting around the pine breakfast table in the kitchen of Susie's spacious ranch with its view of horses grazing in the meadow, drinking their fifth cup of coffee—with caffeine because Delia had said, "What the hell, today we need it." They were having a "meeting."

"Men suck." Delia swallowed a handful of vitamins and washed them down with the caffeine.

"Especially Bill Lewis." Susie stared at Lara, who was slumped over her blue coffee mug, elbows on the table, chin in her hands, no makeup, dark hair dragged back any-old-how, looking bleak and miserable. "That cheating bastard has put years on you in the space of a couple of weeks."

"Must you go on this trip?" Vannie asked gently. "It's so full of memories for you, it will only hurt you more."

"I haven't told you everything." Lara stared into her coffee as though she had not even heard Vannie. "I met a man. I had sex with him on the beach the other night. It was the most beautiful thing that ever happened to me."

There was a stunned silence; they looked at one another, then back at Lara.

She was talking like a woman in a dream. "I didn't know it could be like that. It just took me over. I didn't know where I was, *who* I was. All I wanted was Dan and what he was doing to me, and what I was doing to him."

The Girlfriends caught one anothers' eyes again, brows raised.

"It was all my fault." Lara's voice quivered. "I knew what I was doing when I asked him to stay for supper. I knew I wanted him, even though I didn't admit it to myself. But it was there in my every move, from the candles and the wine to the white skirt and the gold sandals."

"Slut!" Delia grinned admiringly.

"So when do we get to meet the lover?" Susie poured more coffee and brought out the chocolate cake. "It's an emergency," she explained, as the others glanced skeptically at her. "Anyhow, it's only leftovers from the kids."

Since it was only leftovers, they all helped themselves to the cake. "I just had to tell you," Lara said, her mouth full of comforting calories.

"Of course you did," Delia said. "And this is the most exciting news we've had in years. Besides, the hell with Bill. He's a two-timing jerk who deserves a bitch like Melissa Kenney. Tell us about the lover. Who is he?"

"His name is Dan Holland." Lara eyes darkened and she sighed because of the tug of memory that went with just saying his name. "He's the guy who's fixing my deck out at the beach house." She looked guiltily at them. "And he's thirty-two years old."

Their jaws dropped. "Jeez," Susie gasped, "is he housebroken?"

"*And* he's beautiful." Lara ignored her. "*And* the best lover I ever had."

"And what's the count on that, Ms. Lara Lewis?" Delia snorted. "A grand total of two?"

But Vannie reached out and squeezed her hand. "I'm glad you met him, Lara. He's just what you need right now."

They turned on her, astonished. "Vannie the Virgin" had been her nickname and now here she was condoning Lara's fling with the handyman.

"What do you know about it, anyhow?" Delia demanded.

"More than you think." Vannie gave them a demure little smile as they stared at her, astonished. "My sex life is pretty good, thank you for asking. And I can see why Lara would need a man now. Bill has been neglecting her; she's a lovely, normal woman. And if Dan Holland is as good as she says, then my hat's off to her."

"Well!" Susie sank back against the cushions, stunned. "Thanks for sharing that with us, Vannie. I'll think about it next time I have dinner with you and Lucas."

"Okay, so Lara came to us for help and so far we haven't resolved anything," Delia said impatiently. "The score is this. One: Bill has opted out and Lara isn't sure she would want him back even if he came crawling. Two: Lara has a lover with whom she had a wonderful time and who is going to be a great help getting her over this hurdle. I think we should take a vote. Does Lara keep her lover and have herself a ball? Or does she go off to France alone and have a miserable time remembering the way it used to be? Dan? Or France?"

"Dan." Three hands shot up in the air, three smiling faces turned toward Lara.

"It's too late," she said miserably. "I ruined it. He's gone."

"You did *what?*"

Lara explained about the ringing phone, that she had known it was Bill, how confused and guilty she had felt, and how she had turned on Dan. "So he just picked up his shoes and left," she said.

"Jeez, now you may never get your deck finished." Practical Susie shrugged as the others glared at her.

"His final words were 'This is your call, Lara, not mine.' " Gloomily, Lara helped herself to another slab of cake. "And that's the end of Dan Holland," she said, licking chocolate off her fingers. "So now I'm going to Paris. Alone. And that's that."

Vannie removed the plate of cake from in front of her. "You don't need that many calories for comfort. And did you ever think of those little words *I'm sorry?* An apology might be all it would take. After all, you were in the wrong."

But Lara shook her head. "It's over," she said with such a note of finality in her voice they knew it was true.

"Then the hell with it, there's no time to be wasted." Delia slid her feet into her sandals and pushed back her chair. The others stared inquiringly at her. "Well, we can't let Lara go to Paris looking like this, can we?"

They turned to inspect Lara, blushing in her old *Rolling Stones* sweatshirt and ancient jeans, hair a mess and not even a touch of lip gloss.

Lara stared down at herself. She knew she was dowdy, shuffling into middle age. Then Delia hauled her to her feet. "You're up against a sex symbol in a doctor's white coat," she told her firmly. "Think *ER.* You can't win. Not without some sexy new clothes. Get your skates on, girls, we're going shopping."

Chapter Thirteen

The new clothes hung in Lara's closet, the shoes and sandals neatly stacked underneath. The expensive handbag was still wrapped in its own smart little cloth cover, and the new underwear, or rather "lingerie," was quite different from the cotton kind she usually wore, all lace and thongs. The thongs had shocked the hell out of her but Delia had said, "This is a Second Honeymoon, and even if you are going on your own, you never know what might happen." She had held up the miniscule bit of lace. "This thong may turn you around," she added solemnly. Lara looked questioningly at her. "In the nicest sense of the word, of course," Delia added with a giggle.

Personally, Lara thought her butt looked big in a thong and, besides, she doubted she would ever get used to the way it felt, but the Girlfriends had been so eager, so pleased to give her the makeover. Smartening her up. But for whom?

Bill had not called her back. And neither had Dan Holland. In a few days' time she would be leaving for Paris. She would be staying, all alone, in a lavish room at the Ritz—the same hotel she and Bill had stayed in on their honeymoon as a gift from her mother. She would dine in solitary state at a famous Michelin three-star restaurant. She would drive, alone, through the Loire, looking at châteaux, staying in the same little inns, eating in the same cafes and bistros she and Bill had eaten in together.

She would picnic alone by the lake near Limoges, where she and Bill had fed the ducks. She would stay, alone, in that little hotel near Bergerac with the Dordogne River lapping at its walls, and from where you could watch the swans floating past your bathtub. She would drive across country to Avignon, gateway to Provence. She would explore the hill villages. Alone. Stay in an old farmhouse and dine, alone, on stuffed zucchini blossoms and Cavaillon melons awash in sweet Baumes de Venise wine.

Alone, she would plunge south to the coast, to the Riviera. She would stay in the same places, sunbathe on the same beaches, linger in cafes in the blue, blue evenings. Alone.

She didn't want to go. She didn't want to go so bad that she was already reaching for the phone, prepared to cancel. Then she looked at the new clothes, remembered her own confident words to the Girlfriends.

She touched the little diamond necklace that she still wore at all times, the talisman that was supposed to bring Bill back to her. Bill was not coming back, but still, she did not take it off. Was she still hoping? Despite the way she felt about Dan Holland?

Dan had not been out of her thoughts for more than a few minutes ever since he had left her. He was in her head when she was standing in line at the supermarket. She was thinking about him when she was watching the show she had organized for seniors. And she was wondering where he was and what he was doing while she helped serve them lunch afterward.

She was thinking about Dan's strong, hard hands on her rounded body when she soaped herself in the shower and as she inspected herself, naked, in the mirror, searching for flaws he might have noticed. And finding them.

And then in bed she dreamed of his hard young body on hers, waking hot and fluid with desire, wanting him.

The San Francisco house closed in on her claustrophobically. Her hand rested on the phone. She knew Dan's number by heart. With a cry of impatience, she turned away. She threw on a pair of old jeans and a T-shirt, and called to Dex. The dog grabbed his blankie and leapt happily into the passenger seat next to her.

It was already sunset when she drove up the narrow dirt lane that led to Dan Holland's home, a small weather-bleached wooden A-frame with a neat little garden in front and the roar of the ocean behind.

Lara stared at the picket fence and the fragrant star jasmine twining enthusiastically around the porch rails, at the iceberg roses and a little pathway edged in seashells. Dan was an old-fashioned man, all right.

She sat in the car, undecided. *Leave it, Lara. Walk away. Let him go, he's too young, his brother is your son's age. There's no future in it.*

But she got out of the car and walked up the little seashell-studded path. An old ship's bell with a brass chain acted as a doorbell. She pulled it and heard it clang somewhere inside the house. Music drifted out onto the porch along with the scent of jasmine as she waited.

She tapped on the door, opened it a crack, peeked in, called "Hello? Is anyone there?"

A large room soared to the rafters, overlooked by a gallery. There were squashed-looking sofas with dark blue slipcovers and plaid throws, a beat-up wooden coffee table and a large-screen TV, big enough, she guessed, for Dan to watch sports in comfort. A pine table with six chairs, a seagrass rug, a tall white jar with branches of curly willow. Everything was immaculate. As though a woman lived here, Lara thought.

She walked hesitantly through the French windows and onto a sheltered patio overlooking the ocean. The soft sound of bossa nova guitar music from the outside speakers flowed over her. And then she saw them, framed in an archway leading to the side yard, their backs to her.

The woman was blond and slender and Dan's arm was draped affectionately over her shoulders. Even as she looked, he dropped a kiss on her blond hair, and Lara heard him laugh as the woman said something.

She turned to flee. She shouldn't be here. . . . She should never have come. . . . Now she knew she had not meant anything to him, anyway. . . . Oh, God, she had to get out of there.

"Lara!"

She was caught. Mortified, she swung around to face them.

"Welcome." Dan took her hands in his, smiling at her.

Over his shoulder, Lara's eyes met the woman's. She was strong and glowing with health, and looked as though she spent a lot of time outdoors. And she was about Lara's age.

"Let me introduce you to my aunt Jess," Dan was saying. "My mother's youngest sister, and the woman who keeps this place in shape for me."

Aunt Jess shook her hand, taking her in. "He could never manage on his own."

"Lara's a friend." Dan seemed relaxed, easy. "She has a house down the coast from Carmel."

"That's nice." Aunt Jess smiled. "It's a beautiful part of the country to live in."

"Yes. Thank you. It is." Lara was lost for words. Dan was still holding on to her hands and she knew his aunt was well aware of it.

"Well, I'll be on my way," Aunt Jess said briskly. "I've got the kids to feed. And the horses and the dogs, to say nothing of the cats and hamsters." She was laughing as she said it, as though it was all a part of some delightful routine that comprised her busy life. A life that she obviously loved, Lara thought enviously.

When she was gone Lara turned and looked at Dan. "You said it was my call. I've come to say I'm sorry. I was wrong. And besides, I don't know if I can live without you."

She hadn't meant to say that last bit — it just came out, the way truth does, tripping her up.

Dan's hands were on her shoulders, her face tilted up to his, long hair swinging free. "You haven't been out of my mind for a minute since I left you," he said quietly.

"But nothing can come of this." She needed him to know that, needed him to know she expected nothing from him. "I'm too old for you. Look at me; I'm the same age as your aunt Jess. *Look at me, Dan.* See the truth."

"I've always seen the truth." He sounded surprised that she even mentioned it.

She drank in every detail of his strong young face, the faint golden stubble on his chin, the firm, sensual mouth, the straight nose and the strong neck, the broad sweep of his brow and the deep-set eyes, such a dark, intense blue they dazzled beneath the shock of sunbleached hair. He was so beautiful, she wanted to touch him, to make love to him, to be possessed by him.

"We have only three days," she said, determined to make her position clear, "and then I'm going to Paris."

Dan held her away from him, shocked. "You've come here to tell me you're going away with your husband? And you'll allow me—*us*—the three days in between?"

Oh, God, they were fighting again; it wasn't what she had meant at all. "No, no, I'm going alone. I planned this trip so long ago. I have to go."

Then his arms were around her again. His body was warm against hers, his hair smelled fresh of the wind. She didn't know what made her say it, but suddenly she did.

"Come to Paris with me, Dan," she whispered as he bent to kiss her.

They were wrapped so close their bodies felt like one. He picked her up, carried her up the shallow stairs. His bedroom overlooked the ocean. The windows were flung wide and she could smell salt air as he lay her down on the simple pine bed. The white sheets were cool against her flesh, his golden skin hot against hers.

"I've never missed anyone the way I missed you. It was like losing a part of me," he murmured in between tiny soft bites on her mouth. "I told you that night that I thought I had found out what love is. Do you believe me?"

Reality was very far away. It was just the two of them, their bodies, the cool, the heat. "I believe."

He gripped her in a bear hug; the muscles in his arms crushed the sides of her breasts. She could feel the crisp golden hair on his body, the wonderful, wonderful weight of him.

"Oh, God, I'm so glad you came back to me," he whispered. "I thought you still loved Bill. I thought he would come back to you and all would be forgiven."

"And I thought you would marry beautiful Britt. . . ."

But then she forgot all about Britt. All she wanted was to feel his warm, sun-gold skin under her hands, to guide him into her, to feel the slow rhythm of their bodies making love together, and the gentle sea wind wafting in the windows, cooling their heat-scorched flesh.

When at last he was inside her, she knew nothing but the senses, the trembling nerve endings, the mingling sweat of love. And she wanted nothing more than to be in Dan Holland's arms.

Chapter Fourteen

He's going with her," Vannie said to Susie over the telephone the next day.

"Bill is?" Susie asked, confused.

"Of course not, you idiot. The beautiful handyman. Dan Holland."

"Jeez, she's taking him with her? To Paris?"

"No, to Des Moines!" Vannie was impatient when she was rattled. "She called this morning, said not to come and see her off at the airport, she has company."

"So what are we going to do about it?"

"I was hoping you would know." Vannie sighed. "I'm gonna call Delia. I'll get right back to you."

"*Well, well, well,*" Delia said when she spoke to her, and Vannie could tell there was a big grin on her face. She might have guessed which way Delia would vote.

"So what are we going to do about it?" she demanded worriedly.

"Do about it? Honey, we are just going to wish our girlfriend well and hope that she has a hell of a time in gay Paree, to say nothing of the rest of France." Delia was thrilled. "Surely you remember the original bleak scenario? The Second Honeymoon, the faithless Bill? Lara retracing their steps alone, cafe by cafe, hotel room by hotel room. At least now we won't have to worry about her jumping out of the window when the memories get too much for her. Remember, she always said her honeymoon was the happiest time of her life. That everything had gone like clockwork. Perfect hotels, perfect locations, perfect weather. Perfect husband."

"Well, I guess now she'll have something to compare it with."

"Now she has Dan Holland to *share* it with," Delia corrected her. "I wonder if he knows what he's getting into," she added thoughtfully. "I mean, do you suppose Lara told him about the Second Honeymoon? And does the man realize he has a lot of perfection to live up to on this trip?" She laughed. "It promises to be interesting, Vannie. The truth about the past emerging from those oh-so-perfect memories. And also the truth about the present with the oh-so-wonderful Dan. And in the end," she added softly, "will Lara finally have found the woman she was meant to be?"

Chapter Fifteen

San Francisco International Airport was crowded and noisy, full of tired, yelling children and anxious parents. Lara and Dan waited patiently at the counter for their boarding passes.

"The Paris flight is overbooked." The Delta check-in clerk peered morosely at her computer. "We've put you on a flight to Cincinnati."

Lara's horrified eyes met Dan's. Cincinnati seemed an awfully long way from Paris.

"Your flight will board in two hours, at ten forty-five, gate thirty-eight."

"But how *could* you overbook us?" Lara demanded, irate. "I've had these tickets for six months."

Dan raised a quizzical eyebrow. "Better just roll with it, babe. You're getting nowhere."

The clerk slapped stickers impatiently onto their three bags. "I have no control over ticketing, ma'am." She looked at Lara for the first time. "I assume you do want to take the Cincinnati flight."

What choice did she have? And anyhow, why was it, Lara wondered, stuffing documents back into her bag as they walked from the desk with two hours to kill, that somehow the desk clerk had made her feel grateful just to be on a flight that would take her to Cincinnati and not Paris?

"Ohio," Dan said, squeezing her arm cheerfully. "That'll be a first."

"For me too," Lara said with a regretful little sigh as he guided her toward Starbucks.

"Let's buy a newspaper, have coffee, talk about Paris, and all those other wonderful places we plan on visiting," he added.

"And let's pretend we're not still in an airport," she commented wistfully, an hour and three cups of coffee, plus one very solid blueberry muffin, later. They should have been on that Paris flight by now, holding hands, maybe drinking champagne, winging their way to her land of dreams. And memories. The sneaky thought occurred to her that they would never have dared bump Bill from the flight.

She was half asleep, her head on Dan's shoulder when the announcement came that their Cincinnati flight was delayed. At the same moment Lara remembered that because she had used Bill's air miles, they were flying business class and could have taken advantage of the comforts of the club lounge. What an idiot she was. The truth was, she had never flown alone before. In fact, she had hardly flown at all. Her travel had always been vicarious, through Bill.

Dan edged his way through the crowd toward the desk, stepping carefully around a child playing on the floor. He wanted to ask how long the delay would be and explain the urgency of their connecting flight to Paris.

He came back ten minutes later with the gloomy news that

the flight should be boarding in half an hour, which would leave them only forty minutes to catch the Paris flight.

He sank into the hard metal seat next to her and stretched his long legs. "They said no problem, this happens all the time." Lara threw him a skeptical glance and he took her hand reassuringly in his. "It'll be okay, sweetheart," he promised. "We'll get to Paris, all right."

Another half hour passed. It was noon and they were still in San Francisco International. Lara slumped deeper in the hard chair, contemplating the end of her romantic vacation, then finally, *at last*, the flight was called, and they filed aboard like grateful sheep, herded by ticket takers and flight attendants. "We're connecting with the Paris flight," Lara told the pretty blond flight attendant who came to offer her a glass of champagne. "But we're so late we're afraid we'll miss it."

"Don't worry, this always happens," the attendant told her. "You'll make it."

As the aircraft doors were closed and they taxied out onto the runway and finally took off for Cincinnati, Lara hoped she was right.

The flight grew bumpy as they approached Cincinnati. Fierce thunderstorms were plaguing the area and they were descending, tightly buckled, through a mass of dense gray cloud, lurching their way through to a faultless landing. Dan grabbed Lara's hand, already on his feet as the flight attendant made an announcement.

"For those passengers with connecting flights, please see our red-coated representatives, who will meet you at the gate." The blond attendant threw them a tired smile as they ran past her, through the jetway into the terminal.

There was only one red-jacketed assistant and he was surrounded by anxious passengers. "Paris," Lara called out, frantic. "Please . . ."

He caught her eye. "Paris has already departed."

"*Departed?*" They stared at him, horrified.

"Go to the information desk; they might be able to reroute you through London or Frankfurt."

"*Frankfurt?*" Lara's vocabulary had been reduced to single words, thankfully not yet the four-letter kind, but they were already running through the terminal in search of the information desk.

"You don't understand," she said plaintively to the indifferent assistant, who had obviously heard it all before, and too often. "I made these reservations six months ago. I should be on the flight to Paris *now*."

"Lady, I have no control over the weather," the man said coldly. "We might be able to get you out on a flight to Frankfurt tonight, at eleven forty-five. You can connect with the Lufthansa Paris flight there. It'll get you into Paris at one-fifteen tomorrow."

Lara glanced despairingly at Dan. "But that means we lose a whole day in Paris."

The clerk shrugged, indifferent. "If you want, you can wait until tomorrow evening, see if we can get you on that flight."

"What do you mean, *see* if you can get us on it?" Dan demanded.

The clerk tapped at his computer. "All flights for the next week are fully booked, sir. We would have to put you on standby. Meanwhile, we have two seats on the Frankfurt flight at eleven forty-five tonight, one in coach, one in business. Take it or leave it. And I might as well tell you, so many flights have been delayed or canceled because of the weather, there are no hotel rooms left in Cincinnati."

They stared silently at each other. It was a ten-hour flight to Frankfurt and they couldn't even travel together. "We'll take it." Dan sighed.

He put a comforting arm around Lara as they made their way up to the Crown Lounge with another six hours to kill before their flight. "I'm sorry, honey. We'll soon be in Paris, though, you'll see."

They sat in the lounge, nibbling on unwanted sandwiches, drinking yet another cup of coffee, watching lightning stabbing through the ominous sky. I'm exhausted, Lara thought, and, darn it, I'm still only in *Cincinnati.*

It was hardly a great start to a romantic adventure. She stole a glance at Dan, immersed in a baseball game on TV. This was surely God's punishment for an adulterous woman, she thought, especially one who's taking her lover on her Second Honeymoon. I should never have left Carmel, never have asked him to come with me. And besides, she just *knew* this would never have happened to Bill.

A couple of hours passed. Dan went off to check at the desk. After a lengthy conversation with the woman in charge, he returned smiling, with the first miracle of the day. They had seats together in business class.

The second miracle happened when their flight was called, and the third miracle when, despite the weather, they actually took off on time.

They smiled delightedly at each other, as they left Cincinnati behind. *"Finally,"* Lara said, relieved.

The words *at last* and *finally* are becoming regulars in our conversation, she thought. *At last*, twelve hours after we left home, we are *finally* on our way to Europe, and she pushed the nagging reminder that they should have been in Paris by now to the back of her mind. She was with Dan, and they were on their way to Paris.

Well, not quite, but at least they were en route to Europe. Even if it was only to Frankfurt.

Chapter Sixteen

Lara was wide awake the whole ten-hour flight, suspended in space and time with Dan dozing uneasily in the seat next to her. She glanced lovingly at him. He looked so *young*.

She knew she should have told him this was meant to be her Second Honeymoon, but somehow she had thought it better he didn't know, and now it was too late.

She thought about the last time she had flown to Europe, with her brand-new husband.

They had been married the day before with Lara in traditional white—a fluid satin column of a gown with a long train it had taken four little pages to manage. She remembered it had been a size six and thought regretfully there was no way she would have been able to get into it now, though her daughter, Minnie, certainly could have. Lara had worn her glossy dark hair piled up to accommodate a circlet of fragrant gardenias, and with her winged eyebrows and golden brown eyes and the sweet glow of youth, she had looked even more like Audrey Hepburn.

Bill, whom she had only ever seen in a doctor's white coat

or jeans and sweaters, had looked like a handsome, boyish stranger in a gray cutaway, his curly dark hair brushed flat and a white rosebud in his buttonhole.

Her mother had insisted on the works: three hundred guests, the local country club for the reception booked a year in advance, all the little female cousins as flower girls, plus the Girlfriends as bridesmaids. Dinner and dancing, wedding cake and champagne, photographs and speeches. By the time it was all over, she and Bill had been eager to escape to their hotel room, not because they couldn't wait to fall into each other's arms, but because they couldn't wait to fall into bed. They were exhausted from the tension of the weeks leading up to the big wedding, and then the following day Bill had slept on the flight to Paris, just the way Dan was now.

Lara had been too excited, too brimming with happiness to want to miss a minute of it. She had sipped champagne and solemnly eaten every scrap of airline food because she couldn't remember eating a thing at her own wedding and she was starving. She had watched the movie while every other person on the flight slept. She remembered it to this day. *Diary of a Mad Housewife,* it was called.

Perhaps the title had been an omen, she thought now with a wry smile. A prediction of things to come. And if the truth were known; some of those endless weeks when Bill was away and she was left alone with two small children, it had come true. When the kids jammed the faucet and flooded the bathroom and water was pouring down the stairs and she was panicked because she didn't know where the stopcock was to shut it off; and when Minnie hit Josh over the head with a toy train and there was blood everywhere and she had to rush, frantic, to the emergency room to have him stitched up; and when the rent was due and she was counting pennies and buying Hamburger Helper, eking things out. *Those* days she might have qualified for the mad-housewife role.

Then, Bill didn't earn much. He worked all hours and was often away, and her own life was dominated by her young children and the strain of holding their precarious financial life together. But, they had been happy then. Hadn't they? Yet now, recalling the stress and the overwhelming responsibilities that had rested on her young shoulders, Lara couldn't imagine how.

Her eyes lingered on Dan's sleeping face. His head drooped and she moved closer so that he might rest against her shoulder. She saw that everyone else was sleeping or watching the movie and was glad there was no one to observe her infatuation with her lover and to comment on their age difference. Then she reminded herself sternly that she shouldn't give a damn what anybody thought. *Oh, but you do,* the small, treacherous voice inside her whispered, and she sighed, ashamed. And, anyhow, was it infatuation? Or was this love? How was she supposed to tell?

As the plane flew steadily on toward Frankfurt, Lara recalled her and Bill's arrival at the Paris Ritz. She remembered how excited she had been to stay at the famous hotel where Ernest Hemingway had drunk martinis in the bar on the rue Cambon, and where he had "liberated" Paris after the war. And where Chanel had lived in a grand suite with a sweeping staircase. Chanel had shown her collections there, sitting half hidden on the stairs, smoking furiously as she spied on the reaction her new fashions were getting. Crowned heads and courtesans and movie stars had stayed at the luxurious hotel and, years later, the beautiful Princess Diana had eaten her last meal there. The Ritz was steeped in history and Lara had wallowed in its luxury like a happy seal.

Or had she?

Somewhere from the back of her mind, hidden for years, she dredged up a memory of overwhelming fatigue. She had been only twenty and had never traveled farther afield from her California home than Chicago. Bill was twenty-eight and had spent most of his life in school, or as a hospital intern. They were a couple of immature young hicks in a foreign country, unsure of themselves and unsure of each other. She was irritable, he was moody. And their room had surely been the smallest in the grand hotel, looking out onto rooftops.

"Les toits de Paris," Bill had said, flaunting his knowledge of French and for some reason irritating the hell out of her. Why did he always have to be so pompous, so factual? She had stared at him as though she were seeing an alien from another planet.

That night they slept at opposite sides of the *lit matrimonial,* the double bed that Bill had specifically requested; angry, stiff, blaming each other, their marriage still unconsummated. And Lara had wanted to go home so bad she had cried.

Then how had she remembered it all these years as perfection? In her memory were only the facts that there had been flowers in the room, a brass bed, beautiful gold brocade curtains and gilded furnishings, and that the tiny balcony had looked out onto the stars.

The next day Bill had walked her everywhere, guidebook in hand. She thought they might as well have had placards on their backs announcing they were American tourists. She had wanted to browse in every little boutique, sit and people-watch in small cafes sipping glamorous French drinks like Ricard or Pastis, which were the names she saw on those huge yellow ashtrays that graced every outdoor table. She had wanted to *feel* French, and Bill had wanted to *look at* France. That was the difference between them. But, typically, Bill had planned his schedule and he intended to get through it.

By day three, Lara's feet were killing her. She had huge blisters on every toe, and that night they were going to what was then Paris's grandest restaurant. It was to be the highlight of their stay.

She spent hours soaking her swollen feet in ice water, until she feared frostbite, trying to force them into the black suede heels that went with the smart little black dress she had bought specially. It was no good; the only shoes she could get on her feet were sneakers. She longed to stay in bed and just send for room service, but Bill wouldn't hear of it.

"Put the sneakers on, Lara," he ordered impatiently. "We're going to the Tour d'Argent."

Heads had turned her way as she limped, mortified, into the elegant restaurant on the quai de la Tournelle, and she could see people smiling, commenting behind their hands. But the maître d' was full of Gallic charm, sympathetic to her youth.

"Blisters," she explained in a whisper, agonized with embarrassment.

"Ah, madame, Paris can be very hard on the feet," he murmured, understandingly, as he showed them to a table near the window with a stupendous view of Notre Dame.

Food was different all those years ago, especially French food, still all butter and cream and smoothly rich. She had been a student until she married, living as cheaply as possible, eating pizza and burgers, and Bill was an impecunious intern, existing on whatever the hospital cafeteria offered. Now Bill ordered lavishly.

"We'll start with the foie gras," he decided without consulting her. "And with it, a glass of the sauternes."

Young Lara stared at him, all wide smudgy eyes and soft

open mouth, impressed by his sudden knowledge of French food. He even knew the right wine to order.

"Then what?" Bill glanced inquiringly at her. Pushing her long dark hair out of her eyes, she hastily studied the menu, all of it written in French.

"Monsieur should, of course, try the duck," the waiter said helpfully. "The Tour d'Argent is famous for it. After that, perhaps a green salad, a little cheese. And then dessert."

The sommelier was their next hurdle as Bill frantically scanned the wine list, hot under the collar at the prices, searching for a bottle to suit their budget.

"Monsieur and madame are perhaps on their honeymoon?" The sommelier had them pegged perfectly. "Then, of course, you must have champagne." So, of course, Bill ordered champagne, grandly refusing even to look at the cost.

They toasted each other, sipping the delicious bubbles, and Lara remembered thinking how handsome and distinguished Bill looked. Her husband, the doctor. And she could taste, even now, the silky-smooth foie gras as it slid down her throat, followed by the sumptuous sweetness of the golden sauternes.

By the time they had eaten their salad they had also finished the champagne, so Bill had thrown all caution to the wind and ordered a bottle of red wine, Château something or other. It was dark and heavy and expensive and she remembered it had to be decanted over a candle flame by the sommelier.

She could still recall the aroma of the roast duck when they brought it, intact, to their table for them to admire, with its crackling bronze skin and the little numbered tag on its leg to show that it was specially bred and only in limited quantities, like the fine wine.

Somehow that number made Lara remember that this duck

had been a live creature. She pictured it waddling around a country pond, its leg already tagged, not knowing that its fate was already sealed. She took a quick gulp of the wine, trying not to look as the waiter carved the duck. But she couldn't help but see as he put parts of it, along with the carcass, into a huge silver press and squeezed out the bloody juices. Lara swallowed hard as he presented the platter triumphantly.

She could not eat the duck; it just stuck in her throat. Bill, in his new role as Man of the World, was icy with disdain at her gaucheness. The silence between them deepened and the waiter refilled their glasses.

She had forced herself to eat the pungent cheeses, washing them down with the wine, afraid to say no. And they both devoured the chocolate confection that was dessert.

Lara spent that night on the marble floor of their bathroom at the Ritz, throwing up. Bill slept, fully clothed, drunk as a lord and snoring loudly, in the *lit matrimonial.*

How Lara had hated him that night, miserable and alone in that chilly bathroom. Her husband, *the doctor,* didn't even know she was ill. She wished she had never married him. Throwing up again, she wished, tearfully, she were dead.

The next morning, Bill was up bright and early. Lara was lying in bed feeling like hell.

"Car's waiting, honey," he called cheerfully from the shower. "Better get your act together; we're off to the Loire today to take a look at some of those châteaux."

Groaning, Lara heaved herself out of bed, still jet-lagged, still sick, her head still spinning from all that wine. If she knew Bill, they would have to personally inspect every inch of those damned châteaux. "Can't we just stay here another day? Just you and me? Send down for coffee, take it easy?"

He stuck his head around the bathroom door, toweling his wet hair. "Are you crazy, Lara? We're in France. There's no time to take it easy. And who needs room service anyhow?"

I do, she thought miserably, inspecting her blistered toes and thinking that at least she would get to sit down for a few hours in the car. She was to be the navigator and Bill would do the driving. And he was a fast and impatient driver.

It was hell just getting out of Paris; the highways were clogged with traffic. The map was in French, the names confusing, and she lost their way six times that morning, following the *Toutes Directions* signs that always seemed to lead them nowhere. Their destination was Tours but they ended up somewhere near Le Mans without having seen a single château. Bill was furious and Lara sulked, insisting that it wasn't her fault and how could he be this mean to her. And instead of just living with it and finding a little hotel and spending time in the place they were in, Bill insisted on sticking with his schedule and driving all the way back to Tours.

Darkness had fallen, and naturally they got lost again and ended up almost back where they came from. The night had been saved by a stay at Laurent, a family-owned hotel in Loué near Le Mans that they practically fell over. It was pretty and bourgeois and it had a restaurant. They were starving by then and the food had been simple in that wonderful French way; the *Bresse* chicken mouth-watering, the *tarte tatin* sublime, and the feather bed welcoming to a pair of exhausted honeymooners.

The truth was, Lara now realized, amazed, she and Bill had fought all the time in Paris. That she had got drunk, that the staff at the hotel were snooty to a couple of immature young hicks from America, and that mostly they had been too exhausted to make love.

Then how had she remembered Paris as the perfect happy idyll all these years? She shook her head, bewildered at the tricks the mind can play, when you wanted it to.

At least, this time around, she thought, it can't get any worse.

Chapter Seventeen

Dan opened his eyes. He turned his head and studied Lara's profile, taut as a cameo in the dimmed interior of the plane. She was lost in her thoughts and there was such an air of sadness about her it made him wonder if he had done the right thing, going to France with her. Was she already regretting it? Was she embarrassed by their age difference? Or was she merely upset over the endless delays and blaming herself? If he knew her well enough, and he believed by now he did, he would bet on a mixture of all three.

He took her chin in his hand, turned her face toward him. "Love," he told her solemnly, "can survive anything that Delta airlines can hand out to it."

Lara laughed, snapping suddenly out of her somber mood, and he grabbed her firmly in his arms and planted a kiss on her soft mouth. "It's been too long since I did that." He smoothed his palm across her cheek, tracing the outline of her lips with a finger.

The overhead lights snapped on and they moved reluctantly apart.

"Ladies and gentlemen," the flight attendant intoned in that special automaton airline voice, "we shall shortly be serving breakfast, prior to landing at Frankfurt."

Stiff with fatigue Lara said, "I don't think I could handle one more cup of coffee."

"Or even one more dry-as-dust bread roll . . ."

"To say nothing of another ice cream sundae." She remembered, guiltily, that she had consumed two: one on the flight to Cincinnati and one on this flight, and she prayed they would not offer her a third on the Paris flight because somehow, with the stress, all her willpower had disappeared. She was a prisoner to the airlines, a slave who obediently ate what they gave her despite the calories, or even whether she liked it. At least it was something to do. Besides, the wine had given her a headache.

Breakfast was served and rapidly cleared away. They were straightening their seat backs, making sure they were buckled in, and then they were landing in Frankfurt.

"For those passengers with connecting flights, a member of our staff, identified by his red jacket, will be waiting at the gate to assist you. Thank you for flying with Delta." The flight attendant sounded weary.

Lara glanced at her watch; it was now twenty-two hours since they had left San Francisco and they were still only in Frankfurt. She thought wistfully she should have been in that wonderful room in the Ritz by now.

There was no red-coated staff member to assist them in the terminal. In fact, there was no one. Frankfurt airport was as deserted as a school cafeteria after lunch, and as sterile-clean and shiny as an operating room.

Dan took out the piece of paper the airline clerk had given him in Cincinnati with the number of the Lufthansa flight to Paris. He checked it against the Departures monitor. "We've got fifteen minutes," he said, grabbing Lara's hand again. They ran past endless window displays of sleek Escada dresses and leather jackets and Longchamps bags and empty cafes, and of course their gate was at the opposite end of the terminal. They made it with only minutes to spare.

The blond woman in the red glasses at the Lufthansa desk glanced disapprovingly at them, as though there were no excuse for them being this late. Still catching his breath, Dan handed her the piece of paper with their flight reservations. She studied it, frowning, clicking away on her computer keyboard while Lara shifted anxiously from foot to foot. They would be closing the aircraft doors if she didn't hurry up.

The clerk handed the paper back. "You are not booked on this flight," she said.

To her surprise, Lara giggled. It was the final straw. Dan grinned at her, then they both began to laugh. The clerk stared, astonished at them, as Lara leaned against the desk, weak with laughter and fatigue. "It's too much," she hiccuped. *Just too much.*

"Look," Dan explained as reasonably as he could manage. "We've had a long flight—*two* long flights. We should have been in Paris *yesterday.* Can't you get us on to this flight?" He gave the blonde his biggest smile. "Please," he said. "I'd really appreciate it."

She permitted him a reluctant smile, then turned back to her computer. "You might just be lucky. There seem to be a couple of no-shows." She glanced at her watch. "It's too late for them now," she admitted, briskly issuing boarding passes.

They hurried onto the plane and slumped into their seats, exhausted. The doors were slammed, the engines roared. *"Finally,"* Lara sighed.

"At last." Dan grinned. "We're on our way."

Lara smiled at him, elated. She felt like Eve about to enter the Garden. And she just knew that Paris would be their Eden.

Chapter Eighteen

Was it Lara's imagination, or was there a different feel about the arrivals hall at Charles de Gaulle? For a start there was the smell of strong cigarettes in the air and a fluid, elegant bustle about the way the people walked and the way little urban dogs peeked at her from behind legs and baggage. And there was that wonderful language that made even the commonplace *"Bonjour, madame"* sound as though it were being sung.

They were at carousel 22, waiting for their baggage. Lara slid her arm through Dan's. "Hey," she whispered, "we're in Paris."

He grinned down at her. "I never would have known."

She glanced at her watch. "A mere twenty-five hours ago, we were in California. We could have been in Australia by now."

"I'd rather be in Paris. With you," he added.

The carousel began to move. Bags bounced out of the opening, drifting past them, quickly claimed by other passengers. Lara could easily identify her black bags because she had put bright yellow tags on them, and Dan's was a dark green duffel.

She frowned anxiously at the few that were on their third or fourth trip around the carousel. A few minutes later the carousel was switched off.

"Oh, God, *I don't believe it,*" she wailed as it dawned on her that she was in Paris but now she had nothing to wear.

"It'll be okay, honey, I'll take care of it," Dan said reassuringly. "Sit right here; don't get upset and don't move."

Lara watched as he strode to the distant information desk, all the way at the other end of the enormous baggage hall. She knew in her gut it was hopeless. Their luggage might be anywhere. San Francisco, Cincinnati, Frankfurt. Or even in China with Bill.

"But you don't understand," Dan was saying to the Air France attendant at the lost-luggage desk. "We have no clothes. Nothing."

She looked pityingly at the handsome young American as she handed him a blue zippered bag, similar to the ones airlines give passengers on long flights, but larger. "Take this," she said with a supportive smile. "It will have everything you need." And when Dan said he doubted it, she gazed into his eyes and said, "Trust me, m'sieur. And by the way, *normalement* the Lufthansa flights come in at Terminal C. You might look for your luggage there."

Dan hurried back to tell Lara, who was wilting badly by now, then he dashed off again in search of Terminal C, leaving her all alone in the cavernous baggage hall.

Lara watched him disappear around a distant corner, thinking wistfully about her sexy new lingerie and the pretty new dress, and of how good the bed at the Ritz was going to feel when they finally got there. They had been traveling almost twenty-six hours and she'd had no sleep. She felt dizzy, light-headed, exhausted. Half dozing, she waited for Dan to get back.

Terminal C seemed like about a mile away to Dan and he figured this must be French-style "close by." When he finally found it, he was directed to a pile of luggage in a corner. None of it was theirs. He grabbed a passing airline employee and tried to describe his dilemma. Though he spoke no French, the man seemed to understand. Try Terminal D, he advised. But at Terminal D, *"Non, non, m'sieur,"* he was told. "Perhaps Terminal A."

At Terminal A, Dan stopped and took stock of the situation. Time was passing. The luggage was gone. And he had left Lara, waiting, all alone. He had to get back to her. He turned to retrace his footsteps, but everywhere looked the same: the same brightly lit hallways, with the same advertisements, the same endless corridors leading to nowhere. He couldn't remember which way he had come. And Lara was just sitting there, waiting for him, expecting him to work miracles with their lost luggage. . . .

He grabbed another airline employee, asked him which terminal the Frankfurt flight came in at, was told again Terminal C. He clapped a frustrated hand to his head, *"No,"* he explained again in slow, careful English, "it was *not* Terminal C. It was the other, *large* terminal. We were at carousel twenty-two."

The man shrugged. "But there is no carousel twenty-two, m'sieur. You are mistaken. Try the information desk."

There was a long line at the information desk. For a moment, Dan thought of pushing his way to the front, explaining the urgency of his mission, that he had lost Lara, that she was waiting for him, that she was all alone. That they had been traveling for twenty-seven hours, he'd been gone over an hour by now. . . .

He was next. He waited politely for the previous customer to move away, then went to step up to the counter. He felt an elbow in his ribs as someone pushed ahead of him. He swung around, crazy with anger and worry, ready to kill. It was a nun. *A nun in a gray habit had jumped in line, elbowed him out of the way. And he had felt like killing her.* God forgive me, he thought, horrified, giving the nun a forgiving smile.

"M'sieur," the information clerk told him, "I don't know what you are talking about. There is no carousel twenty-two. Here are all the terminals, A, B, C, D. You must be mistaken."

Dan slammed his clenched fists on the counter and the clerk cowered back, dismayed. "How can I be mistaken," he roared. "My woman is sitting there, waiting for me at carousel twenty-two. The Lufthansa flight arrived there. They lost our baggage. *There were twenty-two carousels.* . . . "

The clerk stared worriedly at the crazy man. "Why don't you page madame," he suggested faintly.

Of course. Why hadn't *he* thought of that? Fatigue must have taken away his brain function. But he soon discovered there was no multiple paging system; each terminal had its own. He ran to each of the terminals in turn, paging her. Was he *really* crazy? Had he *imagined* carousel 22? His heart was pounding and he was sweating. *He had lost Lara.* God, what a fool he was. What must Lara be thinking? That he had deserted her, that he had gotten lost—the homeboy abroad—his first time in Paris. He knew the famous doctor husband would not have done this, he would never have misplaced his wife at Charles de Gaulle Airport, he would have swept Lara into a waiting limo, swept her off to a suite at the Ritz. . . .

He spotted the employee he had first asked for directions, grabbed him by the lapels. *"Don't tell me again I'm crazy,"* he said through gritted teeth. "There *is* another terminal. I *know* the Lufthansa flight landed there. There were *twenty-two* carousels. My woman is there, waiting for me. . . ."

The man rolled up his eyes, shrugged, pushed his cap to the back of his head. "But, m'sieur, you must mean the *new* terminal. Why didn't you say so?" He gave that little Gallic shrug, as though it were obvious. "But of course," he said, "nobody goes there."

Dan let go of the man, carefully smoothing his lapels, apologizing for his anger. Then he set off at a run for Terminal F.

He's lost, Lara thought, panicked. I should never have let him just go off like that. Men always get lost. This isn't LAX or San Francisco, he doesn't speak the language, no one will understand him.

She looked at her watch again. A hour and a half had gone by. She was rooted to her seat. She couldn't get up and look for him, she had to stay here. One of them had to be where they started out from, otherwise they would never find each other. . . . *Never find each other . . .*

Dan saw her, still sitting on the steel bench, stiff with anxiety. She heard his running footsteps, leapt to her feet, flung herself into his outstretched arms with a little cry of relief. He clutched her to him. "Oh, God, I'm just so glad I found you. I'm so *sorry*, so *truly sorry,* I thought I was going crazy, they told me there was no carousel twenty-two, I thought I'd never find you again. . . ."

"I knew you were lost." She was clasped so tight against his chest she could feel his heart thudding.

"All I could think about was you sitting here, waiting. . . ."

She touched his hand, found it trembling. "It's all right."

"There was a nun, she pushed in front of me at the information desk, I wanted to kill her."

Lara grinned. "Good thing you didn't. I hear French jail is not too comfortable."

"Will you ever forgive me?" He wrapped her closer.

"There's nothing to forgive."

"Oh, and by the way," he murmured through kisses, "nobody knows where our luggage is."

Lara shrugged, that same little French shrug everyone seemed to have in Paris. "It doesn't matter," she said again. "We've found each other."

Chapter Nineteen

Outside the terminal, they stumbled gratefully into a taxi. *"Le Ritz, s'il vous plaît,"* Lara told the driver, then sank wearily back. She couldn't believe they were really here. "There's so much to see," she said as they lurched through the snarled traffic.

"How about those famous fountains?" Dan asked.

"The fountains?" She was puzzled, was he mixing Paris up with Rome?

And then they were crossing a bridge and threading their way through the streets of the magical city.

Paris. Shafts of sunlight on imposing gray buildings; swooping mansard roofs peaked with dormer windows; elegant residences with tall green shutters; shade trees on the Champs Élysées and round globe lamps on old stone bridges; traffic and noise. Strollers on the boulevards; chic women with good legs accompanied always, it seemed, by well-behaved little dogs; street markets with a pungent, colorful abundance of fresh produce; snatches of music from a window, with lace curtains protecting the inhabitants of the room from prying eyes. Gilded statues at practically every corner; the creamy stone of the Louvre; the gilt-tipped iron railings and the children in straw hats and navy smocks, walking in a line behind a nun, like a drawing out of *Madeline*. The villageyness of the 6th and 7th Arrondissements; the narrow cobbled streets and hidden courtyards behind massive wooden gates; the aromas of good food and soft perfumes. Sidewalk cafes with little round tables and cane chairs where idlers lounged, sipping a café grand crème or tall pale drinks, as though they had all the time in the world. Dark little boutiques and elegant restaurants; the parks and fountains and, always, the magical artery of the Seine, flowing like lifeblood, because Paris was a city where life was lived out on the streets.

Paris. The memories came back to Lara, thick and heavy, like fresh cream in their sweetness. It was as though her heart had been living here all these years, while that other, less meaningful part of her remained in California.

Their taxi pulled up in front of the great hotel and Lara heaved a deep, heartfelt sigh as the doorman hurried toward them. It was like coming home. Heads turned to look as they trailed, crumpled and luggageless through the elegant red-carpeted lobby, past the long aisle of vitrines — the windows displaying the wares of exclusive jewelers and expensive boutiques. But by now she was too tired to care what people thought about her appearance. Or how much younger Dan was. She was looking forward to the sumptuous sanctity of their room, and the hot bath that would somehow revive her travel-stained soul.

"M'sieur, madame?" The desk clerk was irreproachable in a dark suit and a pleasant smile.

"We have a reservation. Mrs. Lewis, from San Francisco."

Lara's smile lit up her face. She glanced around the elegant lobby while the desk clerk looked at his list. He muttered something to his colleague then said, "Excuse me one moment, madame, while I check the computer."

Lara squeezed Dan's hand. "Isn't this wonderful?" she whispered.

"Looks great," he said, but she noticed he wasn't smiling, and guessed it was because he knew how expensive this must be. He had been adamant that he would pay his own way. It was a matter of self-respect, she understood that, and she had finally agreed, except for the grand hotels like this, which she knew he could not afford.

The clerk returned looking disturbed. "I'm sorry, Madame Lewis, but your reservation was for the day before yesterday. When you did not arrive, the room was assigned to another guest."

"The day before yesterday?" Lara looked puzzled. "But how could that be? It says the seventeenth right here on my confirmation fax."

"Today is the nineteenth, madame."

Lara remembered the lost day. "We missed our flight," she explained, adding vaguely, "the weather." And then she realized the travel agent had also forgotten the nine-hour time difference and booked the room for the same date they had left California, instead of the following day.

"I understand, but we weren't informed of your change of plans. I'm so sorry, these things usually do not happen at the Ritz, Madame."

He was so upset Lara felt sorry for him. "That's all right," she said, "we'll just take some other room."

He lifted his shoulder in that shrug that spoke volumes. "*Je suis desolé, madame,* but it is Fashion Week. Every hotel in Paris in fully booked. I already had my assistant call around the other hotels for you," he lifted his shoulder again, looking sad, "but there is nothing."

Dan put a comforting arm around her slumped shoulders. "That's okay. We'll find somewhere," he said. "Come on, Lara, don't worry about it."

Back out on the street they stared at each other, not knowing what to do, then Dan said, "Since we're homeless in Paris, I suggest a glass of champagne."

Lara's jet-lagged spirits suddenly soared and her grin was almost carefree as she linked her arm in his again and they strolled around the corner to the rue Cambon and the famous Ritz bar.

The cozy paneled bar was full of sober-suited businessmen with a sprinkling of elegantly dressed women. Aware of how disheveled they looked, Lara thought how embarrassed "Bill's wife" would have been. But somehow this new Lara was past caring. They were in Paris. And they were at the Ritz.

"Hemingway sat here," she told Dan, elated, as they nibbled on homemade chips. "Probably in the very seat on which you are now sitting."

"I'm honored." Dan lifted an inquiring eyebrow. "Who sat on your chair?"

"Oh, probably Chanel. Maybe Eisenhower or Jack Kennedy, or poor Princess Diana."

"So we're in good company."

Lara laughed; she felt ridiculously happy even though there was no room at the inn, and possibly none in all of Paris. She sipped her champagne lazily, as if they had all the time in the world to decide. "What shall we do?"

"There's always hotels near the railroad stations," he said. "I'll bet the fashion crowd won't be staying there."

They finished their drinks in a leisurely manner, then Dan paid the astronomical bill of fifty dollars, and they took another cab ride to the area of the Gare du Nord.

"*Arrêttez ici, m'sieur, s'il vous plaît.*" Lara stumbled through the few words of French and the cabdriver stopped obediently outside a tall, shabby gray building with a green neon sign that said *Hotel Zorro, Chambres à Louer.*

It was a cheap commercial hotel of the type found near railway stations anywhere in the world. A small thin man with slicked-back greasy hair glanced up from his copy of *France Soir* as they entered. His black sweater had a hole in it and ashes spilled from the stub of cigarette glued to his bottom lip.

He answered Lara's "*Avez-vous une chambre pour ce soir, m'sieur*" with a grudging nod and shoved a key attached to an enormous metal tag across the gray plastic counter. He muttered a price, then seeing her look of confusion wrote it on a scrap of paper.

"Oh, okay." She took the key and started toward the tiny cage of an elevator.

"*Madame!*" Finally, he spoke. He held out his hand, rubbing his fingers together impatiently. "*En avance, madame.*"

Dan got the international message of the rubbed-together fingers and handed over the necessary francs.

Crushed together in the tiny metal-cage elevator, they creaked slowly upward. Lara's eyes met Dan's apprehensively as the gates opened onto a windowless corridor with a worn red-patterned carpet and twin rows of dingy brown-painted doors. The light was on an all-too-quick timer; it clicked off once, and they had to go back, click it again, and then make a run for it in order to find their room before it switched off.

Room 37 was not a thing of beauty. It was maybe eight-by-ten, with grayish lace curtains at the grimy window, a narrow sagging bed, and a too-bright overhead light. A plastic shower cubicle jutted so close you could have jumped straight from the bed into the shower. Another flimsy cubicle contained the toilet and washbasin. This was definitely not Eden.

Horrified, Lara looked around, debating whether to hurl herself onto the bed in floods of tears or simply get the next flight home. Watching her, Dan wished he could think of something to say that would help.

Lara checked her watch. It was 8:30 P.M. Paris time. She had already forgotten what time it was in California except it was probably yesterday, though, wait a minute, wasn't there a nine-hour difference? She gave up the calculation. All she knew was it was either time to sleep, the endless dropping-off-the-edge-of-the-world sleep of the truly exhausted, or it was time for action. She looked at Dan. He held out his arms and she walked into them.

"We happen to have reservations at this sweet little place I've heard of," she said between kisses, "where the wine is superb and, even more wonderful, there is no markup. And the food is delicious."

"But we have no clean underwear," Dan said, grinning. "And you know what your mom always told you."

Lara licked his mouth hungrily. "There's only one answer to that, Dan Holland," she said, hearing him laugh as she pulled herself from his arms and threw off the clothes she had been wearing for what seemed like forever, then headed into the miniscule plastic shower.

Dan suddenly remembered the little blue-zippered Air France bag. "Wait a minute. That woman told me there was everything I would need in here."

He pulled out a large white T-shirt with *Air France* inscribed across the left breast; then toothpaste and a toothbrush that Lara fell upon with glad cries; a packet of tissues, cotton swabs, soap. He looked at the last item in the bag, then up at her. He grinned. "She was absolutely right!" He held up a condom. "Only the French would think of it."

Lara burst into peals of laughter. "Magnum—*Le plus grand. EXTRA. How* did she know what size? Did they measure your shoulders or something?" He snatched her to him again and they fell onto the bed, laughing so hard they were shaking. Life was sweet in Paris, after all.

Forty minutes and thirty sleepless hours after they had left California, they were sitting opposite each other in the tiny stone-walled Les Bouchons de François Clerk, on the rue Hotel Colbert, a narrow cobblestoned street on the opposite side of the river from Notre Dame.

Looking around, Lara thought Les Bouchons was everything a Paris restaurant should be—small and intimate and cozy—and the other diners seemed not even to notice their scruffy appearance, let alone care. It was because they were all so into their own worlds, she thought: savoring the food, tasting the wine, intent upon their conversations, or else it was just French politeness.

Soon the waiter, in a big white apron, was pouring Roederer Cristal into tall flutes. He brought a basket of breads straight from the oven that to two veterans of airline food smelled like heaven.

Remembering she had no underwear, Lara wriggled, not sure

whether she was comfortable or uncomfortable. She wondered whether no bra and pants could become a way of life.

"I would never have dared go out without underwear at home," she confided. "In fact, I've *never* done this before, at least, not since I was three years old and fell into the lake at the Sleeping Beauty ride at Disneyland, and then it didn't seem to matter. And you know what, now I'm all grown up and should know better, it still doesn't matter."

Dan stroked her tired, pretty face, their eyes linked in that deep, intimate contact that only lovers have, and raised his glass to her. "Am I really here, with you?" he murmured. "Am I dreaming? Or is this Paris?"

"It's Paris," she said, still locked into his gaze. "Paris is everyone's dream."

As they sipped their champagne, still holding hands, Lara thought she felt like a different woman.

Dan said it was kind of a letdown, when they returned to their soulless room near the station, and Lara said it felt like a place where you paid by the hour and that she felt like a hooker, and Dan said good and kissed her in the hideous little elevator, just to make sure she was still awake, and besides, he said, he lusted after her. Then he pushed the timer on the light switch and they ran, giggling, down the shabby corridor to their room, just making it before the light clicked off again.

She leaned back against the closed door, watching him, half smiling. He looked so good to her, she could have eaten him for dessert.

They heard a trickling noise from above. They looked at the ceiling, then, questioningly, back at each other. It dawned on them that someone was using the bathroom upstairs.

"Must be the famous fountains of Paris," Dan whispered, and they collapsed onto the bed, yelling with laughter until the man upstairs thumped on the floor for them to shut up.

They were still laughing as he began to make love to her. There was no way to stifle the noise of their passion but it seemed the French did not mind that.

They did not move out of that narrow sagging bed until the next afternoon, sleeping the sleep of the exhausted, making love like there was no tomorrow. And who knew, Lara thought sleepily, maybe in Paris there wasn't.

Chapter Twenty

The next afternoon there was still no word on their luggage, though Delta thought maybe it was still in Cincinnati, so they made their way to the Boulevard St. Germain, heading for Monoprix, an inexpensive all-purpose store on the rue de Rennes, where they purchased underwear alongside women buying cheeses and detergent, bathing suits and bin liners.

At least I've got underpants, Lara thought, relieved, though she had in fact quite gotten used to doing without. And then they came across a wonderful little lingerie boutique. She smiled, thinking of Delia as she went in. She would buy something really gorgeous.

The shop was tiny and elegant, draped with the lacy teddies of which the French seemed particularly fond. Thongs and demi-bras were shown in illustrations on childlike waifs who, Lara thought doubtfully, bore no resemblance to her rounded self.

The gauntly elegant sales assistant swept her with a cold glance, taking in her decidedly down-market appearance. *"Bonjour, madame,"* she said distantly.

"Bonjour, madame," Lara replied. "I need some bras." She spoke slowly in case the woman only understood French.

The saleswoman's eyes fastened disapprovingly on Lara's lavish breasts. "But what size, madame?"

Lara knew the French worked in centimeters but couldn't remember the correct size. She told her the American size instead. "Thirty-eight." The woman's eyes widened in astonishment. "And a C cup," Lara admitted.

The saleswoman sucked in her breath, her disdainful brows rose, she *tskd-tskd,* and shook her head. *"Oh, mais non, madame."* Her mouth pursed disapprovingly. *"Non! Pas ici.* No. *Not here."*

Lara laughed. This was just unreal, so silly, so absolutely Parisian.

"Imagine, being turned down by a bra shop," she said to Dan out on the street again, still laughing.

Later she got luckier and discovered a sale at Max Studio on the rue des Saints Pères, where she thankfully grabbed up a linen-knit twinset in pale cream, a pair of linen pants, some plain T-shirts and camisoles. Now that she had discovered sales were on, she dragged Dan along Boulevard St. Germain, looking for *Soldes* signs. She stopped dead in her tracks outside Sonia Rykiel's elegant boutique, staring, smitten, at a soft silk-georgette dress, cream splashed with deep pink flowers. It was sleeveless, with small ruffles drifting over the shoulders, a low sweetheart neckline, and a skirt that floated like a cloud. It was, Lara thought with a longing sigh, the epitome of summer in Paris. She *had* to have it, and she knew exactly when she was going to wear it. Tonight, at the famous restaurant where she had made reservations many months ago, when she had still been coming to Paris with Bill. Surprised, she realized she was enjoying herself so much, she had temporarily forgotten about Bill.

Who cares about that treacherous bastard, she thought with that little Parisian shrug, he's certainly not thinking about me. And she strode into the store, emerging, beaming, fifteen minutes later with that dress.

Then they went in search of clothes for Dan. Lara insisted on buying him a beautiful deep-blue shirt that she said matched his eyes, and a yellow and blue tie that she picked out herself, though Dan swore he never would wear one, and he chose a nice unconstructed black linen jacket, and also a pair of soft loafers in a smart shop called Westons, which Lara told him she had heard from Delia was the chicest thing in men's footwear in France.

Two hours later, they flung themselves down at a sidewalk table at the Café Les Deux Magots, their packages piled next to them, sipping café grand crème and nibbling on croissants. Saving themselves, Lara said, for the memorable feast to come that night.

Chapter Twenty-one

That evening, as they dressed for dinner in their ugly, cramped room, Lara inspected the new her in the tiny spotted mirror. The floaty dress clung alarmingly to her curves and she smoothed it doubtfully over her hips, thinking it hadn't looked quite so clingy in the shop and wondering if pink was really okay for a woman her age. The sweetheart neckline revealed the upper curves of her breasts and the fluid skirt showed quite a lot of her legs. Underneath she wore a little lace bra from Monoprix that did wonders for her, and a lace thong that left her feeling naked, which, she figured, she almost was. Plus the new four-inch heels that made her look taller and elegant, if a little wobbly.

She bent her knees, trying to catch the full effect in the murky mirror propped on the chipped brown dresser. Dan's face appeared over her shoulder. He was adjusting the tie she had bought for him, and she thought, guiltily, how Melissa had bought a tie for Bill. Was this a mistress pattern? she wondered.

"Only for you would I wear a tie," Dan said, "and there's no need to look in the mirror," he added, dropping a kiss on top of her head as she stabbed tiny pearl and diamond earrings through her lobes and patted her sleeked-back hair one more time. "You look wonderful."

Lara twirled for him, still uncertain about this new self, and he shook his head, bemused. "Is this really the woman I came in with?"

Laughing, Lara kissed him, straightening his new silk tie, admiring him. "See how handsome you are?" she said.

He grinned back at her. "We're so darn chic I'm not sure Paris is ready for us," he said, and they ran hand in hand down the gloomy corridor before the light could click off. They were still laughing as they hailed a taxi and took off for what Lara knew would be a highlight of their stay in Paris.

Lara hadn't been able to face the Tour d'Argent, where she had gone with Bill, and instead had made reservations at Lucas Carton, a Michelin three-star restaurant on the Place Madeleine in the 8th Arrondissement. She glanced around, pleased with her choice. The turn-of-the-century restaurant was beautiful, with mellow belle epoque wood paneling and tall mirrors. Long banquettes were lined up against paneled partitions topped with antique etched glass, and giant urns held trailing greenery.

A cluster of stony-faced, white-aproned young waiters hovered near the door as an unsmiling maître d' checked their reservations. After an assessing glance, he showed them to a remote table near the kitchen. Lara glanced uneasily at Dan. She knew Bill would have complained about the bad table but Dan didn't seem to have noticed.

The unsmiling young waiters surrounded them, wafting

enormous white linen napkins onto their laps. Lara ordered a bottle of Veuve Cliquot La Grand Dame from the sommelier, the same wonderful and expensive champagne Bill had ordered at the Tour d'Argent, though of course Dan did not know that.

She inspected him from under her lashes, hoping she had done the right thing, bringing him to this smart, stuffy restaurant. She wasn't sure, though; this was so much more Bill than Dan. Sighing, she put on the little gold-rimmed glasses that she had been forced to wear ever since she turned forty if she wanted to read anything other than giant type, and turned her attention to the menu.

Dan was thinking how cute she looked in the little glasses. He caught a snatch of her perfume as she looked up. She smiled questioningly at him and he took her hand across the table. "I was just remembering you," he said.

"Surely you can't have forgotten me already?" She smiled with the new confidence of a woman who knows she is loved.

His eyes held hers. "No, ma'am, Ms. Lewis. I could not."

Lara felt that fluid heat in her body, and she was suddenly breathless from wanting him. Their linked hands transmitted tiny electric pulses that turned her knees to jelly. It was as if they were alone in the crowded restaurant, only the two of them in all of Paris. . . . The sommelier came back and reluctantly they let go of each other. He filled a glass and offered it to Dan.

Dan tasted the champagne, his eyes still linked with Lara's. "Delicious," he said. And neither he nor the sommelier had any doubt that he meant the woman and not the wine.

The waiter handed them menus, enormous stiff cards full of items like a pan roast of frogs legs, and thyme-scented potatoes with cuttlefish ravioli. Unable to find anything familiar, Dan gave up and asked Lara to choose for both of them.

He looked around the beautiful dining room, uncomfortably aware of the hushed voices and serious faces of the other diners. No one seemed to be having a good time and the smart restaurant felt like a temple dedicated to the art of eating. He tugged at his tie, feeling out of his league, out of place, too American. Then he dropped his menu and knocked over his glass.

He stared embarrassed at the spreading puddle of champagne and the shards of crystal on the immaculate white cloth. "Sorry," he muttered as the disdainful waiters clustered around. He knew he should never have come here; this was Lara's husband's style, not his. *Bill* would never have knocked over his champagne glass. *Bill* belonged here. It was a place Lara would have come with Bill.

Ignoring his apologies, the silent waiters brushed away the broken glass, mopping and blotting, draping fresh napkins over the damp spot, bringing a new glass, pouring more champagne.

"It's all right, Dan, it doesn't matter," Lara said, suddenly uneasy. His mouth was set in a firm line and there was a steely glint in his eyes. She knew he was asking himself why she had brought him to such a grand place, a place that was so unlike them. He must think she was showing off to him, Dan the blue-collar guy and she, Bill's wife, the sophisticated woman of the world. She thought sadly she hadn't meant it that way at all.

Sighing, she forced her attention back to the menu, knowing the food just was not Dan. It seemed easier to order soup to start; then, because it sounded so different, for the main course she chose veal sweetbreads with crayfish and caramelized popcorn.

They waited in silence for their food to arrive. Lara looked at the other diners and Dan frowned down at his untouched champagne.

When their food did come, the portions were delicate, the presentation exquisite, and it was absolutely not Dan's style. He did not touch the sweetbreads.

The silence between them was now so deep Lara thought it made the hushed voices of the other diners sound positively gay. Oh, God, she thought, this is a rerun of the Tour d'Argent debacle with Bill. Only now the roles are reversed. Now *I* have become *Bill*!

She stared miserably at the dessert, a study in creamy minimalist decadence. Dan studied the pastry on his plate, then looked her coldly in the eyes. "I want you to know that this is the last time I ever order a fifty-dollar napoleon," he said. Then he signaled the waiter for the bill. When it came, he snatched it from her. It was a stunning six hundred dollars. He paid with his green Amex.

Not knowing what to do, Lara let him.

Chapter Twenty-two

They were outside the restaurant waiting for a taxi. Lara's heart was stuck somewhere in her throat. Out of the corner of her eye, she could see Dan's back turned indifferently away from her. His hands were stuffed into the pockets of the khakis that still bore the mark of the spilled champagne, and he jingled coins aimlessly. Oh, God, she thought, this is already a failure. Paris is over before it's begun.

The thought of the dingy hotel room and the two of them not speaking was unbearable, and on an impulse Lara told the cabdriver to take them to the Café Flore in St. Germain. She sat in her own corner of the cab and Dan sat in his. Neither said a word.

The Left Bank streets were thronged, the cafes bursting at the seams. By a stroke of luck Lara snagged a sidewalk table from a departing couple and sank thankfully into the little cane chair. Dan sat opposite. Their eyes met. His were like blue flint.

She gazed somberly back at him, faced with the horrible truth that she could never tell. She could never confess that she had taken him to the grand Michelin-starred restaurant to relive that honeymoon night with Bill. "I'm sorry," she said quietly. "I know you hated it and I don't blame you."

"That's okay."

The busy waiter wiped off the little marble table then placed a saucer in the center for *l'addition*.

Knowing that Dan must be hungry, Lara asked for a *croque monsieur* and *deux fines*.

When the toasted ham and cheese sandwich and glasses of brandy finally arrived, Dan stared at them; then glanced up at her, and that slow grin that had so charmed her in the beginning spread across his handsome face.

"*Now* we're in Paris," he said. "My kind of town."

Lara let out her held breath in a sigh of relief, wondering if there was something to be said for the old, familiar marriage routine after all. Having a lover was like learning a new game: all the rules were different. *She* had to become different.

Dan devoured his sandwich, then ordered a second one. Cautiously happy again, he held her hand, sipping brandy, watching jugglers and fire-eaters performing on the sidewalk and a little terrier turning somersaults.

Later, with the grand-restaurant debacle hopefully behind them, they wandered the streets of the Left Bank. Lara stopped to admire the beautiful shoes in Maud Frizon on the rue des Saints Pères, then she saw a gauzy draped dress in Angelo Tarlazzi that she knew would be perfect for her daughter, Minnie, and then she fell in love with the entire shop window of beautiful lingerie in tiny Sabbia Rosa, especially a silk and lace teddy in a color like whitewashed peaches that looked as though it weighed less than an ounce. She told Dan, enviously, that she had never owned lingerie like that, and that it would be too expensive, and, anyhow, they would never have her size, but she admired it for a long time.

They browsed the chic boutiques on rue Cherche-Midi, and lingered over the window of Debauve & Gallais on the rue Napoléon, tempted by the luscious-looking chocolates, then drifted happily along the rue Jacob with its antique shops and little cafes and small, funky hotels.

Dan stopped outside the Hôtel d'Angleterre, staring through the plate-glass doors at the tough, gray-haired dragon lady in charge of the front desk. He glanced meaningfully at Lara. "Wait here," he said and went inside.

Lara looked at him, leaning against the counter, chatting to the concierge, who obviously ruled the place with an iron hand. He was apparently asking her for a room and she shook her head, brows raised, shoulders raised. He might as well be asking for the moon, Lara thought, turning away with a sigh, remembering their dingy little hotel room with its thin walls and the sound of the trains rushing by. It just wasn't what Paris was about, not for a pair of lovers seeking paradise. She wondered gloomily how long love could survive there. About as long as in a grand restaurant, she guessed.

She swung around as the glass door opened again. Dan took her arm and pulled her inside. "Welcome to Paris, madame," he said with a triumphant grin.

Lara didn't know how Dan had managed it, since he spoke no French and the concierge spoke no English, but she guessed good all-American charm had won through. The dragon lady had given them a room under the eaves—blue-toile wallpaper, dark beams, ancient stone, an antique clawfoot bathtub, lace curtains, and those tall windows with shutters found only in France.

"It's heaven," she cried, bouncing on the *lit matrimonial*, testing it.

"It's *Paris*," he said, laughing at her.

It's Dan, she thought, loving him.

Dan took a cab back to the station hotel to collect their things, while Lara explored their new quarters.

Flinging back the shutters, she saw that their room faced a flowery interior courtyard with little round tables and chairs, where they would indulge in *café complet* the next morning.

She turned down the canopied bed, fluffed up the pillows, inspected the toiletries in the bathroom, which had stone walls and beams dating back to the revolution, and was thrilled to discover from the hotel brochure that she was in what had formerly been the British embassy.

She ran a bath, emptied the little vial of fragrant oil into the water, stripped off her pretty dress and the Monoprix underthings, and pinned up her hair. She was wallowing in the fragrant bubbles thinking what heaven this was when Dan got back.

He leaned against the door, arms folded, looking, she thought with a shiver of anticipation, devastatingly handsome, and adorable, and sexy and *oh, my God, how she wanted him.* She hadn't felt this way in years; she couldn't ever remember feeling this way about Bill.

"You look like a true Frenchwoman," he said.

She threw him a provocative smile, running her hands the length of her body. "How did you know where I was?"

"Easy. I just followed the trail of lacy undergarments and the scent of French perfume." He was pulling at the knot in his tie, walking toward her, unbuttoning his shirt. He tugged it off, let it drop to the floor. She watched mesmerized as he unzipped the chinos and stood naked in front of her. His taut erection told her how much he wanted her . . . she hadn't seen an erection like that on Bill in years . . . in fact she had hardly seen one at all in a long time, and for an instant she wondered if this was a mistress thing, whether Bill reacted like this to Melissa, taut and strong and ready for her . . . the Younger Woman. Well, Dan was a Younger Man and his erection snapped to attention whenever he looked at her . . . the way Bill's used to . . . hadn't it?

She shook her head; right now all that mattered was her lover. Her love . . .

"Room for two in that tub?" Dan asked, and laughing with relief that love was back again, she welcomed him into her world.

Bubbles clung to her breasts, tangling in the fine golden hair on his chest, popping and crackling as their bodies met. Her skin was slick under his hands, smoother than any silk, and her long, dark, softly curling hair escaped from its pins and floated free on the water. He thought she looked like a Pre-Raphaelite maiden in a painting, except that she was warm and alive and slippery as an eel as he tried to hold her, kissing her mouth and her hair and her eyelashes, gently running his tongue along her ears, down her neck, and over the little diamond necklace she always wore.

Crazy for her, he helped her out of the tub, wrapped her in a towel, and carried her to the bed.

He traced the curve of her breasts with tender fingers, ran his hand over her rounded body, kissed the soft curves. He had once told Lara he didn't know what love was. Now as they lay together he asked himself that question again.

She had known he was a straightforward guy who lived a simple life. He'd thought that was what she had wanted too, that they were alike. But she had stepped into that grand restaurant as though she belonged there, and he had suddenly seen a different woman. Was that the real Lara Lewis? Or was it the other, softer woman with the anxious eyes and the too-small red bathing suit, walking the lonely beach with her dog?

Was this just a romance? Was it just sex? A seduction? Paris? Right now, did it even matter? It was what it was.

Caressing her, he was aware that her soft, sensual body was not like Britt's or any other twenty-something he had known. Yet wasn't that also what he loved about her?

Yes, he told himself as he grasped her to him. An overwhelming *yes.* Her arms were wrapped around his neck and her legs gripped him as though she never wanted to let go. Their bodies were hot for each other. Oh, *yes,* he thought, thrusting deeper into her. *"Yes, I love you, Lara,"* he cried out, unable to help himself as they came together in one great trembling, earth-shattering moment.

Chapter Twenty-three

They were up early the next morning, feeling very French, sipping a breakfast café au lait and eating buttery croissants in the little interior garden, inspecting their fellow guests, who greeted them with a polite *"Bonjour, m'sier, 'dame."*

Out on the street again, Lara laughed at Dan sniffing the air like an eager young horse savoring a spring meadow.

His face alight with pleasure, he asked her, "Don't you smell it?" And she closed her eyes and breathed in the sugary vanilla aroma from the patisserie down the street; the heady fragrance from the perfume store; the smell of the fresh cotton from the baby shop over the way, and the garlicky fumes from the restaurant on the corner. There was the bittersweetness of good chocolate from the chocolatier, the musty odor from the antique store. And, over all, she thought, surely there was the heady scent of sex.

"This is Paris," Dan said, snatching her up in his arms and whirling her around, and Lara threw back her head, laughing at his craziness.

A spatter of applause came from behind. Blushing, she gazed into the laughing eyes of the smartly dressed middle-aged man and woman waiting politely to pass by on the narrow sidewalk.

"*Bravo, mes amis,*" the man called as they stood aside.

But the woman's eyes linked knowingly with Lara's in a complicit exchange of glances: admiring, envying, approving.

Lara smiled as she watched her walk away. She knows, Lara thought. She had been there too. She has felt like this. And she suddenly felt as though she had just joined an exclusive women's club.

They took the metro to Les Halles, heading for Pompidou. The modernistic museum faced an enormous square filled with tourists and vendors of cheap tat, with buskers and street artists of all kinds. Hating it, they wandered through the nearby street and alleys until they decided they were starving again. Lara said it must be the Paris air; Dan said it was love. And just then, they stumbled across a tiny bistro on the rue de l'Arbre Sec. It was called Chez la Vieille. "The Old Woman's Place."

Actually there were two women, one in charge of the kitchen, one in charge of the dining room, and neither one of them was old.

The tiny storefront building dated from the sixteenth century and still had the original black-and-white tiled floor and cracked stone walls, each crack embellished with a sticker saying it had been "inspected" and "passed," which Dan said he hoped meant that the walls weren't about to collapse. The kitchen was to the right, and on the left was a tiny dining room with only seven tables. Aromas of roasting lamb and chicken, of herbs and garlic drifted from the kitchen. It was a different world from the chic Michelin-starred Lucas Carton and it was exactly what they had hoped to find in Paris.

The charming motherly owner in a flowered dress and neatly curled hair told them that the tiny bistro had been there since 1958, and that when Adrienne, the original *vieille* of the name, had retired she had waited a long time before choosing a worthy successor. Now she, Madame, took care of her guests in the dining room while the young woman chef upheld La Vieille Adrienne's reputation.

She took them under her wing, bringing them *coupes* of champagne to drink along with slivers of ham and slabs of foie gras and hunks of baguette, still hot from the oven.

Lara wondered what it was going to do her susceptible waistline, but then she thought rebelliously that she'd been eating celery stalks and carrot sticks for years and much good it had done her. This was not a time to think of diets. She was in Paris with a man who loved good food as much as she did.

Remembering last night's disaster, she thought, relieved, that all that was in the past. *Now* she knew what Dan liked. She smiled, reaching for his hand. Dan was not Bill. He was his own man. She had learned one of the rules of the new game.

Madame suggested they try a merlot rosé, Père Puig, Cuvee de la Nymphe. Perfect, she told them, for the warm day. And, *naturellement,* a bottle of Badoit.

An enormous earthenware terrine of homemade *paté campagne* was placed on the table for them to help themselves, along with a huge platter of *tomates farciés,* oozing oil and herbs. Then fried *calamares* light as little feathers, and ratatouille bursting with juices, and herring filets in wine . . . and much, much more. It was good, earthy food, and exactly right, Lara and Dan agreed, for hungry lovers.

Next came the *ravioli d'hommard en bisque,* light and aromatic and stuffed with fresh lobster, in a winy tomato sauce. Then lamb so succulent it melted in their mouths, leaving a lingering flavor of rosemary, and with it came *pommes* roast. More wine; a salad; a selection of cheeses; then a glossy caramelized *tarte tatin* plus a chocolate mousse as well as a deep bowl filled with fresh purple plums stewed in sweet wine, again all placed on their table for them to help themselves.

Blue cigar smoke curled to the ancient rafters amid a murmur of conversation, and Madame hurried back with tiny glasses of an aromatic *digestif*, the specialty of the house.

Lara gave a satisfied sigh. "It was worth it," Dan said, laughing at her over cups of strong dark coffee. And Lara laughed too. Didn't they always say the way to a man's heart was through his stomach? Now she was beginning to believe it.

Paris seemed to wrap itself around them, it embraced them, kissed them on both cheeks. There might have been a sign *Lovers Welcome in Paris* in blazing lights, matching the star sparkle in their eyes. *Nothing*, they said to each other, could beat Paris for lovers. Today it was theirs.

They walked the tree-lined Champs Élyseés; window-shopped the elegant faubourg St. Honoré; visited the Galerie de Jeu de Paume to see the collection of Impressionists. Happy to behave like tourists, they lounged in cafes and wine bars and held hands and laughed a lot. It was, Lara thought, like being young again. Only the first time around, when she really was young, she didn't recall having this much fun.

She almost lost Dan to the Louvre, though.

They walked into the wonderful cobbled courtyard, through I. M. Pei's glass pyramid, and into the soaring sculpture gallery. Dan was like a man who had found paradise. His hands itched to touch the marble pieces, to feel the subtle folds and curves, and he wondered how the artists had managed to carve so much emotion out of an inert piece of stone.

"A man can lose his dreams in here," he said to Lara, who was looking at him looking at *Psyche réarmée par la baiser de l'amour,* a marble sculpture of a beautiful young girl, reclining exhausted, recovering "from Love's kiss"—presumably from Cupid, who, legend had it, visited her at night.

" 'Antonio Canova, Venice 1757–1822.' " Dan read the inscription plaque with a sigh. "No way could I ever have been as good as this."

"But how do you know? You never tried."

"Believe me, I know. Maybe it wasn't a bad thing I had to look after my brother and sister, after all. It let me off the hook from being a failed artist. Don't worry," he added, reading the concern in her eyes. "I haven't lost my dreams. I've just found greatness, that's all."

They went into the museum store and bought a postcard of the sculpture, and Dan said he would frame it so he would always remember this day.

Oh, but will *you remember?* that unsure, treacherous little voice inside Lara asked. *Or will you forget, the way Bill did, too soon, too soon. . . .*

Chapter Twenty-four

That evening, content with each other, they strolled arm in arm along the banks of the Seine, leaning over the Pont Neuf to watch the Bateaux Mouches go by. The brightly lit boats looked festive, crowded with tourists eating dinner and staring at the passing sights.

A while later, they found themselves in the great church of Notre Dame, where they gazed, dazzled, at the vibrant rose window glowing in the sunset. The serenity, the soaring vaulted arches and echoing ancient stones, took them into another world of peace and contemplation. Tourists wandered about and people knelt, heads bowed. Lara lit candles as an offering, then knelt next to Dan.

Listen, Lord, she said directly to Him, I don't feel like a sinner, but if I am, then forgive me. I'm just snatching at happiness, and I'll take whatever I can get . . . please, help me find the truth about myself, about Bill. About Dan . . .

When they emerged it was dusk. Across the river, Lara caught a glimpse of the lights in the Tour d'Argent. She had forgotten the restaurant was there until she saw it again. An image of the young Bill sprang into her mind, gamely ordering the expensive champagne and the duck, and all at once her heart ached for the two young innocents they used to be. She felt sure now he had only wanted to impress her. Oh, Bill, she thought sadly, what ever happened to us?

They wandered across the Pont de la Tournelle to the Isle St. Louis, the tiny island in the middle of the Seine, peeking into the courtyards of ancient stone mansions along the quai d'Anjou, speculating on the celebrities and millionaires who must live in them; then they strolled the rue St. Louis-en-l'Isle, admiring the puppet shop and the cat store and the patisserie with its jewel-like pastries and rich pâtés. They waited in the long line at Berthillon for ice cream, then sauntered down the street licking their cones; Lara had fig and Dan a chocolate nougat and glazed-chestnut mix that he said was the best he had ever tasted.

Later, they sat at an outdoor table at Le Flore en l'Isle, sipping white wine and watching the boats and the world go by. And finally, when darkness fell, they caught a cab back to the hotel to sleep the sleep of the truly exhausted. Lovers, wrapped in each other's arms.

It had been, Lara thought as she closed her eyes, the very best day of her life.

Not counting the days when your children were born, that unsure little inner voice reminded her.

And so why, she asked herself guiltily, must there always be a qualifying clause to happiness? Why couldn't she just accept what she'd got and make the most of it?

. . .

The next day was to be their last in Paris and they were up early, wandering the streets like a pair of excited kids, still thrilled by how French everything looked, from the exquisite little cobblestoned Place de Furstembourg, with its charming, shuttered buildings and graceful, slender paulownia trees, and its shop windows filled with glowing silks and velvets and brocades; to the street market on the rue de Buci, where they paused at a blue-awninged stall to sample fresh Charentais melon and tiny sugary apricots. They sniffed tangy cheeses and admired luscious hams and gasped at the fantastic iced displays of oysters, more varieties than they had ever known existed, as well as the sweetly pungent gray shrimp and a dozen kinds of fish, some huge and ferocious-looking with teeth and stiff whiskers, and other, tiny ones in sunset pinks and golds, but all glittering and clear-eyed with freshness.

A sweet aroma of baking pastry lured them across the street and they admired the window display of *tartes aux fruits,* so perfect they looked like photographs from Martha Stewart's magazine. They tried to choose between a wicked *chocolat daquoise* and a raspberry *mille feuille* oozing cream. Unable to resist they bought both, devouring them happily at a corner cafe, washed down with tiny cups of strong espresso.

Dan insisted on taking a photograph of Lara, stuffed and smiling and with no lipstick on. A waiter kindly offered to take a picture of both of them and Lara lay back in the curve of Dan's arm, "like a cat who's got the cream," she said when she saw the picture later.

They walked in the Jardins du Luxembourg and lingered over

the little boutiques, and Lara found pretty earrings, small gold hoops studded with tiny pearls, for the Girlfriends from a little shop, Biche de Berre on the rue de Rennes. Tired at last, they took a cab back to the hotel, where, good news, their luggage awaited them. It had indeed been left in Cincinnati, they were told.

It was five o'clock and Lara's feet ached. Tugging off her skirt, she lay down on the bed, yawning. Dan covered her with a blanket, kissed her, and said, "I'll be back soon."

"Where are you going?"

"Out for a walk."

She snuggled deeper under the blanket, her eyes already closed. "But we've walked all day long."

He was laughing as he said, "Yeah, but this is Paris, there's no time to sleep." And then the door closed.

Dimly, in the recesses of her mind, Lara heard Bill saying to her again, *Are you crazy, Lara? We're in France. There's no time to take it easy. . . .*

It was just the way Yogi Berra said it, she thought, suddenly worried. It was déja vu all over again.

Lara awoke to the sound of Dan singing in the shower. Eyes still closed, she smiled. Bill had never sung in the shower, he had always been too preoccupied. Turning, she felt something on the pillow. She opened her eyes and stared at the pretty beribboned box. Relieved, she realized it wasn't déja vu after all, Dan had just wanted to surprise her.

She untied the ribbons and opened the box, lifting away the layers of white tissue paper. Inside was the exquisite little teddy she had admired in Sabbia Rosa, the one that must weigh less than half an ounce, the one made of the very palest peach silk and lace. It was beautiful and she knew it must have cost a small fortune.

She heard Dan whistling softly, the way he had when he was working on her deck. Slipping out of bed, she put on the teddy, letting the smooth silk slide over her breasts. She had never owned a teddy before and this one was so soft and so light, she barely knew she was wearing it. Rummaging in the bottom of the closet, she found her new shoes with the four-inch heels and put them on.

She leaned against the bathroom door in a sexy pose. "I thought I'd model your gift for you."

Dan's laughing eyes took in the fact that she was naked under the silk and that the heels made her legs look extra long and slender. And that she was very, very desirable. "Well, now, thank you very kindly, ma'am. I surely appreciate that."

"I love it, it's a wonderful gift," she said.

"One we both can share."

He smelled of soap and shampoo and of himself as he picked her up in his arms and carried her back to bed.

"It's getting late," Lara protested halfheartedly. "I have to shower and dress."

"I'll help you." He was already nibbling on her earlobes, his hands were under the silk . . . and they forgot the time, and that they were in Paris.

Lara made love instinctively, with no plans of seduction because she had never learned such an art. She just did what she felt like doing, touching, tasting, loving him. She whispered that she loved his strong body, that she needed him now. And then at that ultimate over-the-edge-moment, she laughed, stretching her warm, moist length against him, like a contented alley cat.

A few hours later, they were showered and dressed for the evening. Tonight, Dan had taken charge and had made a reservation at Bofinger, the oldest brasserie in Paris, popular with Parisians and tourists alike.

They held hands, gazing enchanted out of the cab windows at Paris by night, speeding across the stone bridge lit by pretty old-fashioned globes, then circling the Place de la Concorde, where the guillotine had been set up during the Revolution and where Marie Antoinette's head had been cut off, as had Louis XIV's and Robespierre's.

Cursing the traffic, the driver raced down side streets and alleys, honking his horn and bellowing curses at anyone mad enough to get in his way, and they felt thankful to arrive still in one piece.

Bofinger was famous for its magnificent turn-of-the-century stained-glass ceiling, as well as for its tall mirrors and tulip-shaped sconces, marquetry paneling and etched glass. The place was elegant, yet easy and informal.

Lara sat with her back against the wall enjoying her favorite Parisian pastime of people watching, while Dan sat opposite, studying the wine list.

"The Brouilly," he told the waiter. "Chilled. And a bottle of Evian."

Surprised, Lara said admiringly, "You're a quick learner, Mr. Holland."

"I asked the dragon lady at the hotel what to order," he confessed.

She laughed. "Oh? And what else did she say?"

"The seafood platter, for sure. It's one of the best. And so is the *choucroute garnie*, and the roasted lobster."

"I want it all," she decided shamelessly.

She sipped the chilled light red wine while Dan studied the menu and Lara studied the faces. Immediately opposite sat an elegant older woman. She was alone. A bottle of champagne cooled in a silver bucket on a stand next to her table.

She was certainly French, Lara thought, envying her effortless chic. And she was also, as the French say, of a certain age. Her gold-blond hair, streaked with platinum, was cut smooth to her skull, and looked exactly right. Her cheekbones soared like a movie star's and her eyes were as blue as Dan's. She was tall and slender in a yellow designer jacket and a short black skirt with very high heels and very good legs. A wispy black and yellow chiffon scarf was twisted gracefully around her neck along with a triple-strand pearl choker.

Lara guessed that with the scarf and the pearls the older woman was hiding the evidence of age that begins at the neck, that downward pull of time.

The chic Frenchwoman glanced restlessly around. She caught the waiter's eye, said something to him, then anxiously checked her watch.

"He's late." Dan was also watching the woman in the mirror.

"What makes you so sure it's a man she's waiting for?" Lara said indignantly. "It could be her daughter. Or even a friend." Dan lifted a skeptical eyebrow. "Just because she's all dressed up? That's just Paris," Lara insisted.

She didn't quite know why she was defending the woman, except somehow it didn't seem right that she should let her anxiety, her *fear* that her man might not show, be so publicly on display.

I could never do that, she thought. And then she remembered now, on the rue Jacob when Dan had snatched her up in his arms, the naked joy she had felt, and how the passing couple had applauded them. She recalled the woman's complicit smile, acknowledging how fortunate she was to be with such a handsome young man. And she thought, Oh, yes, I could. *This* Lara Lewis could.

The woman got to her feet. She paced nervously to the door, peered out, paced back, sat down again. She caught Lara's eye and sighed, lifting her shoulders in a tiny shrug of defeat.

Then, suddenly, he was there. Loping toward her, jacket slung French-style around his shoulders, his dark hair ruffled by the wind. Vital, attractive. And, Lara saw with a little catch at her heart, so *very* young.

The woman's face lit up. In a second, she was on her feet, her arms were around him. He was here, her lover had come for her. *"Mon amour . . ."* she cried, forgiving him everything.

Lara's blood turned as cold as the wine she was drinking. Oh, God, she wondered, do I look like that? The foolish older woman with the younger man?

"See how sweet they are?" Dan was smiling.

"Sweet?" she repeated, amazed. Then she realized that Dan saw the little scene quite differently. He didn't see the age difference; all he saw was that the woman was happy now that her lover was here. And that was all that mattered.

Lara reached for his hand across the table and those tiny electric signals transmitted from him to her, from her to him. And she too felt happy for the other woman. Happy that her lover had shown up. Happy just for the moment. Because she knew only too well how fleeting happiness could be.

"Seize the day," she said as they raised their glasses in a toast to the woman and her lover. Or even just seize the *moment,* she added to herself, feeling suddenly thankful for any extra minute she could have.

"Did you know that oysters are an aphrodisiac?" Lara let a briny Belon oyster slide smoothly down her throat.

"Think you need one?"

She grinned and took another. "No, but I like them."

"Me too. What do you suppose these are?" Dan inspected a round shell filled with greenish objects.

"Sea urchins?" she guessed.

"Want to try them?"

She shook her head. "They look very fishy. I'm leaving them for you."

"Well, thanks." Dan scooped one out and put it in his mouth. "Good," he said, rolling his eyes, "if you like squishy stuff."

She was laughing as she said, "Enough about food. It's time for a little culture."

"Culture? Didn't we do the Louvre, and the Rodin, and the Jeu de Paume?"

"And Berthillon, and Sonia Rykiel, and Tarlazzi, and La Maison du Chocolat, and Sabbia Rosa." She sighed happily, smoothing her hands over her breasts, thinking of the delicious and expensive peach silk teddy under her black sweater. "That's what Paris is all about," she said dreamily.

Paris was their Eden. Paris was perfect. How could it get better than this?

Chapter Twenty-five

It couldn't, she thought gloomily the next morning. First, it was raining. Not just any old shower but an honest-to-God downpour of the biblical kind. Dan was behind the wheel of the tiny rented Renault 106, a two-door hatchback in baby blue with a five-speed stick shift, cramped bucket seats, and no air-conditioning. It wasn't the vehicle Lara had requested but the unobliging man at the rental company had told them it was all he had and since they were here on the wrong date—again— they were lucky to get it.

Map in hand, Lara stared through the sloshing windshield, unable to see anything except red taillights immediately in front of them.

"Tell me when to turn." Dan's eyes were glued to the road. He was stunned by the wildness of the Parisian drivers as they crisscrossed in front of him. He shifted down and felt the car jump. This was their third trip around this roundabout and Lara still did not have a fix on which street to take and he still not have a fix on the gearshift.

"Oh, what the hell," Lara said, defeated, "let's just get out of here, any way you can."

Dan edged the tiny Renault into the right lane, cursing as yet another vehicle swerved in front of him, sending a wave of water over his windshield. He made a swinging right turn into a narrow street. From behind him, he heard a horn blasting.

"The bastard is leaning on it," Dan said, unnerved. "What the hell's wrong with him? Why is he driving up my tail anyhow?"

Lara turned to look. The driver of an ancient Citroën truck waved his fist at her, mouthing what she knew must be obscene curses. She peered anxiously over the mound of baggage piled behind them to see what was wrong.

"Oh . . . my . . . God . . . Dan," she said slowly. "I think you'd better stop."

"What, and give that idiot the satisfaction?" Dan was bristling with anger now. "He's been honking me out of his way for five minutes now and I'm damned if I'll move over."

"Dan . . ." Lara placed a restraining hand on his arm. "Dan, you have to stop."

He glared at her out of the corner of his eye, negotiating his way uneasily down the narrow street with cars tightly parked on either side, but then something about the look on her face made him take notice. As he braked he heard the rending sound of his back bumper crumpling. "Oh, *shit*," he groaned, "now look what you've made me do."

Lara glared back at him. "Before you decide what *I* have done, Mr. Holland, I suggest you get out and take a look at what *you* have done."

Rattled, Dan got out, slamming the door behind him.

Lara took in the scene. The metal front bumper of the ancient

Citroën was firmly attached to the back bumper of their little Renault. And, as far as she could make out from the driver, it had been ever since Dan had turned off the roundabout. The fact was, they had been driving with the Citroën and its irate driver attached to them for almost five minutes.

She peered out of the rain-streaked window. The driver was shouting at Dan in rapid, angry French. He even went so far as to shake a fist. Arms folded, Dan glared angrily back at him. Rain dripped down his nose and he wiped it impatiently away with the back of his hand.

"Obviously, you rear-ended me," he was saying, reasonably enough, because he figured how, otherwise, could the Citroën be stuck to their rear bumper?

"*Non, non, non.*" The Frenchman was huge. He put up his fists, looking for a fight. "No rear-end."

A traffic jam of epic proportions was piling up on the narrow street behind them. The blare of horns and angry voices mingled with the splashing of the rain. And then the high *uhuh uhuh uhuh* of a police car.

"The idiot says it's my fault," Dan said indignantly.

"Well, was it?" Lara asked in what she considered to be a reasonable tone, though secretly she thought it might be his fault.

Dan glared at her as though she had committed treason. "Of course it wasn't. They were all driving like madmen, you saw that. He rear-ended me!"

A pair of gendarmes approached, *képis* tilted sinisterly over their eyes, black raincapes swirling importantly.

"M'sieur, madame, it is necessary to pull to one side," the first gendarme commanded.

"Sure." Dan was tight-lipped. "Just show me which side."

Cars were parked nose-to-tail the length of the narrow street and obviously there was nowhere for him to get out of the way. Meanwhile, the Citroën driver, with much snorting and waving of hands, was regaling the other gendarme with his account of the story and the infamy of the *tourists américains*. And, Lara noticed, with a sinking feeling, the *flic* was writing it all down in his little notebook.

Dan showed the first gendarme the back of the Renault with the Citroën firmly attached to its bumper. The gendarme took out the notebook again. *"Votre nom, votre permis, carte d'assurance, et votre passport, s'il vous plaît, monsieur."*

Lara took the documents from the glove box and handed them to Dan. "Is it going to be okay?"

He shrugged. "How do I know? I'm having enough trouble trying to understand what he's saying."

With a rending of metal, the Citroën was lifted off their bumper. Ten minutes later, Dan climbed back in the car.

"The bastard tried to claim it was my fault," he said, still fuming.

"Then we're not going to jail?" A smile lurked at the corners of Lara's mouth.

"It was touch-and-go, I'll tell you. If they had believed him, I would have been there."

"That would have been a different way to see Paris." Lara was unable to stop the giggle, it just burst out of her.

Baffled, Dan glared at her out of the corner of his eye. "What's so darn funny? That I might have seen Paris from the inside of a jail cell? Hah! That's some sense of humor you have, ma'am."

"Don't call me *ma'am*," she snapped, angry that he was still angry and couldn't see the funny side of it.

"Sorry. *Mrs.* Lewis."

She slumped in her seat, shocked. It was like a slap in the face. He *never* called her Mrs. Lewis. *Ms.* Lewis was what he always said. Was it a deliberate dig to remind her of who she was and that she was not Mrs. Dan Holland? Their wonderful romantic trip seemed suddenly trivialized and hollow and she wanted to cry but knew she must not, she couldn't let him see the hurt. Great, she thought miserably, it's history repeating itself. This is exactly what happened with Bill. The lost way . . . the fight . . . not speaking . . .

A *Toutes Directions* sign appeared through the murk. "Follow that," she told him sullenly. She didn't know where it led but anything was better than winding their way around the back streets of Paris in an area of warehouses and crumbling buildings she had never seen before.

They were on the Périphérique, the motorway encircling Paris. Relieved, she thought surely from there she would be able to find the right exit for Tours. Soon, they could be in a nice warm hotel room and, maybe, when Dan had had a hot shower, he would come to his senses and see the funny side of it.

Her mouth curled into a smile as she recalled *les flics* striding toward them—the two rain-sodden and angry *criminels américans*—while the Citroën driver had his dukes up ready to fight it out.

"I thought it was pretty funny," she said with that unrepentant giggle. "I thought he was going to punch you right there and then."

A rueful grin curved Dan's mouth. "I figured I was either gonna end up in hospital or in jail."

"Nobody would ever believe it," she gasped between shouts of laughter. "Never in a million years . . ."

He shot her a penetrating look. "For a minute there I thought you were taking his part."

"Who, *me?*" Eyes open wide, Lara gazed innocently back at him. "*Never.* It was obviously the other guy's fault." But she was smiling as she said it. She could almost hear Delia saying. *You're learning, Lara!*

Chapter Twenty-six

They had been on the Périphérique for over two hours.

"I've passed this sign twice," Dan said. He swung onto the exit ramp, made a right, and pulled over. "Give me the map."

Silently, Lara handed it over.

"God, it's so simple, why didn't you see it? Right here; look." He pointed out the route on the map, then disgusted with her incompetence, took off again.

Lara stared out the window in rebellious silence. She didn't know why she hadn't seen it, she just hadn't, that's all. Maybe it wasn't just Bill, she thought, it was truly that all men were alike. They could all read maps in a flash—when they were parked on a quiet street. Huh, she thought, just give a man a map when the car is racing down the motor-way at seventy miles an hour and the signs are flashing by and the driver expects an immediate answer. *That's* when the trouble starts. Of course she should have planned the route beforehand, she admitted that, but still, there was no need for Dan to be so mean about it. After all, they were on the right road now.

"I can't believe we spent two hours on that motorway," Dan said, "when all you had to do was look at the map."

"I looked," she snapped. "You should try searching the small print at seventy miles an hour."

"Kilometers," he corrected her. "And you should put on the bifocals."

"They *are* on!"

She glared furiously ahead at the rain-smudged fields as they splashed down country lanes.

Half an hour passed in silence. "Why are we out in the middle of the countryside?" she asked finally. "We should be on the main route to Tours."

"I'm taking the green-arrow roads instead."

"You're taking the *scenic route*? On a day like this?" Lara threw up her hands, stunned.

Dan's chin was set in a stubborn line, his eyes fixed grimly on the winding country road ahead. "Just leave it to me, Lara, why don't you?" he said in that same cold voice. "I figured there would be less traffic."

"Of course there will. No one takes country roads in this weather. Look, there's a gas station. Let's ask for directions."

"Too late. We're already past it."

"Then, dammit, turn around," she said, exasperated. "Unless, of course, you know where we are."

Dan shrugged. "Beats me."

"Why is it men never want to stop and ask directions?" she demanded through gritted teeth. "It's a failing of your sex, you know that?"

There was a frigid silence in the car. Is this what real love is, she asked herself? Not romance, not flowers and perfume and high heels and sex. Is it fighting and stubbornness and a refusal to see reason—me as well as Dan, I suppose. Yes, of course it's me as well. I'm just as stubborn as he is. And I'm a woman too—that's worse, at least in a man's eyes it is. They never think we act reasonably. Especially in a car.

She sneaked a glance at Dan. His face was impassive, his mouth tight. She told herself, doubtfully, it was just that their nerves were frazzled, the stress of driving in a foreign country, the accident, the everlasting rain. But doubt quivered in her brain like the first rumblings of a volcano, and the tremors grew stronger with each silent, dreary, rain-sodden kilometer.

Panicked, she asked herself if she had made a mistake. A great, huge, terrible mistake. The mistake of a lifetime? Wait a minute, though, only weeks ago she had thought that her marriage to Bill took the Great Mistake award.

She huddled farther into her cramped seat, dwelling miserably on the trembling volcano of thoughts, wondering when they would erupt and end this so-called romantic idyll. She hardened her jaw, pressing her teeth together to stop from crying. She thought longingly of home, of the peace of being alone with just her dog for company, no fights, no mood swings—no mistakes. All she wanted right now was to be at the beach house. Just her and Dex, watching the sunset. Yet only hours ago, she had loved Dan so much she couldn't keep her hands off him, couldn't envision life without him.

All you have to do, girlfriend, is act reasonably, that inner voice told her. Yeah, but you know what, I'm sick and tired of acting reasonably. If this is love, do I want it? Yes, yes, I do, darn it. *Oh, stop being so stubborn, Lara. Face it: of course you want it.*

Another half hour passed and they were in a village of sorts — a straggle of houses along a bleak, lonely road edged with flat, drenched fields. Dan slammed on the brakes and swerved under an arch into a sodden courtyard fronting a ramshackle farm-house. Mud and clucking hens scattered from beneath their wheels and a black dog with liver-colored eyes barked and showed its teeth at them.

"Get lost," Dan snapped as he stepped out of the car, and the dog ducked its head and slunk out of his way.

"So now you're mean to animals as well as women," Lara commented. He turned and glared at her. She glared back. "Anyhow, where are you going?"

He pointed to the handwritten sign at the entrance. *Gîtes. Chambre à Louer.* Room for rent! Did he mean for them to stay *here* tonight? Dismayed, Lara stared at the yard. It was a sea of mud and cow pats, and the dreary old gray stone farmhouse had a definite list to the left and looked about to fall down. Through the sheet of rain she could see Dan talking to a thin, inhospitable-looking woman with scraped-back steel-gray hair and a blank expression.

The woman disappeared into the house then returned with a key. Throwing an old coat over her basic black, she shuffled around the corner with Dan following. He came back a few minutes later. "We're at least seventy kilometers from Tours and the weather's getting worse," he said. "This is it for tonight." He hesitated, then said glumly, "I'm sorry, Lara."

She glared silently at him from beneath her lashes, unforgiv-ing, despite the advice of her inner voice.

He drove the Renault around the back of the farmhouse and stopped in front of an ancient barn. Small windows had been punched through the crumbling stone walls and the roof was missing several tiles. Still silent, she followed him inside.

The room was open to the rafters and furnished, if that was the correct word, with the same small *lit matrimonial* that the French seemed to prefer. This one was covered with an orange and brown chenille spread that matched the orange and brown polyester curtains. The bed and the pine dresser had obviously seen many years' service in the farmer's own bedroom until *gîtes* and unwary tourists and the good times had rolled around. Lara guessed that now he had a shiny new bedroom set from the local discount store. There was a flimsy table, a couple of old cane-bottomed chairs, and a worn, colorless rug on the uneven stone floor. A miniscule gas heater vainly puffed clouds of warmish steam into the icy room.

Lara thought longingly of the sweet little Hôtel de Groison in Tours, warm and cozy, waiting for them. She kicked the table leg angrily, then yelped with pain, hopping on one foot, frustrated, angry, tired, and cold.

"Great," she snarled. "Looks like we'll have a perfect night."

Dan shoved his hands in his pockets. He said, "Aw, come on, Lara, roll with it, can't you? I've said I'm sorry."

She threw him a baleful glare; he was still dripping water onto the flagstones. Turning away, she opened up the bags. "You'd better take a hot shower and get into some dry clothing."

She unlocked her suitcase then peeled off her own wet clothes. She was looking forward to that hot shower. It might be the only highlight of her day. She took out her little portable radio, turned it on.

Tina Turner was singing "What's Love Got to Do With It."

What, indeed, Lara wondered resentfully. She was still thinking about that when Dan emerged from the tiny bathroom. He was holding an extremely small blue towel and looked even colder and wetter than he had before.

"Forget the shower," he said. "There's no hot water."

Lara stared at him, stunned. They could have been in Tours by now, bathing in hot water, dressing in clean clothes, dining in some cozy bistro. . . . Furious, she slammed the suitcase shut. Too late, she heard the lock click, remembered the key inside on top of the neatly folded clothes. Groaning, she sank into the old cane chair.

There was a rending sound and the seat gave way. The chair tipped over and she was on the floor, her bottom jammed into the broken chair, legs sticking into the air. Shrieking with frustration and fury, she kicked her feet, ridiculous, humiliated, and fcd-up.

"*Fuck,*" she yelled since it seemed the only appropriate word. "*Oh, fuck fuck fuck . . .*"

Dan's mocking laughter echoed from the icy rafters. "Never thought I'd hear you say that word, Ms. Lewis."

She glared at him. Naked, he looked so beautiful she almost forgave him. *Almost*—but not quite. She said angrily, "It's all your fault."

He knelt over her and pulled her with one hand, pressing the broken chair down with the other. She popped out so suddenly that he fell backward with her on top of him.

Lara felt a draft as the door opened. They turned their heads and their eyes met those of their hostess.

Madame Defarge stared at the naked woman straddling the naked man. Then, "M'sieur, 'dame," she said with great dignity,

"I've brought you a little of my home-brewed calvados. To take off the chill."

Lara felt the hot blush not just in her face but in her entire naked body. She hid her face in Dan's chest. She heard the tray being deposited on the table then the sound of the door closing behind Madame Defarge.

"*Oh . . . my . . . God,*" she wailed, horrified. "What must she have thought? I'll never be able to look her in the face again."

She struggled to get up but Dan only gripped her tighter. Laughter rumbled in his chest and she glared at him, then suddenly she saw the funny side of it too. They rolled over and over on the old rug, still wrapped in each other's arms, hooting with laughter.

Dan brushed the tears of laughter from his eyes. "Do you really care what Madame Defarge thinks? After all, you'll never meet her again. And, anyhow, she's probably seen it all before."

"Not like you, she hasn't. She'll be dreaming about you for years." Lara snuggled hungrily into his arms. "I know she's never seen a naked man like you."

"Oh? And how do you know?"

"Because neither have I. And I, my friend, am a woman of the world."

Dan's shout of laughter set her off again, but he pulled her to her feet. "Come on, woman of the world, let's have a drop of that warming calvados."

He poured the cloudy, brownish-green liquid. Lara stared doubtfully at it. "*Santé,*" Dan said, having learned the French for "cheers" early on in the game. They drained their glasses. Lara clutched her throat. They stared at each other, wide-eyed and speechless.

"Fire," she gasped, "it's fire water. . . . Oh, my God, I'm dying."

Choking, Dan ran to get her a glass of water. She drained it in one gulp, then, still coughing, said, horrified, "Oh, God, I forgot. We shouldn't be drinking tap water."

"Don't worry, no bug could survive the calvados."

"Dan?"

"Yeah."

"I've locked my key in my suitcase."

He groaned as he pulled a sweater over his head. "I'll ruin it if I have to force it open."

Lara looked doubtfully at her nice new case.

"Tell you what, we'll get a locksmith when we get to Tours." He pushed his duffel across the bed. "Meanwhile, feel free."

She picked through his clothes, pulling on a T-shirt, and his gray sweats, and a pair of his white athletic socks, thanking heaven for sneakers as she laced hers up. She rubbed her long dark hair dry and pushed it up beneath a Lakers baseball cap. She looked like the Michelin Man. "Ready for dinner, Mr. Holland?"

His guilty eyes met hers. "It's like this. Madame Defarge doesn't do meals."

"Probably just as well, if her cooking's anything like her calvados." Lara added a touch of Bobbi Brown "Bare" lip stain, studying the effect in the tiny mirror. "We'll find a cafe in the village."

"As a matter of fact, there is no cafe in the village."

She swung around.

"Though there is a bar. Madame said we could get a meal there."

Lara beamed at him, relieved. "Let's go for it, Mr. Holland.

I just hope it's not too dressy, though, or maybe they won't let us in."

"I wouldn't worry about it," he said gloomily.

They stood in the entrance to the Bar Jurassic, taking in the purple and turquoise Formica decor. The tiled floor around the bar was ankle deep in peanut shells. French pop music blared from the jukebox, and the local population of spiky-haired, black-leather-jacketed young layabouts swung around on their purple plastic bar seats, staring at them. They should have known from the motorcycles outside, Lara thought, staring back through the pungent blue Gitane fog.

"Bonsoir, messieurs," Dan said politely.

"B'soir." The owner was a gruff, graying man with sharp eyes who looked as though he had his hands full with his rowdy clientele. *"Qu'est-ce que vouz voulez, m'sieur, 'dame?"* His eyebrows were raised in a question.

Lara had to think of the French. *"Vouz servez le dîner, m'sieur?"*

He shrugged, pointing to the blackboard in back of him. *"Seulement les sandwiches."*

The entire bar was riveted by this halting exchange.

"Okay, a sandwich," Dan agreed. "What have you got?"

The *patron* ordered the leather-jacketed customers back so they could view the glass display counter. *"Du jambon. Ou du fromage."*

"Jambon et *fromage, s'il vous plaît, monsieur."* Lara was starving. *"Et vous avez du vin?"*

He plonked a bottle on the plastic counter along with a pair of thick tumblers.

Clutching the wine and the tumblers, they shuffled back through the debris and took a seat at the Formica table farthest from the bar. The bottle had no label and the wine tasted as though it had been made yesterday. They drank it anyway.

The *patron* arrived with the *sandwich*—a whole baguette sliced lengthways. Inside were one thin slice of ham and one thin slice of cheese. There was no butter on the bread. Lara's eyes met Dan's. "I guess it's a French sandwich," she said doubtfully.

She asked the *patron* for butter. He looked at her as though she were a mad foreigner. *"Pas du beurre, madame."*

She took a bite of the dry bread. Her eyes met Dan's. "It's really not that bad," she said, swallowing hard.

Dan pushed back his chair. He walked across to the bar and spoke to the *patron*. He came back holding a squeezy bottle of Savora mustard and plonked it down in front of her.

"How about napkins?"

"You can't have everything, Ms. Lewis."

"I don't want everything," she whispered, reaching for his hand. Their eyes locked in that deep gaze and they failed to notice they had company.

"Where you come from in America?"

They glanced up at the four cocky young men standing too close, Lara thought nervously, to their table. They wore identical leather jackets studded with steel nail heads, had identical haircuts cropped to the scalp, identical tattoos and blue-black stubble. And they emanated attitude.

"Uh-uh," Dan whispered to Lara, "the local chapter of the Hells Angels." Then, "We're from San Francisco, my friends," he said, and their pallid faces lit up.

"California?"

For a minute Dan thought he saw dreams in their drink-reddened eyes. "You ever been there?" He took a sip of wine, looking benignly at them.

They shrugged in unison. "*Mais non, non*. . . . Someday, I hope," the tallest one ventured in English. He snatched off Lara's baseball cap, and her eyes popped in alarm.

"Lakers," he said admiringly.

Dan took off his own baseball cap and handed it to the tall guy, who he could tell was the boss. "Forty-Niners," he explained, "the San Francisco football team. It's yours, my friend." He turned to the patron. "*Cognac, s'il vous plaît,* for *mes amis.* And now we'll say good night."

Still hungry, Lara grabbed the rest of the sandwich and stuffed it in her pocket. Dan was already easing her out of there as he laid money on the counter for the brandy.

"*Merci, monsieur.*" Their thanks floated after them into the rainy night. "*Et bon voyage.*"

"You've just gotta know how to handle these things," Dan said smugly as they climbed into the Renault. Then he laughed. "I thought we were about to get blasted by the natives, when all they wanted was our baseball caps. Poor kids," he added, thinking of the dreams that, for them, would never come true.

"You're a nice man, you know that?" Lara leaned her head on his shoulder as he drove.

He glanced affectionately at her. "You didn't think that earlier in the day."

"Well, of course not. *Then,* I hated you."

He laughed. She was a very contradictory woman and he knew it.

. . .

That night they huddled in the old narrow bed like animals seeking warmth from each other's bodies. Lara's eyes were closed and Dan wondered if she was sleeping. He smiled thinking about the disastrous day, and how somehow it had turned out all right in the end. The way it always seemed to on this trip. Because of Lara, he thought. Lara, who with one look from those smudgy topaz eyes could make him weak at the knees. Was topaz the right color? Wasn't it more citrine, especially when the sun caught them in its glitter? And amber, perhaps, in the softness of twilight, copper by candlelight.

He laughed at himself, the working guy, the builder, acting like a poet about his love's eyes.

His *love*. Not just his lover. Because Lara was no mere conquest. She had sneaked into his head, into his dreams, and, somehow, into his heart. What was love, anyway? he asked himself. Then he smiled, remembering the red bathing suit, her shyness, their fights, the laughter.

How do I love thee, let me count the ways . . .

His fifth-grade English teacher, Mrs. Purley, would be proud of him, quoting Browning's *Sonnets from the Portuguese*. . . . Now he knew it had to be love.

He counted the ways he loved her: the sweetness of her expression and the slow smile that exposed the tiniest dimple at the left corner of her mouth. The way she held herself, slightly self-conscious, like a girl still coming to terms with a woman's body. Her breasts, the deep upward curve, satin under his touch. The spicy taste of her; her damp skin with its faint pearly sheen of sweat after they had made love. And, oh,

God, how he loved making love to her. Then it was all passion and fire and nothing else mattered except the way she felt under his hands, and what she did to him, what he did to her. And afterward, the exhausted, tender silence while the hearts that had thundered together gradually slowed, and with it the awareness of having just encountered another's soul, in some far-off place we search so hard to find.

That was it. Lara fitted his soul. She had fallen into his life, invited him into her world, and now he never wanted to leave. Whatever that inexplicable thing that love was, he welcomed it.

It was almost dawn and Lara lay sleepless next to Dan. He snored lightly and she smiled; it was such a comfortable sound. A man in her bed, holding her, snoring, content.

Gray light slipped past the orange poly curtains, still unable to lend the cold room even a vestige of sun color. Shivering, she slid her leg over Dan's, hugged closer to him, letting his warmth permeate her chilled limbs.

Dear God, she thought, watching his face, so close to hers, as he slept, please take care of him. Don't let him leave me . . . not now that I've found him. You know what, God, I'd forgotten how to feel like this. I've found how to laugh, how to be silly, foolish, sexy; how to be *young* with him in a way I never was with Bill, even when I really *was* young. Let me love him, please, even if I can only have him for a little while. . . .

Chapter Twenty-seven

It was ten o'clock the following night and they were comfortably ensconced in the charming little Hotel de Groison in Tours. They had explored the city, had an early supper, and now Dan was sleeping like a dead man in their pretty room overlooking the beautiful garden.

Lara was using the public telephone downstairs to call Delia, partly because she didn't want to disturb Dan, but also because she knew that Delia would want her to tell all and she couldn't exactly do that with Dan around.

She dialed and heard the phone ringing, imagining Delia rushing to answer. Delia always rushed everywhere, she was in perpetual motion, or at least she had been until the bout with chemotherapy had slowed her down a bit.

"Ohhh, it's you at last." Delia was breathless with excitement. "We're gasping to know what's going on. Vannie says we're like a Greek chorus, moaning and worrying and predicting disaster in the background. So? How's it going?"

"It's going good."

"*Good?* What kind of adjective is that? I had expected at least a superlative. *Great,* maybe. Or even better, *stupendous.*"

They were both laughing now. "You know what I mean," Lara said, suddenly shy with her best friend.

"No, I don't know what you mean. Do *you* know what you mean?"

Lara sighed. "We fight all the time," she admitted. "Or, at least, yesterday we did. And once in Paris. Big fights."

"That's good; at least he's not perfect. *Then* I would have been suspicious."

"But sometimes—most times—it's wonderful."

She heard Delia's sigh of relief. "Well, thank the Lord for that. At least it's taken your mind off Bill the Bastard."

"Delia," Lara hesitated to admit it, but this *was* her best friend, "it hasn't—you know—taken my mind off Bill. At least not completely. I keep remembering stuff—things we did together."

"Of course you do. Aren't you retracing your footsteps? Visiting the same places, staying in the same hotels? What did you expect?"

"But the odd thing is, now I'm remembering it the way it really was. Not this sort of glowing, golden version I must have polished up over the years. And you know what else, Delia? It's uncanny the way this trip with Dan is sometimes so like what happened when I was with Bill, I might be with the same man."

"Except you are not. And just remember one thing, honey: men are all alike. They're a different breed from us women, who, naturally, think for ourselves. They have the same archetypical reaction to certain circumstances."

"It's like, press their buttons and watch what happens," Lara said, amazed. "I mean, why won't they stop and ask directions? Why won't they read a map? Why do they get pissed off when we make simple mistakes?"

Delia was laughing. "Oh, my, trouble on the road, huh? So tell me about Paris."

"Paris was wonderful. Mostly," Lara added, remembering Lucas Carton. "Delia, I'm having fun with Dan, just walking the streets. We hold hands all the time. He makes me . . . he makes me feel beautiful. *Paris* makes me feel beautiful. Delia, it's not hormone replacements I need, it's *femininity* replacements. Give me the same flirt pills these French women have and age doesn't seem to matter. I'd forgotten how to feel that way. Sometimes I can't believe it's me, acting so sort of . . . shameless."

"So it's just sex between you, right?"

"Yes . . . no . . . I mean, how do I know? Right now it's all I can think of. When I think of leaving, him not being there anymore, it's not only my heart that sinks, it's all of me—heart, sex, everything. I mean, Delia, how are you supposed to *know?* Do you think he loves me? Just a little bit?"

"Doesn't he tell you that? Lara, you have to have more confidence in yourself. You can't let Bill take that away from you."

"Maybe right now he loves me," she said, still unsure. "But what if I'm just a passing fancy—a holiday romance? Maybe, when we get home, he'll go back to Britt. . . ."

Delia sighed again. "So, you obviously haven't discovered who you are yet."

"I'm still looking. I just wish I didn't keep tripping over memories of Bill wherever we go."

"Oh, yeah? Remember Bill? The louse in Beijing with Melissa Kenney?" Delia wished she were there to shake some sense into her. "And you're in—where are you, anyway?—somewhere in France with Dan. Your wonderful lover. Remember him?"

"I could never forget him," Lara said simply.

"Great. Now let's get to the important stuff. Did you go shopping in Paris?"

"I bought you some earrings, brushed gold studded with tiny pearls. I got the other Girlfriends earrings too. And I bought a dress for Minnie, and a sweater for Josh. Oh, and a wonderful old print of Paris . . . and I guess that's about it."

"Nothing for yourself?"

"Underwear. The airline lost the luggage."

"Oh, my God! So, what else did you get?"

"Delia, there wasn't much time."

"Huh." Delia snorted. "I can't imagine what else you were doing. . . ."

Lara was laughing now. "Actually, I bought a pink-flowered dress. And we ate ice cream cones on the Isle St. Louis and walked around the Left Bank, and visited museums and ate too much good food. I bet I've gained five pounds."

"It's worth it, hon. Keep up the good work."

"Okay. I'd better go now. Love to the girls, Delia. And I love you."

Delia's smacking kiss came down the line. "Love you too, honey. Keep in touch; remember, we are dying to hear how it goes."

Clouds blanketed the Loire Valley the next morning, promising more rain, but still they set off early for Chambord and Blois.

It had rained too when Lara was there with Bill. She remembered staring, frozen and wet, at the magnificent Château du

Chambord through a sheet of water. It had looked like a ghostly vision arising from the past and she had been swept back in time, imagining knights in armor charging their horses into the courtyard and King Louis, or maybe it was Charles, in his gold crown urging his men on to battle. But Bill, the medical man, had wondered out loud about the sanitation and the living conditions underneath all that gloss and grandeur, bringing her back to the present with a thud. She had been so lost in the wonder of how they had built such palaces in the year 1498, and all Bill cared about were the toilets.

As a matter of fact, she remembered now, she too had learned to care about toilets. It had happened right here, in the Loire.

They had stopped for gas at a station in a small town. While Bill filled up, Lara had hurried to the rest room. She swung open the door and stared in astonishment at the concrete floor with a hole in the center and at the two slabs in the shape of large feet.

"Oh, my God," she'd muttered, horrified. But she had to go.

She balanced herself precariously over the hole, then looked around for the flush. She found a lever and pressed it. Water gushed at her from every angle. Shrieking, she danced on tiptoe trying to escape; the water was splashing over her shoes, on her legs. She ran out, stunned.

Bill took one look at her shocked face. His brows rose and his mouth turned down at the corners in that resigned "what did you do now" look. He'd even said it. "What did you do now, Lara? You only went to the rest room."

"Have you *seen* that rest room?" she'd demanded heatedly. "It's from the Middle Ages, it's . . . it's *disgusting*."

Bill had not even laughed, though thinking about it later, Lara had. He had merely sighed. "I had no problem myself."

"But then you wouldn't, would you?" she had said furiously. "Mr. Perfect Know-it-all."

They had not spoken for the rest of the day.

Arms around each other, Dan and Lara sheltered beneath a big burgundy-and-green-striped umbrella, purchased that morning in town.

"It makes you wonder how they ever built this place," Dan the builder marveled, touching the worn stones reverently, inspecting joists and beams and admiring massive oaken doors like a man in love. "I can just see you hanging out that turret window," he added, "letting down your long hair like Rapunzel snaring her lover."

Lara's dark hair was beaded with crystalline raindrops and her amber eyes smiled at him. Her cheeks were pink from the wind and her mouth soft with love. Bundled up in sweaters and a bright red anorak, she looked like the roly-poly teenager she had told him she used to be.

"Did I ever tell you, Ms. Lewis, ma'am, *Lara*—that right now you are more beautiful than Chambord? Or Blois? Or Chenonceau, or Amboise? Or even the naked woman in my bed last night?"

She blushed. "The rain's clouding your vision. This is the real me you're looking at."

"Both are the real you." He kissed raindrops from her eyelashes and the tip of her nose, burying his face in the fragrance of her neck, where the tiny pulse beat beneath his lips. "You're beautiful, Lara Lewis," he murmured. "Never forget that."

I won't, she told herself, lost in his arms, his kiss. Brimming with happiness, she stored those words in her memory bank. I'll never forget you said that.

Chapter Twenty-eight

They were sitting in a tiny movie theater in Blois watching an old Gérard Depardieu film in French without subtitles, just to escape from the wind and the rain.

"What are you thinking about?" Dan whispered in her ear.

She stared at the screen, where a grizzly murder was taking place in a storm. "Sunshine," she whispered back.

"What d'you say we get out of here? Head south?"

She turned to look at him. "I was hoping you would say that."

Angry hissing noises came from behind them and people glared their way. Clutching hands they edged along the row, stumbling over feet in the darkness, giggling like two children.

The Holiday Inn was not where Lara had stayed with Bill. In fact, they had not stopped in Blois, but because of the weather she was willing to make a small exception to her honeymoon itinerary and, anyhow, it was the first hotel she had come across in the Gault guide. It was functional and comfortable, and it was *warm*. If they went south tomorrow, they would miss the famous gardens at Villandry, as well as the fabled châ-teau of Azay-le-Rideau, but, somehow, she thought they would return someday.

Meanwhile, she soaked in the Holiday Inn's tiny tub while Dan pored over the map, tracing their route down through Poitiers and Angoulème to Bergerac.

"Why such a convoluted route, anyway?" he asked when she emerged wrapped in a towel, her long wet hair draped around her shoulders like seaweed on a mermaid. "We could be in Pro-vence, in the sun. In fact, why don't we just drop off the car and fly to Marseilles?"

"Oh, but that's not the point," she said, alarmed that he wanted to change her honeymoon route. "It's not the way we . . . the way *I* want to do it. Besides," she added quickly, "it'll be too difficult to cancel all those reservations and get flights. And I know you're going to enjoy seeing it all."

Dan said he surely hoped she was right and that the rain would quit. Meanwhile, he called room service and ordered steak-*frites* and a half bottle of a local Saumur. The white wine didn't go with the steak but he thought they ought to try it anyway, since that's what the area was famous for. Plus a slab of apple tart with vanilla ice cream.

They sat at the little table. Lara's wet hair was wrapped in a white towel-turban, and she was wearing her blue cotton robe and terry slippers. Dan had on gray sweatpants and a white T-shirt. On the TV, Canal Plus blasted them with the news in French.

"Just like an old married couple," Dan said with a grin.

It was exactly what Lara had been thinking, but she hadn't dared say it.

"I feel guilty about being in a Holiday Inn, here in France," she said.

"It beats Madame Defarge's barn."

She had to agree with that.

The thin steak was what the French call *saignant* — "cooked," if that was the right word, for a minute on each side, so rare the blood still ran, and the *frites* were soggy. But the apple tart was a wonder to behold. It was more than just an apple tart, it was the local specialty, known as *pithiviers,* a fluffy, flaky pastry layered with rich almond paste and topped with concentric swirls of sugary apples. The vanilla ice cream was no match for Berthillon's, but they didn't care. They washed it down with the Saumur wine, which turned out to be sweet and syrupy and perfect with the dessert.

After supper, Dan dried Lara's hair for her. He smoothed the soft ripples with his hand, spreading it out around her shoulders the better to admire it. "Like waves of silk," he said, bending to drop a kiss on the top of her head. "Beautiful."

A little thrill of happiness shot up Lara's spine. It was the second time that day he had told her she was beautiful.

Naked, they lay propped up in bed, the blankets up to their chins, watching what must have been a very old interview with the French singer and man about town Serge Gainsbourg. Lara knew it was old because Gainsbourg had died several years earlier. And, of course, it was in French, but they were getting used to that and they enjoyed the music. Eventually they turned out the lights, kissed, and slid farther down under the covers. Silent. Introspective.

Does he really think I'm beautiful? Lara was wondering.

How can he think you are beautiful? the nagging little voice of her conscience—or was it her alter ego, or maybe reality?— reminded her. *You've never been a beauty. You were an overweight teenager who only slimmed down at college because you hated the food. You were at your peak when you married Bill and then you were only twenty. Now you look in the mirror every morning and see the truth.*

But my hair, she thought defensively, he said that was beautiful too.

Sure, I'll give you that, the mean little voice admitted, *but, hey, let's face it, you're no girl anymore. This is the Second Honeymoon, only without the first guy. The one who has grown old with you. That's when you become the matched set, the same vintage, so to speak. It kind of equals things out and you don't notice the deficiencies so much because you both have them. Except now Bill's turned you in for a younger, perkier model. And you are here in France with a young lover who must surely see the flaws. Besides, you've gained weight since you got here—you'll never get into that red bathing suit now. . . .*

Lara tossed restlessly in his arms and Dan moved away, giving her room.

"You okay?" he whispered, turning on his side, away from her.

"I'm fine."

There, you see that, the evil little voice said triumphantly. *He doesn't want to make love to you. You should never have worn the robe and slippers. He likes it better when you're in the Sabbia Rosa and the lizard heels. Young men like hot women, not women who remind them of their mothers.*

Lara's heart sank. Maybe that was it. And when they got back to California he was just going to say a polite good-bye and "It was fun and I'll never forget you"—and go and marry beautiful blond Britt, who was young enough to be her daughter.

She sighed. If all it amounted to was a quick romantic affair, at least she would have the memories.

Dan caught the sigh and wondered if she was thinking about Bill. Maybe she was wishing it was her husband lying in bed next to her instead of him. He frowned. He didn't know Bill Lewis, but he certainly didn't like what he had heard about him. And he knew Bill didn't deserve a woman like Lara. She was special, different; she kept him guessing all the time.

Like now, for instance, he was wondering why she seemed so distant. Why sometimes she seemed to go off somewhere inside herself, shutting him out. She was insecure—it didn't take a genius to figure that out—and he didn't know how to make her feel better about herself. He guessed that's what happened to a woman when her husband left her for someone else, though it hadn't sounded like a great marriage to him, anyway. She had said Bill was hardly ever there.

Had Bill ever loved her? He supposed he must have, when they were young—he could have kicked himself for thinking that last bit. Lara would always be young; she was that kind of woman. He had meant it when he told her she was beautiful. To him, she was far more lovely than lean, hard-bodied young Britt with her breast implants and her size-two dresses. Lara was a real woman, rounded, female, slender where it counted and with nature's curves in all the right places. And, call him an old-fashioned guy, but that was what he liked about her.

He said softly, "Lara? Are you awake?"

"Yes." Her voice was muffled by the blanket that almost covered her head.

"You know what?" he said. "We're a lot alike, you and I. In a way, our lives have paralleled each other's. We both brought up children alone, made a home for them, sacrificed the way a good parent does for them. It's normal, natural. Except for men like Bill."

Dan didn't know why he mentioned Bill, except it just angered him that Lara seemed to keep her husband on a pedestal: the great self-important surgeon too busy with his career to bother much about his own wife and kids.

"Bill was a busy man; he wanted to save lives," Lara said, suddenly realizing how many years she had been saying exactly that. And believing it. Defending Bill was a reflex action. "He was always a distant man," she added, remembering the first time she had met him, when she had held his hand while he shed tears for his dead mother. Even then, he hadn't really shared his feelings with her. It was she who had shared her feelings with him.

"When Josh was born, Bill was at a medical conference. He knew I was due but he said it was more important that he be in Atlanta." She shrugged, adding, "I'm sure it was necessary." Though now she wondered.

"Bill didn't want to see his child being born?" Dan said, astonished. "*His own son?* He wasn't there to help you? Jesus Christ, how old were you? Twenty-one or -two? You were just a kid yourself."

"It was okay. The Girlfriends were with me. And my mom, of course."

"Who are the Girlfriends?"

They were sitting up now. Dan's arm was around her shoulders, her head nestled into the curve against his chest. His warm body had a faint tang of grassy cologne.

"The Girlfriends are Vannie, Susie, and Delia." She smiled as she told him their stories. About their quirks and their humor and their loyalty. "I don't know what I would do without them," she finished guiltily, because though she had spoken to Delia, so far she hadn't so much as sent the others a postcard.

Dan tilted her face up to his. "Did you tell them about us?"

"I did."

"And what did the Girlfriends say?" He didn't know why it was so important to have the approval of her best friends, but it was.

Lara laughed. "They said, *'Go for it, Lara.'* "

Dan laughed too. Then, "Are you going to divorce Bill?" he asked out of the blue.

She took a shocked breath. "I haven't gotten around to thinking about that."

"You can't live your life in limbo forever," he said abruptly. "You're going to have to make a decision sooner or later."

Lara pushed back her hair worriedly, the romantic mood gone. "Why are we having this conversation in the middle of the night, anyhow?"

"I couldn't sleep." Throwing back the covers, Dan walked to the window. He gazed out at the slumbering town of Blois.

Lara watched him for a minute, wondering what answer to give him about the divorce. Then she turned over and buried her head under the blanket. Damn him, she said to herself. I don't want to think about it, I don't want to go there. Not now. Not yet.

Chapter Twenty-nine

The next morning, early, they sat crushed in the battered little Renault, whizzing down the autoroute, past miles and miles of empty countryside, past manicured rest stops with playgrounds for children and restaurants that served coffee and snacks and instant meals.

Last night's conversation still hung between them. But what had Dan been getting at with Bill? Lara thought worriedly. It was nothing to do with him, none of his business.

Oh, yes, it is, the little voice retorted. *You're a married woman and he has a right to be concerned about what your husband thinks. And what he might do. Bill could sue you for divorce naming Dan as the other man.*

Wow! Lara drew in a deep breath. She had never thought of herself as the guilty party. No, I'm not, she told herself indignantly. Bill was unfaithful first. He made the choice. If he hadn't, I wouldn't be here now with a stranger. I would be here with my husband.

A stranger? Is that how you think about him? Her alter ego was not letting her off the hook this morning. She remembered those long afternoons on her deck, watching Dan work, admiring his hard brown young body. She thought of those little electric signals that passed between them, like the lightning in the old RKO pylon logo. Zigzagging his way into her head, into her sex. Into her heart. Did electric zigzags mean love? She wondered.

After a couple of silent hours, they pulled into a motorway cafe. They sat opposite each other in a red plastic booth, sipping surprisingly good coffee and sharing a passable croissant.

Dan looked at her across the table. She was wearing an oversized blue rollneck sweater and jeans and her dark hair was pulled back in a ponytail. She looked adorable, wide-eyed and apprehensive. "I'm sorry, Lara." Their hands met over the croissant plate. "I didn't mean to bug you about Bill. It's just that"—he searched his head for what it was exactly that bothered him—"he gets in our way," he said finally. "Somehow, he's always there."

"Not *always*," she said softly, squeezing his hand. "But I'm sorry too. Let's just forget about Bill. We're on vacation, we should be enjoying ourselves."

"I *am* enjoying myself," he said, shaking his head in wonderment, "despite how aggravating you are."

"And how adorable you are."

He laughed then and Lara laughed with him.

"Not exactly the way I would have described myself," he said.

"No, but I bet Britt would." She bit her lip. She wished she hadn't said that.

His eyes still held a glint of laughter. "Let's not go there, shall we?"

"Certainly not. And I apologize one more time." They were back on even keel again. Happy.

Later, zooming down the autoroute, Lara spotted a familiar exit sign. *Limoges*. She remembered it perfectly. "Oh, Dan, we have to get off here," she cried, excited. "There's this lake somewhere around here; I remember it has swans on it."

"How do you remember?" he asked, surprised.

Too late, she realized Dan didn't know she had been there before. She added quickly, "Oh, I was here once, years ago. I traveled a bit when I was younger."

"Then this is kind of a memory thing for you?"

She gave him a guilty smile. "I'm just recalling my youth, I guess. But you'll see, it'll be a good place for a picnic."

In the end they didn't eat their picnic by the lake outside Limoges because Lara couldn't find it. She scrutinized the map while Dan drove around in circles, until he finally said, "The heck with it; let's eat the stuff in the car." So they pulled over to the side of the country road, and munched on a long thin bread called a *ficelle* and a hunk of Gruyère cheese bought from a tiny store in a small village a few miles back, washing it down with cold Evian water.

As they drove off again, Lara looked out the windows at the wisps of fog drifting from the moist brown fields. Wasn't it exactly here, in this very avenue of poplars they were driving through, that she had *left* Bill? The memory stabbed at her like a knife wound. How could she ever have forgotten?

Of course it couldn't be the same avenue of poplars, but it was very much like it. She recalled the scene in perfect detail. They had been sitting on a crumbling wall, all that remained of an old bridge, eating bread and cheese, just like now. It had begun to rain and the picnic, wrapped only in a brown paper bag, was getting wet. Bill was bustling around, organizing them.

"Get back into the car," he'd ordered, wrapping up the food. "We're getting soaked."

But Lara had lingered, entranced by the scene unfolding on the lake. A pair of swans, startlingly white on the carbon-gray water, were gliding toward them followed by three tiny brown chicks. The lowering sky pressed against the drooping willows and their long, delicate green fronds floated sideways in the sudden wind, like a girl's long, fine hair.

Fishing the camera from her bag, she clicked away, laughing as the swans paddled nearer. "Ready for their close-up," she called gaily to Bill.

"Come on, Lara. You're getting soaked." He marched grumpily back to the car.

Ignoring the rain, she snapped happily away. When she finally came back, Bill was already behind the wheel with the engine running. He glanced at her, then at the camera, and said scathingly, "Lara, you left the lens cap on."

She stared at the camera. Damn it, he was right. *As usual.* And she had taken a whole roll of film with the lens covered. She groaned. Over her shoulder she could see the swans were still there, she could still capture that image. "I have to go back and take more."

"Oh, come *on*, Lara. You've seen swans before. Just get in out of the rain and let's get going."

"Philistine," she said scornfully. "These pictures are meant to be a wonderful memory of France. We can show them to our children, and our grandchildren, tell them all about our epic journey."

"Oh, sure," Bill said, ignoring what she said. "Meanwhile, let's go."

Snatching up the bag of bread and cheese, Lara turned her back on him and marched back to the edge of the lake to feed the swans. They fluttered around her, the little chicks cheeping, trying vainly to scramble up the slope. Enchanted, she took her pictures.

Bill was leaning on the horn. "Lara," he yelled, "for Christ's sake, come on."

"This is my honeymoon as well as yours, Bill Lewis," she yelled back. "And tell me what difference does ten minutes make, anyway?"

"It's getting dark, you idiot, and I have to drive through this godforsaken countryside not knowing where I am because you can't read the goddamn map."

"*What* did you say?" She marched toward him. The swans tagged after her, making angry swan sounds, abandoning their chicks in their greed.

"We should have set off at six." Bill glared at her. "Only *you* wanted to sleep late. *Then* you insisted on having breakfast. *Then* you lost our way—not once, but three times."

"So what's wrong with sleeping late?" she yelled back. "What's so wrong with having breakfast? We're not on our way to work, dammit. We're on vacation."

"We have a schedule," Bill said stiffly. "And I for one intend to stick with that."

"Then stick with it on your own, Dr. Lewis." She threw the Michelin road map at him. With her bad aim it hit the dashboard and she heard it rip. "And be your own navigator. Just try reading that map yourself when you're whirling around corners on two wheels at seventy miles an hour."

"Kilometers," Bill corrected her through gritted teeth.

"Ohhh. . . . fuck you." Furious, Lara stomped off down the road.

The wind was blowing hard now, cutting through her hooded sweatshirt, and the rain was coming down in sheets. She strode on, still fuming. Why was Bill so damn serious all the time? Why couldn't he take time out to admire the swans? What was wrong with him, anyway? Him and his fucking schedule. All he thought about was getting from point A to point B when the whole point was to enjoy France, not pass it by without so much as a glance. How could he accuse her of losing their way three times? It was only twice today, and both had been minor, and, besides, it was just that the French roundabouts were such a bitch. . . . She never wanted to see him again; he could go complain to some other woman. She'd had it.

Hunched against the wind, she marched on. She was soaked now. And miserable. The fight was going out of her.

She heard the car behind her, *phutphut*ing the way small French cars did. She slowed but did not look back. She told herself Bill would have to *beg* her to get into that car. But first he would have to apologize. Then *maybe* she would think about it. . . .

The car drove straight by her. Lara stared after it, stunned. It disappeared from sight and she was alone in the deepening twilight. The narrow tree-lined road stretched in front of her, the wind rustled eerily in the trees, and a white mist spiraled off the damp brown fields. There was no human habitation, no farm with smoke curling welcomingly from its chimney. Even the swans had gone back to their lake with their chicks. Except for the wind, there was just empty silence.

Fighting back the tears Lara marched on, head down. "Fuck you, Bill Lewis," she muttered. "I never want to see you again, *never. . . .*"

But what will you do without him? that little voice asked nastily. *Where will you go? This road goes on forever, no cars have passed since you came here. You're all alone somewhere in France and he's not coming back for you. Maybe you got what you deserved; maybe he was right and you shouldn't have stopped to feed the swans when it was getting dark and you had to get on to the next town.*

Lara stamped her foot, furious. "I was *not* wrong. I had *every right* to feed those bloody swans."

Tears spurted from her eyes, rolled down her icy face. They dried quickly in the harsh wind, chapping her cheeks. Sniffling, she marched on down the empty road. She had never felt so alone. So *abandoned.*

She must have walked almost half a mile when she saw the car parked in a muddy gateway that led to yet another brown field. Inside she could see Bill, warm and dry, arms folded, staring at her. Ignoring him, she marched straight past on the other side of the road.

"Lara! For God's sakes." He stuck his head out the window. "Get in the car."

She swung around, spitting mad. "Why?" she hissed. "So my loving new husband can prove to me how much he cares about me? Bah!" She continued her lonely march, straining her ears for the sound of the car's engine as he came after her. *Nothing.* Blinded with tears, she marched on.

"Lara!" Bill caught up to her, took her arm, pulled her to him. "My God, Lara, what are we doing?" he groaned. "Why are we fighting like this? I was just worried about reaching civilization before it got dark and we got lost again."

For a second Lara considered arguing the "getting lost again" scenario, then sensibly decided against it. "And I just wanted to take pictures of the swans," she said, her voice muffled against his shoulder. "I'm so sorry, Bill." Her arms were around him now; she was safe against his manly, anoraked chest.

It wasn't until she was lying in bed, warm and secure next to her husband later that night, in the very hotel he had intended for them to stay in, that she remembered. Bill had not said he was sorry too.

You've been sleeping." Dan's voice had a smile in it. "Wake up and look at what I found for you."

Lara glanced around. They were in the courtyard of a small stone auberge. Through the open door she could see a fire burning in the massive grate, and from somewhere came the rattle of pots and pans and the aroma of something good cooking.

"I figured what was the use of pressing on any further in this bad weather, when there's a great little place right here."

"How did you find it?" she asked admiringly.

"Oh, I just kinda fell over it." He grinned as he hauled their bags out of the hatchback. "It ain't the Holiday Inn, lady, but you can bet it's French."

"And *good*," she added, following him into the welcoming portals of the tiny inn, remembering that after the fight with Bill, which had somehow conveniently been blocked from her memory bank until now, he had still insisted on finding the hotel they were booked into.

Again, she wondered how she had recalled the sweet bucolic vision of the two of them on the bank of the lake, feeding swans under blue skies, laughing and loving on their wonderful French honeymoon.

She was beginning to think it was a good thing Bill hadn't come with her. If things hadn't already been over between them, these memories would surely have done the trick.

Chapter Thirty

It was late the next afternoon and they were sitting on the shaded stone terrace of the fourteenth-century Hôtel Le Château, in Lalinde near Bergerac, which by some miracle Lara had found without a hitch. The Dordogne River swirled lazily past, bearing flotillas of mallards and moorhens downstream, as well as the occasional kayaker and fisherman. A young waiter was opening a bottle of Ruinart champagne, the sky was an amazing azure blue with only one tiny puff of cloud, and the sun shone, as it had all day long.

Lara heaved a contented sigh. "Perfect," she murmured, accepting the glass of champagne. She raised it in a toast: "To us. And to the sun, finally."

Dan's eyes met hers. "To us. And thanks for the great navigating."

She lifted a nonchalant shoulder. "It was nothing, m'sieur. I do that every day. In my sleep."

"That's usually what it feels like," he agreed. "Now there's just one problem."

It was the same mistake as at the Ritz—they had been booked in for the previous night. Lara guessed this was going to happen all through their trip and that she would have to enlist the proprietor's help in telephoning the other hotels where they had reservations to ask them to make the adjustment.

"If the other people don't show up by six, we can have their room," she said optimistically. She wasn't about to let it worry her, she was having too good a time. The sun was warm, the champagne cold, and the river a pageant of color lapping almost at their feet.

They had been on the road for seven hours and Dan was amazed that Lara looked as fresh as a daisy in crumpled pale-blue linen overalls. Her hair was piled on top of her head for coolness and she wore no makeup save for a dash of lip gloss. Her pale skin was turning pink under the sun's kiss and her dark curling lashes gave her a sultry look that turned him on.

He looked longingly at her. "I wish we had that bedroom now."

She caught the electric zigs and zags and smiled. "Finish your champagne. There's time enough for that."

"Yeah, if we have a room."

"There's always the backseat of the car."

"In a Renault 106?"

She laughed with him. "Don't worry, it'll be okay," she said confidently. Somehow she just knew it was one of those days when everything would go right.

It was impossible to guess from its narrow welcoming hallway and the curved oak staircase that the little hotel had been a prison in the thirteenth century. Rebuilt in the nineteenth, the tiny turreted château had only eight rooms and was more like a bourgeois house located on a side street, right on the Dordogne River, in the small town of Lalinde.

It had changed since Lara had been there with Bill, with a new chef-proprietor and a little swimming pool artistically surrounded by rocks and plants. The two small yellow dining rooms were models of French bourgeois taste and the food was based on local delicacies like foie gras and duck confit, rich and full of good flavors.

Content, Lara sat back, thinking how angry Bill would have been about the mix-up with the reservations, how he would have been pacing by now. Or worse, he'd have been back in the car on his way to find some other place to stay. "It will all work out" seemed to be Dan's philosophy, and he was right. After all, in a pinch there was always the railway hotel.

"A centime for your thoughts, madame," Dan offered.

"I was remembering the railway hotel near the Gare du Nord and the sound of the trains going by."

"And the famous fountains of Paris."

They were laughing when the desk clerk came bustling toward them to tell them that the other guests had telephoned to cancel and the room was theirs.

"Great timing," Dan said.

"I told you, you could trust me."

"Anywhere except in an automobile," he agreed. Their gaze locked, shutting out the rest of the world. He reached out, took her hand, dropped a kiss on her cheek. "Consider that a deposit. . . ."

They were still laughing as they made their way up the oak staircase and through dim spacious hallways to the third floor.

Thankfully, their room was not the same one Lara had shared with Bill. She unlatched the tall windows that opened inward, French-style, pushed back the green shutters, and gazed down at the Dordogne River lapping at the stone walls. She thought of the long-ago men who had once been imprisoned here, and how they must have stared hopelessly out to the opposite bank and freedom. But there were no bad vibes left over from the past in the simple, sun-filled rooms with their cheerful Oriental throw rugs and the old-fashioned furniture that looked as though it had come from somebody's grandmother's place. As did the big fluffy bed. Which was where they landed when Dan swooped her away from the view and into his arms.

Lara had come to terms with her rounded figure. She knew Dan loved her body; after all, he told her so, often. She told herself she no longer wanted to look twenty years younger for him . . . well, maybe five would do. Right now, age didn't matter; time was suspended as he rolled her over until she lay on top. She stretched her body luxuriously along his length, enjoying her power as she felt him harden against her, smiling that secret little smile of a woman who knows a man wants her. And this time she was going to take him, make him her own.

She straddled him, pausing for a moment as their eyes collided. She ran a hand down his strong neck, across his chest, feeling the muscles tense beneath her teasing fingers, knowing how urgently he wanted her. "Beautiful," she murmured, depositing tiny, light-as-air kisses where her fingers had touched. "I've never seen anyone as beautiful."

His hands found her nipples and she flung back her head, groaning with pleasure, pressing down on his hardness; she had to touch him, to touch herself, feel with every fiber of her body what was happening to her, to them.

He was strong when she took him in her hand and sank down on him. He trembled beneath her, gripped her hips as she moved over him—*God, oh, God,* she heard him mutter—and she felt empowered, the arbiter of his fate for this one delicious moment.

They tangled like animals on their big soft bed, then Dan was on top, exploring, savoring. . . .

"I didn't know I could be like this," Lara whispered as he held still over her. She could feel those seismic tremors quivering through his body.

"Open your eyes, Lara, look at me," he urged. And the last veil of her inhibitions was drawn aside as she drowned in his eyes, hurtled over the edge by the sensual drive of his body into hers.

Afterward, they lay entwined. His skin was damp with sweat, salty under her tongue as she tasted him. She pushed the dark gold hair back from his eyes, still locked in his embrace, still in that other world of the senses. "Darling Dan," she whispered, "I love you."

Watching him walk naked into the bathroom in the little tower, Lara asked herself if she *really* loved him. Or if she was *in* love with him. Was there a difference?

Of course there's a difference. The voice of her alter ego was back again just when she least needed it. She turned her head into the pillow and covered her ears, as if to shut it out. *How could he love you? He barely knows, you. This is the classic shipboard romance, Lara—like on* Love Boat, *right? Proximity, a carefree vacation . . .*

Not exactly *carefree,* she thought. I'm here to find myself. To reconcile myself to being without Bill, without a husband. To start over again.

Alone, the nagging voice reminded her.

Alone, she sighed. If I have to.

You mean you're still holding out some hope that Dan won't be going right back to Britt as soon as you get back home? Come on,

Lara, grow up, why don't you. I mean, how old are you now? Don't you ever learn?

Dammit, how can I learn? This is only my second time around. . . . I'm a virtual novice.

Darn right you are, lady. But not this guy. Not Dan. He's probably had more girlfriends than you've had hot dinners. . . .

"Lara," Dan called from the turret bathroom, and she ran to him.

He was leaning out of the tiny arched window, and she stopped to take in the long lines of his hard young body, the taut buttocks, the lean flanks and muscular legs. The maple-syrup tan gained from working shirtless outdoors ended where his shorts fitted then started again halfway down his thighs, under a fine layer of golden hair. Lara put a hand on her still-pounding heart, struck with the physical force of how her body reacted to him. He was, she thought with a little catch in her throat, like a great golden bear.

He swung around, saw her, held out his hand to her. "You've got to see this."

The sun was setting across the river, burning the brown waters a rippling red, tipping the trees on the far bank with crimson, hiding in a rosy gold lining behind the purplish clouds of approaching dusk. And, down the center of the river, like a painting by Corot, floated a pair of swans: regal, proud, the keepers of the great river, their white feathers now a blush pink, fading to mauve as the sun dipped finally behind the horizon.

"I'll never forget this moment as long as I live," Dan said quietly. "Our lovemaking, the swans, the sunset, and you here with me now. It's . . ." He searched for the right word. "*Perfect*," he said humbly. "Yes, that's it. *Perfect*."

For once the nagging little voice that was either Lara's conscience or her alter ego had nothing to say.

Chapter Thirty-one

Dan lay back against the pillows on their bed, his hands behind his head, watching Lara get ready for the evening. It had taken him five minutes to shower and throw on a clean shirt and pants, but he knew that even a woman as unserious about her appearance as Lara needed at least thirty, and a woman like Britt took forever. Polishing up the image for her public, he guessed.

His skin was cool from the shower; Lara's familiar perfume tickled his nose and he anticipated, pleasantly, a simple meal and a bottle of wine out on the terrace overlooking the river. What more could life offer a man?

Diamonds glittered at Lara's throat, matching the band of diamonds that encircled the third finger of her left hand—and which, Dan had noticed, though he had said nothing, Lara had not yet taken off.

Did that mean Bill Lewis was still on the scene? He frowned, suddenly uneasy. He didn't even want to think about that. That other life seemed so remote, that reality too far away even to contemplate. Still, he had to ask himself the question: Did he love Lara? Love her in the way you were supposed to when you knew this was it? Knew this was your one and only? Your life-time partner, your friend, companion, lover?

Oh, yes, he loved her. But how did he love her? And why?

The answer to the first question was easy: Lara was unique. She was beautiful, intelligent, wounded. She was gentle and vulnerable in an old-fashioned way. Had he simply taken her in his arms that first night at the beach to comfort her? The hell he had not—he had wanted her the first time he saw her in that skimpy bathing suit.

He had never met anyone like her, so untouched by the day-to-day material rules that dominated the lives of most young women he had dated. The truth was, he told himself, that Lara simply didn't care about such things. Or did she? After all, she was a woman with two homes and a successful husband who had given her a lifestyle many women would envy. Bill had given Lara far more, materially, than he would ever be able to offer.

And, yes, that worried him. Could there be a future for Lara and him in his scaled-down, simple life? Could she give all that up for the local builder/handyman? And what about her chil-dren? They were old enough to resent losing their mom to the blue-collar guy who came back to his modest home covered in dust and sweat every night, instead of to a Pacific Heights man-sion in a custom-tailored suit and a designer tie. It was a deeply troubling thought.

His eyes rested on Lara, still hesitating in front of the mir-ror. He smiled as a snatch of Eric Clapton's song ran through his brain. The one about his lover preparing to go out, putting on her makeup, brushing her long blond hair, and then asking,

"Do I look all right?" And he tells her she looks wonderful tonight.

He knew Lara was wondering if she looked all right. And that Eric Clapton had got it right. This woman looked wonderful tonight too, though his enduring image of her would always be in the too-small red bathing suit with her breasts spilling out and that shyly embarrassed look on her face.

Lara hadn't even suspected the power of her attraction, and that was what had made him fall for her. He wanted to take her in his arms right now and cover her with kisses, except he knew that when a woman had spent half an hour primping, he'd better be careful not to muss her up. Though he'd bet Lara wouldn't mind, she would just laugh and kiss him back, then put on fresh lipstick.

The image of Bill in his designer suit and tie was stuck in Dan's mind's eye. He owned only one tie, the one Lara had given him. He had worn it on that disastrous night at the Paris restaurant and odds were he'd never wear it again. Except, perhaps, to his wedding . . .

Jesus, there he went again. Full circle. Were he and Lara really meant to be? He still didn't know the answer to that, but one thing he did know: he loved her. And he didn't want to lose her.

Lara looked at her man, handsome in a loose white linen shirt, sleeves rolled up, golden hair still wet from the shower. At the bright blue of his eyes, at the strong mouth that knew how to tease her, how to taste her; at the hands that knew her body better than she knew it herself. She had never felt this *intimate* with Bill, had never known a man the way she knew Dan, even though she had known him such a short time. But it wasn't time that mattered, she told herself, it was the emotions. You just knew when it was right. And this was *so* right. She was smiling as she took his hand and walked down the old oak staircase out onto the terrace.

She wore the pink-flowered dress—her "Paris" dress, she called it, and tonight she had no qualms about its appropriateness for her age. It was the perfect dress for dining on a summer terrace: soft, pretty, and sexy.

The big brown river swirled past and the restaurant was crowded with guests and locals—she picked out a British voice here and there among the French. But she and Dan were quiet tonight. Contentment lay amicably between them, comforting as a soft blanket. They needed no one else. An air of tranquillity still lingered, as did the image of the rose-colored swans on the melting-gold river. A bottle of the local rich red Pécharment wine eased the pang of sadness she felt as she counted the days they had left. Exactly twelve.

This was, she thought, taking Dan's brown hand in hers across the table, the kind of night you never wanted to end.

They lay together in the big old-fashioned bed, her leg flung over his, his arm under her shoulders. The busy Dordogne River lapped its way soothingly past their stone walls and, somewhere in the woods opposite, an owl hooted, reminding Lara of ghosts and demons and witches. Safe in her lover's arms, they held no terrors for her tonight, and she slept.

Dan watched her smooth, sleeping face for a long while. Filled with tenderness, he recalled their evening together, how she had looked, what she had said, the joyous smile that had lit her eyes with sparkles. He lay back against the pillows, his arm still around her, and the final lines of the Eric Clapton song still running through his mind. Lara had looked wonderful tonight.

Chapter Thirty-two

They were back at the car at ten the next morning, piling in their heavy bags one more time, reminding Lara once again that, of course, she had packed too much. She'd bet now she could have gotten away with just the stuff she had bought in Paris, her luggage could have stayed lost forever.

"This is beginning to feel like one long Greyhound bus trip," she complained. "We've not even explored the countryside and it's so lovely, around here."

Dan shrugged. "I was just going along with your schedule, Ms. Lewis."

She stared stunned at him. She was the one with the schedule now. Not Bill. *She*, Lara the lazy one, who wanted nothing more than to mooch around unspoiled French villages and linger in the tiny squares; to bid bonjour to the polite school-smocked children and chat as well as she could in her limited French with the woman in the pastry shop while deciding which delicacy would best accompany a café grand crème. *She*, who had only wanted to explore cobblestoned alleys and massive-gated courtyards and romantic, balconied houses and musty an-tiques shops and even the *quincaillerie*, the hardware shop, because she loved the way the name sounded, and loved the dark old-fashioned store with its smells of tar and sawdust and rope. *She had become Bill.*

That did it. Mentally throwing the schedule to the winds she took another step toward freedom from the ties that still bound her. "Why don't we just cruise around the countryside for a while," she said. "Check out some of those medieval villages where Richard the Lion-Hearted once ruled, find a little place to stay that's different and off the beaten track."

So they climbed into the dusty Renault and took off for who knew where. The beginning of an adventure, Lara hoped, pleased with herself and starry-eyed and bubbling with a new joy. Had she finally left Bill behind?

The Dordogne is a land of ancient watermills perched over tranquil little tributaries; of turreted pigeon towers filled with cooing doves; of medieval stone villages with streets so narrow the houses seem to lean into one another. Of cloistered squares and towns once ruled by the kings of England. Magical, mys-tical, it dreams on, a still-quiet backwater on the tide of tourism.

"*This* is France." Lara squeezed Dan's arm, and he turned and gave her the grin that lit up his face so boyishly. She smiled, reminding herself that Dan had been a boy not so many years ago. But not even the question of age could bring her down today. The sun was shining and birds sang in the hedgerows as she pointed out turreted mini-châteaux on the sides of steep-sloped green hills and straggling farms crowded with clacking geese and underwear-pink piglets, and the bustling Saturday market in Bergerac that offered everything from local goat cheese and farm-fresh produce, foie gras and Agen prunes, to antiques and linens.

It was Lara's turn to drive and she wound around the narrow country lanes, past vineyards and tiny hamlets — mere straggles of pale stone houses not big enough to bear the name of "village" — past ancient watermills looming over brooding brown rivers, and finally into the central square in the old village of Beaumont.

It was so perfect, it could have been a movie set on the back lot at Universal City: an old columned open market; houses from different centuries; mansard roofs and red-tiled roofs; ancient half-timbered walls; honey-colored stone; a church tower; a blue-awninged greengrocer with fruits and vegetables piled in crates outside; a fragrant patisserie; a couple of cafes with green plastic chairs; and a crush of cars parked at nonchalant angles in the center of the square.

It was deserted save for a lone man reading a newspaper and smoking a Gauloise at a corner cafe. A couple of dogs lounged lazily in doorways, hardly bothering to raise an eyelid as Lara and Dan sauntered past. They stopped, as they always seemed to, outside the patisserie, where they bought a fresh tomato and onion tart, which they shared at the corner cafe with a café grand crème for Lara and a Stella Artois for Dan.

Dan heaved a sigh of pure satisfaction and said, "If you say 'Now this is France' one more time, I may have to leave you," making Lara laugh.

And then they were in the car again, bouncing their way down potholed lanes, through villages with strange names like Naussannes and Issigeac and Nojals-en-Clotte.

It was at the crossroads of two tiny lanes that Lara saw the house. She stopped the car and stared at it, instantly in love.

Half hidden by trees, it sat solidly atop a small hill, built of pale golden stone topped with a *pigeonnier,* a square tower where in the old days farmers had raised pigeons for the cookpot.

A good-looking gray-haired man was coming down the curving driveway, a bright red power saw in one hand. He was wearing shorts, sneakers, and a baseball cap that said *Lost Balls Retirement Golf Club,* and he looked tanned, fit, and very American.

"How're y'doin'?" He raised a hand in greeting.

"Great. Just admiring your home," Dan called out. "That's some place you've got there."

"You should have seen it before my wife got her hands on it. There were cows bedding down in what's now our bedroom." He held out his hand. "Hi, I'm Jerry Shoup."

"Lara Lewis, Dan Holland." They climbed out of the car and shook hands.

"Where are you guys from?"

"San Francisco." Lara smiled at him. He was friendly, easy. "You're every American's dream, doing up an old farm, making it into a wonderful home in the middle of the French countryside."

Jerry laughed. "There's dreams and dreams. What with French rules and regulations and bylaws and zoning, you need to know more about local politics than building, as well as be on good terms with the mayor, to get anything done around here."

He gestured down the road at a neighboring farm. "That

place was for sale. Friends of ours bought it. Their daughter, an architect, came out from L.A. to figure out how to expand the old farmhouse. They had it all planned, were all set.

"The farmers' union told them the rule was they must wait sixty days before the transaction could be completed, and that any farmer had first option to buy. There was no problem; no local farmer wanted the place.

"It was at six o'clock on the evening of the sixtieth day. We had just broken out the champagne to celebrate their new home, when a call came from their *notaire,* the local lawyer. A farmer had come in from out of town and wanted the property. There was no appeal. He had prior right." He shrugged. "So there you go. You've just got to get lucky, I guess."

Lara didn't care about problems, she was in love with the place. The sun beat down and the only sound was the buzzing of bees and a songbird winging by. The place was enchanted, a dream from which, too soon, she would wake up, only to find herself back in the dusty Renault on their way to yet another town.

Dan was asking Jerry how he had found their place.

"We have a friend here owns a vineyard, turns out a pretty good Bergerac wine. We were just driving by and my wife said 'Stop.' So I stopped." He grinned. "All there was, was a pile of tumbling old buildings with geese and pigs and chickens and laundry hanging around. We spoke to the old couple who lived there. They were anxious to quit, wanted a modern place closer to town with hot and cold running water and a bathroom, I guess. We made a deal there and then, shook hands on it. Then we went home and I told my wife, 'You know what? We're crazy.' 'You know what, Jer?' she said. 'We've always been that way.' "

Lara laughed. "Sounds like a woman after my own heart."

"Hey, come on in and meet her," Jerry said. "She'll show you the house. We're real proud of it."

Red Shoup was a tall, slim, attractive woman with the red hair of her name. In yellow shorts and a big sun hat, she was weeding flower beds in the courtyard. "Hi," she said, coming toward them with a big smile. "Sorry I can't shake hands, but I'm a bit weedy. Welcome, anyway." She glanced at her husband. "Where did you find them?"

"Admiring your house. I thought they looked like they needed a glass of wine and a tour."

Red laughed, a big hearty laugh that made them smile too. "Okay, first things first. The big old barn behind you is now the main house. When we saw it the walls were crumbling, there was no roof, and pigs still lived in it. The small house on the right was the original farmhouse where madame and monsieur lived until they went on to more modern and better things in Bergerac. Now it's a guest house. The *pigeonnier* on the other side of the courtyard was the first building we converted so we would have somewhere to live while the major work on the barn was carried out. The old bakery, on the far side of the courtyard, is now Jerry's office and our game room, with a pool table. And over there," she waved an elegant arm, "is the nine-hole golf course. The 'Lost Balls Retirement Golf Club,' Jerry calls it. It's rough, but he and our sons built it, complete with sand traps. And I designed the swimming pool using concrete pipes."

The long, narrow, deep-blue pool bisected the house and looked like something out of *Architectural Digest*, right in the middle of the French countryside. Dan said he was a builder by trade and he was in awe.

"Sounds easy, doesn't it?" Red grinned. "You'll never know the truth," she added feelingly, waving them inside the old barn.

They stared thirty feet up to the raftered ceiling with its ancient beams; at the stone walls and the *colombage* and the massive limestone fireplace; at the country kitchen that led to an open dining area; at the antiques and rugs and the flowers. Lara sighed and asked if by any chance they took boarders.

Red laughed. "Unfortunately not paying ones, though as usual we have a full house."

From the terrace in back came the sound of voices and soon they were being introduced to four handsome grown-up children and a bunch of grandchildren. Chilled white wine, fresh-made lemonade, bowls of nuts and biscuits and slices of rough local sausage were brought out.

One daughter, a beauty, was standing at an easel painting something exotic and quite wonderful. Another elegant daughter was supervising the children in the pool, and the two handsome sons joined them on the terrace, along with a fabulous-looking young Asian woman whom one introduced as his wife.

Red asked where they were staying and when Lara admitted they had no idea, she said she knew just the place.

Within minutes, it seemed to Lara, their lives were organized. They were staying at a local château and dinner was arranged there later that night with the Shoups.

They wound their way up a little hill to the château, parked in a dusty, unpaved area, then walked across the wooden bridge over a tiny stream, where a great black dog sprawled, on guard. He raised his head, gave a flurry of barks, then settled back down.

The English *patron* hurried toward them. "He's not really our dog," he apologized. "Or at least he wasn't. He's just sort of adopted us and now he's become territorial and considers the place his own."

They were in a long lofty room with an enormous oak refectory table. Tapestries hung on stone walls and off at one end Lara caught a glimpse of an enormous kitchen with copper pots and pans dangling from a rack over the vast wooden counter. Upstairs was another grand room with painted beams and heraldic shields, Persian rugs, and elegant furnishings. And somewhere beyond that, she assumed, were the family quarters.

They were shown to their own quarters, off the paved courtyard, up a winding stone staircase in a little round tower. It was like being in someone's pretty home, with a brass bed covered in English flowered chintz and fluffy swagged curtains to match.

"Don't forget, aperitifs and canapés on the terrace at six," the owner beamed as he left.

Which was where they met their fellow guests later, over an exotic drink that tasted of raspberries. "We mix a different brew every day," the *patron* told them as his charming wife proferred a tray of olives and fresh-from-the-oven cheese straws.

The sun was just beginning to set on the valley and Lara could see cars winding past on the curving road below and hear the bleat of a lone sheep on the hillside. The other guests, all British, mingled sociably, asking where they were from and how they were enjoying France, keeping a strict eye on their young offspring racing dangerously close to the edge of the pool.

A frazzled-looking young mother in a print skirt and striped T-shirt sighed as she told them, "Sarah has fallen in twice already. And always when I've just got her bathed and into something decent in time for supper," and Dan said he thought it looked pretty much like Sarah was about to do it again.

Seven-thirty was dinnertime. Lara was wearing the Paris dress again and the lizard sandals in honor of the grand dining room.

"Beautiful," Dan whispered to her, smiling as he remembered the roly-poly woman bundled up in his sweatpants and layers of clothing that freezing night in Madame Defarge's barn.

Red and Jerry Shoup arrived in a group of six, and then two other pairs of guests arrived. With Lara and Dan and the patron and his wife, that made fourteen at the long table.

Somebody was a cordon-bleu cook, Lara couldn't remember whether it was him or her, but the food was simple and good and elegantly served. The wine flowed and the conversation was brimming with humor and punctuated with laughter. It was like a very nice English dinner party.

They were given all kinds of advice on what to see and where to go. You mustn't miss Monpazier, they were told. It's a thirteenth-century bastide, a little fortified village built by England's King Edward the First, who was married to France's Eleanor of Castile. It's perfectly preserved and on the list of the hundred most beautiful villages in France.

And then there's Domme, of course, off in the other direction, though, past Sarlat, but it's probably the prettiest of all the Dordogne villages.

And you shouldn't miss the Countess's château, just down the road, in the Lot region. She produces the finest prunes—the famous prunes of Agen. Hers are boxed like fine chocolates and they sell them in Harrods. Of course, it's better when they are in season, but the Countess always has boxes for sale.

And then there's the Moulin de Moulède, a little watermill

near Montflanquin, where Madame serves a fine prix fixe lunch, all the locals go there.

"We could stay here forever," Lara said, "there's so much to see."

"Well, why don't you?" Red Shoup's shrewd blue gaze settled on the pair of them. She smiled at Lara. "Hang on to him, honey," she whispered, "he's a gem."

Once again there was that complicit exchange of glances between women. And once again the smile lightened Lara's already light heart until she almost levitated. She *knew* she had made the right choice, done the right thing. And she wasn't even missing Bill one bit. At least, not tonight.

"Why don't we buy a place here?" she said, brimming with enthusiasm as she stumbled up the spiral stone stairs with Dan later. She could already see them on some enchanted tower in the woods, with a view of the great river curving through the valley below. She put a hand over her mouth to stop herself, knowing she was talking commitment. "That was the wine talking," she apologized. "Forget I said it."

"Why should I forget?" He was following her up the stairs; his hand slid up her skirt, and she laughed.

"Whatever will the neighbors think?" she whispered, melting into him.

"After Madame Defarge, what does it matter?"

He carried her up the remaining steps, fumbling with the key while she leaned against him, laughing. Soon she was naked and he was on top of her.

"The bed squeaks," she whispered.

He lifted his head. "Do you care?"

She shook her head. "Not one bit." And she was laughing again as he made love to her, squeaky springs and all.

San Francisco—and reality—were so far away. . . .

Chapter Thirty-three

Two days later, they were on the road again, whizzing down the Autoroute des Deux Mers, the "Highway of Two Seas," stopping every now and again to find the francs necessary to pay the tolls, then zooming on. Monpazier, the Shoups, and the Dordogne were behind them, and three boxes of the Countess's Agen prunes wilted in the backseat.

They were singing along with the radio, the Stones and "Brown Sugar." Lara had first heard it when she was in her teens; Dan must have been just a kid.

"Take me dancing tonight," she said suddenly. "I want to dance with you."

He glanced at her, smiling at her enthusiasm. "Okay," he agreed.

Uh-oh, now you're acting like a teenager. The voice brought her nastily down to earth. *When did you ever dance with Bill?*

Never, Lara thought airily. I never danced with Bill. He was always too serious. And now I want to dance, so there. . . .

The walled city of Carcassonne appeared, shimmering in the

sunlight atop the hill, its ramparts and towers silhouetted against the blue sky.

"It's a mirage." Lara breathed, awed. "It can't be real."

They got off at the next exit and chugged up the hill. The only entry was over the drawbridge. They had to park the car outside the walls and walk across, which they did, hand in hand.

They were in a medieval fortified town, on a cobblestoned street so narrow they were forced to press themselves against the walls to allow the few cars permitted in for deliveries to squeeze past. They climbed onto the ramparts and strode along the battlements imagining the knights of old watching their enemies massing on their horses, battle standards flying as they crossed the River Aude and charged up the hill, bows drawn, arrows ready. And the defenders of Carcassonne spilling vats of boiling oil on them.

Lara snapped away with her little Nikon (it had no lens cap to cheat her this time) while Dan admired the massive stones, wondering how they had built all this without machinery. Sheer power of labor, he guessed, hundreds of men working at once.

They found a room at the Hotel Dame Carcas, with a huge cherrywood bed and flowery wallpaper, and after a shower, they explored the town, then lingered over a citron *presse* in an outdoor cafe, watching the world go by.

Later, they found a bistro that served *cassoulet*, the local stew of preserved goose, with Toulouse sausages and thick white beans in a rich tomato-based sauce. It came in individual clay pots, crusted on top from the wood-fired oven, and they washed it down with a local rough red *vin du pays*. Lara thought it was heaven until Dan suddenly said, "So, are you going to leave Bill?"

What could she tell him? That she didn't know yet? That she

had to find herself first? That she had to know the truth about who *she* was?

"Must we talk about this now?" she said coaxingly. "It's such a lovely night, all I want to think about is us. *You*."

"You have to think about it sometime, Lara. I need to know." She could see he was deadly serious and didn't know what to think. Was he asking for a commitment? She just couldn't cope with that.

"I will," she replied. "Just not now, not this magical night."

Fool, the voice murmured. *Oh, you foolish woman* . . .

They held hands on the way back to the hotel, and Lara thought thankfully that everything seemed all right again. High up on their hill, the sky was ink blue and spattered with tiny stars. "As though God had thrown a paintbrush out there," she said dreamily. And the narrow streets smelled of wood smoke and of Armagnac and geraniums. Secrets hung in the air, intangible, yet you felt them there. She thought that in France there was no need to go searching for history in museums; you lived with it every day. It was in the street you were walking down, in the old stone walls, in the turn-of-the-century brasseries and the ancient beams in the ceiling above your bed at night. In France, Lara thought, the past was always part of the present.

And so, she was soon to find out, was her own past. Because it was about to come back to haunt her.

Lara was wide awake. The *cassoulet* was sitting too heavily in her stomach. She turned her head to look at Dan, curled around her, one leg flung across hers. His mouth was slightly open and his hair was silver in the moonlight streaming through the open window.

Leaning on her elbow, she studied him, noticing for the first time the tiny creases around his eyes, the as-yet-faint furrows on his brow, the golden stubble on his chin. Her heart melted at how vulnerable he looked.

Guilty at watching him when he was unaware, she slid from the bed and went to the window. She gazed out at the night sky, black as satin, pinned with a giant opal moon. The ancient town slept. Everyone, Lara thought restlessly, but her. She turned to look at Dan. He was lying on his back now, snoring softly.

Sighing with loneliness, she tiptoed into the bathroom and took a Zantac to quell the *cassoulet*. Then she found a crumpled copy of the *Herald Tribune* Dan had picked up in a cafe and went and sat by the window. There was enough light from the moon to read by and she smoothed out the pages, indifferently studying the headlines about train crashes and bull markets. Nothing that was going on in the world seemed to touch her charmed life; she was in a time warp, secured by the drawbridge in her walled city. The world could get along without her for a few weeks.

Not even a few weeks, anymore, the voice reminded her. *What is it now? Ten days?*

Lara shivered and pulled her robe closer. She didn't want to think about reality.

Halfway down the next page she saw the photograph. *Famous doctor and his assistant open new cardiac wing in Beijing*, the caption read.

For a second, she didn't get it. Then it hit her. Her hands trembled as she stared at the picture of Bill and Melissa Kenney. Bill had obviously not known he was being photographed. Either that or he didn't care. His arm was around Melissa's shoulder, his lips close to her ear . . . as though he were about to kiss her, Lara thought, sickened.

> World-famous cardiac surgeon, Dr. William H. Lewis of San Francisco, seen here with his assistant, pediatrician Dr. Melissa Kenney, were guests of honor of the Chinese government at the opening of a new cardiac center in Beijing. Dr. Lewis has won acclaim for his lifesaving heart and lung transplants on children, using pioneering techniques. The couple will continue on to New Delhi, where Dr. Lewis will cooperate on designing a new children's surgical facility and hospital. Dr. Lewis says, "My work is the most important thing in the world to me. Saving lives, children's lives, is why I became a doctor in the first place. Nothing can give a man more satisfaction than that. I consider it a job well done."

Lara's flimsy bubble of happiness collapsed like a punctured party balloon. Anger choked her, sorrow clawed at her heart, self-pity overwhelmed her, and jealousy dug a ferocious acid pit in her stomach. Dan did not exist. France did not exist. All there was now was Bill and the past. Their entwined lives of twenty-five years, their long-ago youth, their children. And her own pain. The new woman she had become fell apart, as insubstantial as her alter ego had assured her she was all along.

When she could summon the strength, she went downstairs to the darkened lobby.

The sleepy young man on night duty stared at her as though he were seeing a ghost. He shuffled upright in his chair and got to his feet, smoothing back his hair. "Madame?"

"Telephone?" she asked, unable to think in French, even though the word, fortunately, was identical.

He gestured to a small wooden cubicle under the stairs.

Lara stepped inside, closed the door, and sank onto the tiny cushioned seat. Automatically, she dialed Delia's number. She needed the Girlfriends.

The line was bad and there was what sounded like thousands of miles of ocean roaring at her when Delia answered. "Well, hi," she said. "We hadn't heard from you, so we assumed no news was good news and that you were having such a great time, you hadn't given us a second thought. Or even a *first* thought."

"Delia, I'm in Carcassonne."

"Sounds like some kind of rich French casserole."

"Oh, Delia." Lara's voice shook. "I just saw Bill's picture in the *Herald Tribune*. He was with the pediatrician and he looks as though he's just about to kiss her."

Delia's sigh sounded wobbly as it struggled over the cable. "So what do you care, Lar? I gather you're getting plenty of kissing yourself."

"That's not the point. . . ."

Lara's voice trailed off and Delia said quickly, "Okay, so what *is* the point? I'm assuming you must have one since you're calling specifically to tell me about it."

"I mean . . . well, it just proves it's true, doesn't it?"

"But, honey, you already knew it was true. You can't let seeing a picture of them together put you back to square one. Remember, you're on a voyage of self-discovery—not spying on Bill and his bimbo."

"But, Delia, I *am* back to square one. I mean, I knew Bill

was with her, but seeing her in that picture, standing next to him as though she belonged, it just suddenly made it all so real. Delia, I *earned* that role. *I* was the good wife. *I* should be the one there at Bill's side sharing his achievements when the world acknowledges him as a sort of patron saint to children. Oh, I'm not knocking him on that score; he really is almost that. Dammit, Delia, I guess what I'm saying is that *I* should be the one Bill loves. Now all I can think about is him with her. And about my children and what they are going to think when their father tells them he's leaving us for another woman. What will become of me when I get back and I'm just plain old Lara Lewis again?"

"Don't you understand?" Delia wondered impatiently why she had to bludgeon Lara into seeing reason. "You were wronged, sure. But so have millions of other women been wronged. But you and Bill have not been in love for years, Lara, admit it."

Lara was silent and Delia said sternly, "I hope you're not crying, Lar, because it's time you started counting your blessings instead. You have two great kids who are grown up enough and independent enough to cope with the situation. You are only forty-five and in good shape, though I admit you could lose a few pounds. And you have a guy who's crazy about you. So come on, Lar, for God's sakes, give yourself a break. Get a life before I lose patience with you."

Lara smiled sadly. "Sounds like you already did that."

But Delia had an answer for everything that ailed her, even a broken heart. She said, "I get the feeling that you need new shoes. Sexy stilettos with peep toes, as expensive as you can find. Go for it, girlfriend."

Lara promised to buy the stilettos and heard Delia's gusty

sigh of relief echoing down the transatlantic line with the sound of ocean waves whooshing over it as they said good-bye.

She was freezing by the time she slid back into bed. Keeping as still as she could so as not to disturb Dan, she lay with her eyes open, staring at the flowered wallpaper until dawn came. But she wasn't thinking about the shoes, or Delia, or Dan. She was thinking about Bill.

Chapter Thirty-four

When Dan awoke the next morning, Lara was gone. No note, no cheerful morning-naked face peeking around the bathroom door. She simply was not there. He dressed hurriedly and ran downstairs to look for her. Then, in the small square outside the hotel, he spotted her outside at a cafe.

It was only eight-thirty but already the sun blazed down. Still, Lara looked cool in white linen shorts and a black-and-white-striped camisole with black espadrilles laced around her ankles and tied in a little bow. Dan guessed she had bought them at the store down the street. She also wore huge dark sunglasses that he hadn't seen before—she usually wore little rose-tinted wire ones. And she was staring into space, an empty coffee cup on the table in front of her.

The metal chair scraped noisily on the flagstones as he took a seat next to her, and she frowned, as though the noise hurt her head. "Sorry," he said. "And *bonjour,* Lara." She glanced at him but he couldn't see her eyes because of the huge sunglasses.

"Oh, hi, Dan." She sounded as though he were the last person she expected to see instead of the guy she came in with.

He waved to the waiter, ordered croissants and coffee, and the usual grand crème for her.

"No." She stopped him. "I'll have another espresso. Double, please."

He looked at her, astonished, as she continued to stare into space, lost, he assumed, in her own thoughts. She was not wearing makeup, not even lip gloss, which she always did because she said it kept her lips from chapping.

The waiter returned with the coffee and croissants. He glanced up at the sky with an ominous shrug, "Today, m'sieur, 'dame," he told them, "we have the mistral. Soon, you will feel it."

Dan had heard about the infamous mistral, the gale-force wind that blew from the Russian steppes, gaining strength as it funneled through the Rhône Valley all the way to southern France. "Is it that bad?"

Again the waiter shrugged, something it seemed the French could not talk without. "Is bad, m'sieur. Bad for business. Bad for families, bad for the"—he sought for the English word—"the harmony. You know?"

"The harmony?" Dan repeated.

"It drives people crazy." The waiter snapped his fingers against his head. "You have to watch out in the mistral."

"I'll watch out," Dan promised as the first gust of wind swept across the square, sending their paper napkins flying and rattling the umbrellas in their heavy stands.

Lara seemed unaware of their conversation. She finished what must have been her fourth double espresso, got up abruptly, and said, "I'm going to pack. You stay here, enjoy the sunshine. No, don't worry," she held up her hand, "I'll take care of it."

Ten minutes later when Dan returned to the hotel, he found her downstairs with their luggage, and the hotel bill already paid.

"I thought you liked this place," he said, surprised. "Now you can't wait to get out of here."

She shrugged, looking around the foyer as though seeing it for the first time. The porter wheeled their luggage out to the car and she climbed silently into the passenger seat.

Perhaps the mistral was getting her crazy, Dan thought, rolling up the window to shut out the gritty wind. Or it might be that time of the month. Or even the full moon.

"You sure you're feeling okay?" he asked after they had been driving in silence for half an hour.

"I'm fine." She sat slumped in the hard little bucket seat, still in the dark glasses, inscrutable as Cleopatra.

They were on the A 61 heading for Avignon, City of the Popes. Dan had been reading up on Provence and liked what he'd read. It was a land of harsh rocks and strong light, beloved of artists, as dry and rugged as parts of his own California, filled with vineyards and sunflowers, truffles and olives, and blue, blue skies haunted by high-hovering hawks.

It was astonishing, he thought as he drove, how *much* of France there was—and with absolutely nothing on it. They had passed miles and miles, acre upon acre of nothing but green fields bordered by trees. He had not realized France was so immense, so free of overbuild, so absolutely gosh-darn beautiful. He glanced at Lara. She wasn't looking at the scenery. Her lips were closed in a tight line and she was staring straight ahead.

He fumbled in his pocket, took out a ten-franc piece, laid it on her knee. "I'm upping the ante," he said with a sigh. "*Ten* francs for your thoughts." Still she said nothing. "Silence could make you rich," he promised.

"I have a headache. I couldn't sleep. . . ."

He inspected her face anxiously as he slowed down into the waiting line of cars approaching a tollbooth. "Maybe you shouldn't have drunk all that coffee."

She lifted a weary shoulder, indifferent.

"How about Advil?"

"I already did that."

The drive was taking longer than he'd thought. Lara seemed disinterested in navigating and he was forced to stop a couple of times to consult the map, and finally ended up lost in the urban sprawl around Montepellier. He parked outside a sidewalk cafe and they took a seat and ordered two Oranginas and two *croques monsieurs*. He downed the cold, fizzy drink thirstily and ordered another, watching Lara, a silent enigma behind the big sunglasses.

Lara wasn't aware of Dan's attention. Her thoughts were on Bill and Melissa in India together. And on the mess her life was in. She was back to square one and in a total funk.

Dan carefully cut the crusts off the bread and then cut it into four triangles. "Eat something," he coaxed her with the childish sandwich. "You look as though you need it."

Obediently, Lara ate. The food did make her feel better. Not inside, where it still hurt, but it made her feel stronger so at least she could walk back to the car without stumbling.

She took the wheel and drove the last part of the route into Avignon without getting lost once. The unair-conditioned car was hot as hell and the silence was tangible.

But when they finally got to Avignon the hotel wasn't at all like the sweet little French hotel Lara remembered. It looked awful, inhospitable, commercial, and dingy. Its grimy, tattered shutters were closed tight against the mistral and the stucco walls were flaking. Could she and Bill really have stayed there? Had she gotten it wrong again? Back home she had the receipt that told her they had; that's how she had tracked down all their hotels, and the restaurants. Bill had kept everything. If nothing else, he was an organized man.

Dan got out of the car. "I'd better check it out," he said.

A tear bumped from Lara's eye. She was looking at the truth. Her honeymoon had never been the wonderful trip she remembered. All these years, she had lied to herself about it. And now *she* was the one who had brought them here, the one who had insisted on sticking with her schedule. She had become exactly like that bastard Bill. He *was* a bastard, wasn't he?

Yeah, but you know you still care. The inner voice was goading her on again. *He's still the man you fell in love with at the age of seventeen, he's still the guy you married, the father of your children, keeper of your happiness and guardian of your heart. . . .*

Dan got back into the car. He didn't notice her tears behind the dark glasses. "You wouldn't like it" was all he said. "Come on, honey, move over. I'll drive."

While Dan negotiated his way through the maze of narrow streets, Lara gazed unseeing at the stern stone walls of the ancient palace where, in the fourteenth century, seven popes had opted to live instead of in Rome. They could have been in Pittsburgh for all she cared.

They ended up at the Hôtel du Mirande, an exquisite small hotel in a converted town house, luxuriously furnished with beautiful antiques and artwork. Their window looked out over the roofs of the old part of town, glowing like jewels in the setting sun, but Lara wasn't interested. Her problems crowded in on her. Her life had been a sham; the past she had treasured did not exist; there *was* no present, no future.

When their bags had been stowed and the amenities explained by the bellhop, Dan perched next to her on the bed. "Okay, Lara, let's have it," he said. She looked back at him, her eyes big and dark under the delicately winged brows.

"I think it's over between us, Dan!"

He stared at her. The lump in his throat was so big he couldn't speak. She was looking at him as if he were a stranger. He was looking at her as though she had just shot him. His shoulders slumped, his strong workman's hands lay limp in his lap. He bowed his head.

"Are you going to give me any reason for that?" he asked finally.

"It's Bill."

"But Bill has always been there. He was there when we met. He was there when we fell in love. He was there when we left for this trip. Why Bill *now*? What happened, Lara?"

She shrugged again, avoiding his eyes, saying nothing.

"For God's sakes, Lara, don't I have a right to know?"

There was a steely edge to his voice that shocked her. She pressed her hand against her heart to stop it from thudding. All the lightness had gone out of her and she could not even recall what it had felt like that day at the Shoups' house when she had been so buoyant with happiness she had thought she was about to levitate.

She walked across to the table, took the page from the *Herald Tribune* from her bag, and handed it to him.

Dan looked at the photograph of Bill and his mistress, scanning the text quickly. "So?" He didn't get it.

"Don't you see. That's *Bill*—he's with *her* in India. He looks as though he's about to kiss her. . . ."

He looked up at her, shocked. "Don't tell me you're going to play the jealous wife at this stage of the game."

She heard the contempt in his voice, and she nodded, acknowledging her treachery. "I'm sorry, I can't help it. I'm jealous. I admit it."

"Okay, so how do you think Bill would feel if he saw the photograph of the two of us in Paris? The one the waiter took of us where you look like the cat that's got the cream and I've got my arm around you? Would he be jealous?"

Lara slumped despairingly onto the bed. "You don't know what it's like. It's twenty-five years of my life, *his* life. . . . There are things between us, a whole lifetime of things. . . . It's hard not to be jealous, not to be hurt."

"So now you propose to go on being hurt forever, is that it? You choose martyrdom while Bill has fun. Great. I didn't realize you were a masochist as well as jealous. *And* still in love with your husband."

Dan shoved his hands in his pockets, staring down at her. "I can't handle this, Lara. I don't know what to do. I need to clear my head."

Her eyes tracked him as he walked to the door. "Where are you going?"

"A walk, a drink . . . oh, God, I don't know. . . ."

He was gone, closing the door quietly behind him as he left, and Lara thought, agonized, that a part of her soul went with him. *That part that doesn't belong to those twenty-five years with Bill*, her conscience added nastily.

. . .

Lara asked herself a lot of questions in that hour after Dan had gone, standing under the shower, letting the cool water run over her aching head, over her closed lids, over the body that had born Bill's two children, the body he no longer wanted.

It's your pride that's hurt, stupid, the voice inside said, surprising her. *When did you last make love with Bill? When did he last look at you the way Dan does? When did he last consider your feelings before his? When did he last show up for an event that was important to you but not to him? Ask yourself these questions and you'll soon see how those twenty-five years shrink, honey. Maybe all the way back to a total of six or seven when you thought you were happy—or at least thought you were going to be happy someday. And now you are prepared to give up Dan's love, your happiness, for selfish Bill, who doesn't give a goddamn about you, anyway? And maybe never did. Fool . . . fool . . . fool that you are, Lara Lewis . . .*

Dan was sitting at a sidewalk cafe table with his third or maybe fourth glass of Pastis when he saw her.

She had changed into the white skirt and shirt she had worn the first night when they had made love on the beach. She wore the gold sandals and the gold hoops in her ears and she had pulled back her hair, still damp from the shower, into a knot at the nape of her neck.

She looked, Dan thought morosely, like a Spanish noblewoman in one of the Goya court paintings he had seen in the Louvre. Cool, untroubled, her brow clear.

"Thank God I found you," she said.

He pulled out a chair for her, waited icily polite until she was seated. "Can I get you something?"

"A glass of red wine, please."

He signaled the waiter, ordered the wine, sat in silence studying her long feet in the strappy gold sandals and her glossy dark-red-polished nails.

"I'm sorry, Dan." She was staring at him in that Audrey Hepburn way she had of looking, all big topaz eyes.

She said quietly, "I was wrong to say what I did."

"Not if you meant it, you weren't." He took another slug of the Pastis.

The waiter arrived with the glass of the Côtes du Rhône for madame. He placed it in front of her and added another slip to the mounting pile in the saucer for *l'addition*.

"It's not easy to leave half a lifetime behind, Dan, please understand that." She gazed pleadingly at him.

"I understand."

He was impenetrable behind his barricade of hurt and pride. "I've hurt you and I don't know why I did it. I don't know how to ask you to forgive me. All I can say is I'm sorry. I asked myself the questions you were asking me, and you're right. I have to come to terms with the past, know the truth instead of deluding myself that my marriage was all one golden stretch of time playing happy families. I always thought my honeymoon was so wonderful, but now I know—" She stopped herself just in time.

"Now you know *what* about your honeymoon?"

Lara crossed her fingers as she lied. "Now I know that honeymoons should be like this. Like what we have." She stared into the glass of red wine as though it fascinated her. Tears glittered in her eyes.

"Don't ever do that to me again, Lara," Dan said quietly. "You'll never know what these past few hours have cost me."

She no longer cared who saw her tears, and now they ran down her cheeks and plopped off her chin. "I promise."

He lifted her hand to his lips. "It's you and me, Lara," he said. "That's where it's at. Just you and me."

Lara remembered the woman in the Paris brasserie, the chic, older Frenchwoman with her young lover, how her face had lighted up when she saw him. She felt that same glow in her own face now and finally understood. That woman had not cared who saw, who noticed. She was in love and that was all that mattered.

Arms around each other's waists, they walked back to the Mirande, where they fell into the big soft comfortable bed and into each other's arms. Too exhausted to make love, they slept like the dead.

Chapter Thirty-five

Avignon and the terrible fight were behind them. They were on a dusty road, swirling around the town of Cavaillon, looking for the N100, the road leading to the Luberon, one of the most beautiful parts of Provence.

The car windows were open, letting in the hot air and dust from the *garrigue,* the dry scrubland dotted with massive limestone rocks that rose on either side of the road. Tacky billboards advertising supermarkets and cafes, *pensions* and pizza joints littered the landscape and Lara was thinking sadly it didn't look like much of anything. And then the French did it again. The same miracle they always pulled off.

There, perched up on top of a sheer rock face, was a medieval stone village complete with church tower and ramparts. Silhouetted against the whitewashed blue sky, it looked like a painted backdrop for the story of the knights of King Arthur.

Dan was busy avoiding the slow tractors as well as the enormous trucks and speeding motorists whose main purpose in life seemed to be to pass him, preferably on the wrong side and with only inches to spare. He swung the Renault left under the wheels of a pickup trailing a wooden cart piled high with the local Cavaillon melons, whose sweet perfume filled the air, then chugged up the winding white road that led to Gordes. Past clusters of pale houses fastened to the hillside. Past tiny vineyards, and the Village des Bories, with its ancient circular stone shepherds' huts. Past tiny farms with clucking geese. In the distance the green Luberon Mountains loomed and the air was clean as purest springwater. Bees buzzed in the wild iris, lupine, and lavender. Palm fronds rattled in the mistral and overhead the sky was the palest whitewashed blue.

Lara drank it all in, heady as wine. In her bag were two books: M. F. K. Fisher's *Two Towns in Provence,* and Laurence Wylie's *Village in the Vaucluse.* She had intended to read them as they wended their way south but somehow there had not been time. Now, she promised herself she would do that. In fact, she would read them aloud to Dan so they could enjoy them together. Fisher's book told how it was for a young American woman with two small children to uproot herself from the United States and her estranged husband (had Lara bought it because of the similarity in their histories? she wondered) and go to live in Aix-en-Provence in the fifties. She had painted a memorable picture of the people and places—local characters, artists, cafes, churches, and landscapes; told how it felt to be poor in another country and yet gain all the bounty of the beauty and culture that came free. And *Village in the Vaucluse* was a living history of life in the old days, before tourists discovered the delights and pitfalls of life in Provence.

They strolled down Gordes's narrow alleyways, skidding on the slippery cobblestones, peering over low stone walls at the distant valley, and poking around tiny dark shops selling the distinctive sunshine-yellow, cobalt-blue, and dark-red patterned fabrics of Provence. Dan bought her lavender sachets wrapped in pretty fabric and she said they smelled of summer, and Lara bought him an old sepia photograph of Gordes, the way it used to be before it was restored and people like themselves came to buy souvenirs.

Pleased, they took a seat under a cafe umbrella in the Place du Château and ordered a carafe of the local rosé and salade niçoise.

The pace had definitely slowed. Life was simpler here, out of the fast lane, away from the grand restaurants and the unending motorways. Delighted with each other, they held hands. The sun warmed their pale skin, the tail end of the mistral flapped the fringes of the green umbrella and blew Lara's long hair horizontal, and they breathed the aromas of garlic and rosemary, of baking bread and sweet, juicy melons.

"Are you going to say it or am I?" she asked him with a grin.

"*This*"—Dan waved his hands expansively—"is Provence. A whole different world from France, with a soul all its own."

Lara was glad that he sensed it too. They were united again. Together. A team. Lara and Dan against the world and to hell with Bill Lewis and the bimbo. Remembering Delia's words of wisdom, Lara wondered where she could buy some stilettos around here, the symbol of her newfound independence and, hopefully, of her new confidence in herself as a woman.

They drove on, through silent, windswept country lanes where the hedgerows were filled with the tiniest purple irises, brilliant blue scabious, and wild yellow broom. Little black-and-white birds darted fast as space shuttles in front of their windshield, tiny brown rabbits scuttled from under the wheels, and hawks hovered over the white rocks in search of prey.

At the ancient Abbeye de Sénanque, silence hung, tangible as the spiritual presence of the monks who, centuries before, had worshiped there. The buildings were simple and unadorned and they strolled in cool cloisters where the flagstones had been polished to a sheen by the pacing of decades of pious feet. Surrounded by its fields of lavender, the abbey was a step back in time to a quieter, more inward life, and they sat for a while, letting the peace of the place sink into their souls.

Back in Gordes and too tired to go farther, they checked into the Hotel la Bastide.

The hotel was part of the original stone fortress, clinging to the edge of the sheer cliff overlooking the valley and the winding road they had climbed in the puffing little Renault. Coming in from the heat of the afternoon, the cool stone hallways felt calm and refreshing. Their room had lofty beamed ceilings, tiled floors, and *toile de jouey* wallcoverings. Shutters opened onto the wide valley view, where a thousand starlings congregated in the treetops, twittering and singing in the twilight.

Sighing with pleasure, Lara turned from the window, right into Dan's waiting arms. "I'm dusty," she protested between kisses. "I'm hot, sweaty—"

"I love my women hot and sweaty and I'll forgive the dust." He was kissing her breasts now and she threw back her head, laughing. Why, oh, why had she always thought lovemaking was such a serious thing? Why had she never known it was joyous, that you could laugh when you were doing it? Laugh at each other while you were loving each other?

The big bed was a treat, no squeaky springs here, just big soft pillows and crisp white sheets and their own heated bodies, though Lara did take a minute out to think worriedly that she must feel plumper under his hands; she was sure she had gained at least five pounds.

But Dan didn't care, he loved her roundness, her smooth skin, her long limbs, and the satin feel of her as he buried his face in her softness. His hands were under her, lifting her to his mouth, and the faint exotic scent of her was the only element that mattered to his senses right then, right now, forever. . . . She writhed under his tongue, and he gripped her tighter, forcing her into even dizzier heights, until she yelped with pleasure and then cried out *no more, no more, enough . . . I can't bear it.* And then he took her and made her his own. Again.

The thought of those extra pounds did not put Lara off dinner that night, though, in the vaulted twelfth-century cellar. Candlelight flickered off the creamy stone walls, and there were bunches of perfumed yellow roses in deep-blue vases on the tables, and tiny *amuses bouches* to tempt the appetite. It was cool and elegant but comfortable, and it was busy. Many of the diners had that glossy Parisian look about them, expensively dressed in clothing they considered suitable for *la campagne,* white or black silk outfits as austere as a Japanese haiku, with the added flash of substantial diamonds. There were a few tourists, like themselves, gazing around with that same bemused look on their faces, as though they had landed in another world and maybe, just maybe, it was paradise.

Tonight, Lara looked a completely different person from the sad, insecure woman in Carmel. She wore her long dark hair loose and flowing, something she hadn't done in years because she'd thought it too young. And there was a special glow about her, a new confidence. She looked like a woman who had just been made love to.

And so did the young woman at the next table, Lara thought, studying her. Homely was Lara's first impression of her. A strong nose, chin too square, short dark hair, tiny round glasses. But the girl's three male companions seemed completely under her spell. They were hanging on to her every word, and her smile lit up the room.

The girl's looks weren't that important, Lara realized suddenly. Her nose was her nose, her chin, her chin, but her self-confidence and femininity were unquestioned. And her charm was all her own. She watched her enviously.

"See how she has all the men enchanted," she whispered to Dan. "She has them under her spell."

"She's a sorceress, like you," he agreed, kissing her hand, and she smiled because she had never thought of herself as a sorceress before. It wasn't the Lara Lewis she knew—or, at least, the old Lara, the woman she used to be.

Dan ordered a local rosé, and tiny mussels in a tangy sauce, with crusty bread that Lara said was to die for, and they liked the mussels so much they ordered them twice. Then the local lamb from the steep hills of Sisteron, tiny loin chops studded with slivers of garlic, rosy as the sunset and twice as delicate, served with creamy-smooth mashed potatoes rich with sweet butter and cream and far better than anybody's grandmother could make. A tray of local cheeses came next, and with them they drank a glass of spicy, delicious Chateauneuf du Pape, Le Vieux Telegraphe.

Afterward, they strolled up the street to the Place du Château, where they sat at the Renaissance cafe sipping coffee under a bowl of stars that were more sparkly than the smart Parisians' enormous diamonds. The mistral had departed, leaving only a breeze to ruffle Lara's long hair. From all around came the pleasant murmur of multinational voices: the local Provence patois, the rapid Parisian chatter, the high-pitched voices of British women, and the guttural laughter of the Germans. They were a world away from reality, in a kingdom more magical than mere Disneyland.

Unable to believe he was really there, Dan said, "Shouldn't I be in Monterey putting up a taco stand? Or off building a ranch in the hills of Carmel? Can this be *real*?"

"I'll pinch you if you like." Lara laughed, but she understood exactly what he meant. This hill village was so remote from their own reality, from Dan's daily life and work, from her own lonely home in San Francisco and the lostness of her life, it seemed to promise new beginnings.

They lingered into the night. Dan was so easy to talk to; he really listened, tried to understand, and the thoughts just came out of her mouth, off the top of her head completely unedited. Things she hadn't even thought about in years, but were just lurking there. About how she had adored her father and her desolation when he had died lingeringly of lung cancer when she was sixteen. About her mother, who had married again and gone to live in Florida, leaving Lara a lonely young-married, with no one to give her advice and help with the children. About never knowing much about sex except what she had gleaned from the Girlfriends. She told him she had never "known" anyone but Bill, never known any of the men with the predatory hands and a sense of entitlement to her body, the way Delia had told her she had.

"None of our mothers had told us about sex," she said. "It wasn't considered a proper subject in suburbia."

And she told him about how she felt now about her home,

her children, her fears and hopes for them. Bit by bit, she told him her life.

They slept that night, the way they always did now, wrapped around each other, as though the big bed were a small one, with the shutters flung wide to the starry night and the cool breeze. And Lara's dreams were of sunlight and wine and love.

Lara canceled the rest of their reservations, deliberately avoiding the hotels where she had stayed with Bill, determined to put him — and their life — behind her. The next day, they chugged back down the hill, drove for a while, took a couple of wrong turns and ended up in a hamlet — just a few houses and barns strung along the narrow road. A signpost showed they were in Joucas, and, curious, they followed another sign pointing to the Mas des Herbes Blanches.

When they found it, it was a honey-colored Provençal farm-house converted into a hotel, and it fit as snugly into the land-scape as though it had grown out of it. The low terra-cotta-tile roofs stuck out at many angles, and a courtyard terrace over-looked a deep blue swimming pool and parklike grounds where the white grasses, the *herbes blanches* that gave the hotel its name, grew.

Lara unpacked for the first time since they had left Paris, hanging up the creased garments, sending things out to be washed and pressed so they could be repacked and creased all over again when she did her on-the-road nightly shuffle through them to pick out something to wear. Being on the road had its drawbacks as well as its fascinations.

Then they drove into the nearby small town of Apt. The

morning market was still in full swing and they were instantly lost in the smells of Provence: the hovering aroma of rosemary and thyme and mint, the sharp tang of dozens of different types of olives, and the sweet scent of melons mingled with the tempting smell coming from a pizza truck. They bought a melon and ate it with the juice running down their chins, watching the local women picking through every vegetable and fruit until the perfect ones were found. Baskets of speckled brown eggs were displayed next to live chickens and quacking ducks, and overall hung a pungent odor of cheese—rounds of creamy-white goat and sheep cheeses, and cheeses that looked as though they had been around for a hundred years, hard, black, and crusty. There were tiny fresh-picked lettuces and little leeks; yellow zucchini blossoms and knobby green-red tomatoes; enormous white radishes, tiny purple aubergines, and fat red peppers.

There was another truck with roasting pork, and the aroma tempted them into trying succulent slices on hunks of fresh bread.

In the medieval stone village of Bonnieux, they rented bicycles and helmets and peddled into the green foothills of the Luberon Mountains, puffing through tiny, windswept Ménerbes, passed periodically by yellow-and-black-Lycra-clad *cyclistes* like swarms of bees.

Lara's calves ached and the sun scorched down and she wished she had put on more sunscreen. Finally, hot, exhausted, and sunburned, they dropped their bikes in the shade of a scrub oak and flung themselves panting to the ground.

She groaned, arms outflung, "Why did I ever suggest this? I haven't even been on the treadmill in over a year."

Dan was flat on his back, arms pillowing his head. "Look at it this way: going back it's all downhill." He massaged her aching calves, until she could bear it no longer, then he kissed her sun-pink knees and hauled her to her feet again.

The heady smell of wild thyme crushed beneath their feet followed them as they wandered deep into the forest. After a while, they stopped and stood, hand in hand, listening to the silence. The arcing branches filtered the greenish light, and it was like being in a great outdoor cathedral. Very gradually, they became aware of the sounds of life: the scuttle of a small animal through the underbrush; a flutter of unseen wings; the cooing of a bird; and somewhere far off in the distance, the barking of a dog. It was, they agreed, awed—magical.

But when they finally returned to the place where they had left their bicycles, they were brought back to reality with a thud. The bikes were gone.

"Stolen," Dan said with a sigh.

"Now what do we do?" Lara tugged at her shorts, hot and sticky and, predictably, hungry once again.

"Guess," Dan said. Then he took her hand and they began to hike down the steep hill. When they reached the road, they looked left and right. It was as empty as an out-of-season football field.

"Better start walking," Dan said. "Soon as we see a car coming, stick out your thumb."

"You mean we're going to *hitchhike*?" Lara was dumbfounded; it was exactly what she had warned her own daughter never to do.

"What do you suggest? That I get on my cell phone and call a taxi? Come on, Lara, of course we're going to hitchhike. And you'd better start praying a car comes by soon because I seem to remember it was a long way back to Ménerbes."

Lara stomped along the road, head down, furious with herself that she had been naive enough to leave the bikes unpadlocked and unattended. She would *never* have done that in California.

It was that magic hour between twelve and two when the whole of Provence locked up and went for lunch. She knew no sensible farmer or businessman would be on the road now. He would be in the local restaurant eating the menu of the day and washing it down with a bottle of red from the local cooperative near Bonnieux. The midday sun scorched down and she rammed her sun hat on her head, wishing she had worn a long-sleeved shirt instead of just a tank top.

"Which way?" Dan asked when they came to the fork in the road.

Lara had about as much sense of direction as a turned-around road sign. "Right," she said positively, and they trudged down yet another empty, dusty white road.

"Come on, Lara." She was flagging and Dan urged her on. "We'll never get there at this rate."

Lara was thinking that the road had a familiar look about it, but, then, all the country roads looked alike to her. Still, it did look very much like the one she and Bill had driven down, searching for a tiny restaurant he had heard about, and, as usual, was determined to find at all cost. That was Bill, dogged as Dexter, never giving up on anything.

Especially on children's lives, the voice reminded her suddenly. *He never gives up on those kids, either, you know. That's what makes him a great doctor.*

True, she admitted silently. Though Bill was never such a good father to his own children. But then, they were never sick, at least not seriously, like his patients.

Lost in her thoughts, she didn't notice that the road was

getting narrower and that the soft verge was crumbling. Not until she tripped over it, that is.

"Ow! Now look what I've done," she cried, surprised to find herself sitting in a rocky ditch.

Dan hurried to help her up. "Are you okay?"

She put her weight on her foot, testing it, then sat down again suddenly. It hurt like hell. "I think I must have sprained it." She stared doubtfully at the foot that suddenly felt too big for the sneaker. "I'm sorry," she added, looking back up at Dan.

"What d'you mean? I'm the one who's sorry. You're the one who's hurt. Look, you're obviously not going to be able to walk on that foot. I'll go on and get the car. You'll just have to stay here and wait for me."

He helped her into the shade of a mangy scrub oak. "At least you're out of the sun," he said, patting her hair as though she were a child. "Don't worry, honey, I'll be back before you know it."

"Before I can count to ten?" she asked with a smile, remembering how she had promised the same thing to her kids when they were small and ten seemed an eternity away. Like now.

Dan stood, arms folded, looking down at her. "Before you know it," he promised. Then he dropped a kiss on her upturned face and set off at a jog down the heat-shimmering road.

As he disappeared from sight, Lara recalled carousel 22 at Charles de Gaulle. Every time he disappeared like this she found herself hoping nervously it wasn't déjà vu all over again. Again.

Chapter Thirty-six

She suddenly realized she was alone on a small, silent back road somewhere in Provence. The only sound was the everlasting wind whistling through the scrub oak. Even the birds were taking a siesta.

Lara thought worriedly about the bicycle thieves. What if they came back to rob her? Not that she had anything to steal except maybe her old watch. Oh, and the necklace. She ran her fingers over the diamonds; perhaps she should take it off, hide it in her pocket . . . but she had promised never to remove it until Bill came back. It was her talisman that would bring him back to her.

Well, so far, the talisman's not working too good, the voice reminded her edgily.

Oh, God, was she back to that again? Admitting that she still wanted him?

She tugged off her sneaker and inspected her swollen foot. It was already turning purple, and she realized too late there was no chance she could get the shoe back on. "Oh, *shoot,*" she said crossly. "It'll be a repeat of the Tour d'Argent, only with me in my best black and bare feet instead of the lizard heels." Gloomily, she contemplated the foot, wondering what her husband, the doctor, would have done in this situation.

She stared into the lush, green valley below. *Wasn't this the road you were on with Bill?* The voice surprised her. *Remember the field of poppies?*

And she was instantly catapulted back in time.

Bill and Lara were driving along a twisting sandy road, searching for a restaurant. Rocks loomed on the right. To the left lay a valley, soft and green. They might have been the only people in the world. There were no farmers working in the vineyards, no people walking their dogs, no cars passed them. Then, suddenly, below them in the valley was a field of scarlet poppies, a solid mass of red, a lavish Oriental carpet shimmering in the breeze.

Mesmerized, they took the winding road down into that valley. Taking off their shoes, they ran barefoot and hand in hand through the waist-high poppies, sank down into them.

Lying on her back Lara could see the scarlet petals, delicate as butterfly wings, wafting in the breeze; she could smell the crushed grass, feel the itch of pollen in her nose, hear the buzz of fat bumblebees, the whir of tiny wings, the scratching of field creatures. They were one with the earth as they made love, sheltered from view by the poppies, embraced by nature, clasped in each other's arms.

Oh, Bill," Lara whispered now. "It wasn't all bad, was it? There were times when I knew you loved me, when I really loved you. Don't let me believe it was all bad, and that the past years have been a sham, a waste; please don't let me. . . . I couldn't bear it. I couldn't bear to be left with nothing."

Sure, there were good times. Her alter ego had turned nasty. *Count 'em, baby, on the fingers of one hand.*

Not true, she thought despairingly. There were lots of times. . . .

Yeah, when he still came home nights, before he got too big for his boots, too self-important to care anymore. Maybe he's making love to Melissa right now in some Chinese rice paddy. Maybe she's thinking like you did, Hey, there's another side to this man, a sensual side, a softer, more loving side. . . .

Lara was jolted out of her dream. A cold wind sent shivers down her spine and goose bumps popped up on her arms. The temperature must have dropped twenty degrees. Solid black clouds were massing quickly over the tops of the mountains.

She stared anxiously down the empty road, praying Dan would hurry back.

She watched the clouds rolling down the mountains, saw the rain falling on the upslopes, then a dazzling neon stab of lightning followed seconds later by a giant roll of thunder. A lone cypress went up in flames with a great sizzle.

Oh, my God, she thought, this is dangerous. I have to get out of here. She looked around, saw a broken branch, pulled it toward her, yelping as a small scorpion rustled away into the underbrush. She managed to haul herself to her feet and put her swollen foot cautiously on the ground. Of course, it still hurt like hell.

What did you expect? the voice said nastily. *A miraculous recovery so you could run down the road away from the storm? Too late, look what's coming your way now.*

A solid sheet of rain stung her sunburned shoulders, blinding her. In an instant she was soaked. Leaning on the twisted branch, she began to hobble down the road in the direction Dan had gone.

"I'm damned if I'm going to get burned up by lightning out here on my own," she muttered. "Not now, not when I've found him. . . ."

Her long wet hair swung around her shoulders and rain dripped off the end of her nose. Lightning flashed dangerously close and she counted off the seconds. She had only got to three when the thunderclap sent her hobbling, terrified, even faster.

The rain had turned to hail the size of marbles. Solid lumps of ice bounced off her head and she didn't see the van's headlights until it was almost on top of her and she heard it skid.

"*Madame, q'est-ce que vous voulez ici?*" a shocked voice asked. "*Viens, viens vite . . .*"

Blinded, she held out a trusting hand. "*Au secours, monsieur,*" she said, remembering the handy little phrase from the Berlitz guidebook: "Help me."

"*Ah, madame . . .*" He half lifted her across the road and pushed her into the van. Stacked behind them Lara caught a glimpse of bidets and toilets in shades of pink and green.

"*Merde,*" her savior said, plus a few other fluent phrases that thankfully she did not understand as he drove slowly through the storm.

She looked at him just as he glanced at her: she, the bedraggled foreign witch-lady in soaking-wet shorts and flimsy top, one shoe off and one shoe on, and one foot purple and swollen. He, short and sharp-eyed in the bright blue overalls French workmen wore and a battered wide-brimmed hat in camouflage green.

"*Touriste.*"

It was a statement not a question, but she said politely, *"Oui, monsieur. Américain."*

"What were you doing out there, alone, in the storm?" he demanded, in French, of course. "And what happened to your foot?"

She tried her best to explain what had happened and that she had been walking down the road to Ménerbes, hoping to meet up with the monsieur.

"Bah," he exclaimed, "madame was going in the wrong direction. Now we go to Ménerbes. There I will see to it that madame gets help for her poor foot," he added more kindly. "It does not look good."

Lara stared at the foot. It did *not* look good. In fact, it looked awful. Sighing, she stared out the windshield. The hail had changed back to rain again and the thunder was behind them. As they swung into the muddy parking lot, overlooking a sheer drop into the valley below, she saw Dan.

He spotted her, flung open the van door, and she fell into his arms. "My God, Lara, I couldn't believe I'd left you there in that storm." Her rescuer waited politely, clutching his battered hat in one hand, scratching his bald head with the other.

"Madame needs attention for the foot, m'sieur," he interrupted their emotional reunion. "Is bad, the foot."

"Is bad?" Dan stared at her swollen ankle, then grabbed the man's hand and shook it heartily.

"Merci, monsieur . . . monsieur . . ." He glanced at the inscription on the side of the white van: *Pierre Etienne Garnier, Équipement Sanitaire. "Merci, Monsieur Garnier. Merci* for both of us. *Un cognac, monsieur."* He waved toward the tiny corner bar and after a few polite protests, Monsieur Garnier agreed to a small *marc,* just to take away the chill of the rain. The weather was

unpredictable near the mountains, one minute sun, the next—pouf—it was like a magician waved his hand and there was snow or thunder or hail.

Half carrying Lara between them, they entered the bar and were at once the center of attention. Shocked voices exclaimed in rapid Provençal patois over madame's foot, ice was brought wrapped in a clean dish towel, brandy was served, and advice offered by the bristled elders, who were the bar's habitués and who were grateful for the distraction because the storm had interrupted their usual afternoon game of *pétanque*.

"Wrap the ankle tightly, madame," someone said. "But first soak the bandage in ice water. Cold is the only thing for a sprain. In a day or two it will be as good as new."

They smiled their thanks, and Dan ordered *marc* for everyone, and amid an *entante cordiale internationale*, they were helped into a taxi, which would take them back to Bonnieux and their bike-rental agency, and their car.

Chapter Thirty-seven

Back at the Mas, Dr. Montand was sent for. He was very young and walked soundlessly across the room on thick rubber-soled shoes as if walking on air, nervous as a novice midwife at a first birth. He peered at the foot that now closely resembled mortadella from the supermarket deli section, a dark liverish pink mottled with spots of white.

He pulled an ugly piggy-pink elastic support sock over the ankle, ruining, Lara thought gloomily, any possibility of her ever appearing chic again. Then he elevated it on two pillows and proposed calamine lotion for her sunburn.

She began to enjoy all the attention. The hotel manager sent flowers to their room along with a delicate meal suitable for an invalid and a bottle of delicious local rosé wine; the maids fluttered around making sure she was comfortable; and Dan hovered anxiously, wondering if he should take her to the hospital.

With her ankle wrapped in ice bags, she slept alone in one of the twin beds Dan had requested, so he would not disturb her. She missed having him next to her. But still, somehow, it was Bill and that field of poppies she dreamed about that night.

When she awoke the next morning Lara knew she had to find that field. Suddenly, it had become the most important thing in her life. She had to *know* that she had been there with Bill, that they had lain together in that field, that their hearts had once beat in rhythm, that their bodies had twined passionately around each other. She had to know that once upon a time they had really loved each other and that the past twenty-five years of her life had not been a sham.

You have the children, the inner voice reminded her. *Josh and Minnie are not a sham, they are the fruit of your love. You don't have to see that field. . . .*

Oh, but I do, she told herself. I need to know it existed. That *I* existed. . . . I need to find myself. And she needed the Girlfriends, needed to speak to them, needed their reassurance that she was right. So while Dan was swimming she called Susie.

"Don't look for that field, Lara," Susie told her sternly. "Forget about it. Reality is not the past, it's where you are now. *Who* you are now. What you have now."

Reluctantly, Lara admitted Susie was right. "I won't look for the field," she promised. But as she put down the phone she thought sadly that now she would never know whether Bill had loved her.

Dan had insisted on their spending the day lounging comfortably by the pool where she could keep her foot elevated. Lara pulled on the red bathing suit, then stared doubtfully at herself in the mirror. There had to be a payoff for eating her way through France and now it showed. She was spilling out all over. Thinking of the Riviera yet to come and all those gorgeous girls in tiny bikinis, her heart sank. Promising herself to eat nothing but fruit and maybe a small salad, she put on a more discreet white suit, wrapped a black pareo around her more ample than she liked hips, and, with Dan's help, limped out onto the terrace.

There is a quality of silence in Provence. Maybe it's the shadowing Luberon Mountains that enclose the villages and valleys, sheltering them from the noise of autoroutes and aircraft and police sirens, but stretched on her lounger by the pool, with her eyes shut, Lara could almost *hear* the silence. Occasionally, she picked up the call of a voice, miles away across the valley; heard the bleat of a goat on the foothills, the clangor of a distant church bell.

But still, she was restless, anxious to get into the car, find that secret place. She thought she knew approximately where it was. . . .

The next morning, even though her foot was still red and swollen, she insisted they travel on. She flung clothes into the suitcases with an urgency that surprised Dan, snapping them firmly shut.

"There's a little restaurant I heard about," she said. "If we hurry, we could make it in time for lunch." She was breaking her promise to Susie and she knew it.

They had been driving for an hour, circling an area that was without a sign of habitation, not even a farm, let alone a restaurant. They wound around rocky bends while Lara peered out the window as though she had lost something precious to her.

How could she tell him she was looking for a dream, when she and Bill were young and life was full of promise?

And how many of those promises have been kept? the voice asked her. *And why, if the dream were true, do you feel that life cheated you after all? Didn't it thrust you into the background, make you dispensable? The forgotten woman. The lost woman.*

"Why are we doing this, Lara?" Dan asked finally, fed up. "Why is this place so important? I don't get it."

"It's just somewhere that I remember as being wonderful."

His eyebrows lifted in surprise. "I didn't know you'd been there."

"I haven't been there." It was almost a lie and she crossed her fingers. "I just meant I remember I was told it was here somewhere. There should be a field of poppies. . . ."

They rounded yet another tight hairpin bend and Lara peered into the valley. A few poppies speckled the ground but not enough to make a carpet. It was there, that place, wasn't it? Or perhaps it was just around the corner? Oh, God, it was here somewhere. Surely she would remember; it had been the highlight of her honeymoon, of her life with Bill.

But she couldn't be sure it was the same place; she and Bill had never found the little rustic restaurant, and now she and Dan couldn't find it either. . . .

Now she would never know the truth.

Chapter Thirty-eight

Her mood changed the next day, though, and she fell in love all over again in Aix. And in love with the little city that personified the heart and soul of Provence.

Double rows of plane trees cast a dappled canopy of shade over the broad sidewalk and onto the dignified flat-fronted seventeenth- and eighteenth-century town houses lining the main street, the Cours Mirabeau, topped and tailed with ornate fountains.

The remnants of the mistral blew a welcome spray over them as they strolled past the fountain where, long ago, Marie de Médicis had been carried by liveried flunkies in her sedan chair; where van Gogh had walked; where Frédéric Mistral the poet, who gave his name to the wind, had lingered in sidewalk cafes; where Cézanne and de Sade might have partaken of glasses of cloudy absinthe.

Arched, shadowy alleyways led into tiny sun-splashed cobbled squares where too many little boutiques took up too much space in the lovely stone façades of the old buildings. But there was a grace about the city, a dignity and also a joie de vivre, a joyous mingling of the well-worn old with today's youth. Multinational and multilingual, the local university students posed on brightly colored little Vespas, the girls' long hair flowing behind them in the breeze, the narrow-hipped guys with cigarettes hanging deliberately casual from the corner of their mouths.

Walnut-skinned farmers in town for the day drank deeply of rough red wine, berets tilted rakishly over the left eye, while their wives in best black studied the shop windows, perhaps looking for another little black number much the same as the one they were wearing. Local businessmen lunched in the same cafes they had frequented every day for years, solemnly reading the daily newspaper, and schoolchildren, reprieved for the afternoon, darted among the pedestrians, tripping over their own feet and hurling insults at one another at the tops of their voices. Across the way, a fat ginger cat sunbathed on a tiny iron balcony, taking in the scene. And the crumpled, sunburned tourists in bright colors and dark glasses wrote postcards home saying "Wish you were here."

Dan and Lara joined the throng at the Café Deux Garçons, where Lara rested her foot and sipped lemonade and wrote sunflowered postcards to the Girlfriends, while Dan downed an icy Stella Artois and people-watched—happily wasting away the day. Which, he guessed, was exactly what such a day in Provence was about.

"We're coming back here," he said positively to Lara. She glanced up from her postcards, smiling. "Will you come with me, Lara?"

"If you ask me, I will."

"I'm asking you now. I need a commitment."

Lara took off the bifocals. His deep blue eyes linked with hers, shutting out the crowds, the buzz of the Vespas, the flirting students. Last night's doubts disappeared. "I promise I'll come back here with you, Dan. Someday."

He pressed his lips to her warm cheek. How he loved the many scents of her: her perfume, the delicate undertone of her skin, the moist scent like warm lilies under the mass of soft, dark hair at the nape of her neck, and her own delicate aroma; the special *taste* of her.

His eyes were still linked with hers, and she smiled reading his look. "We have no hotel room. We're not stopping in Aix, remember?"

"Let's stay, enjoy the magic. Enjoy each other."

"Okay," she joyously agreed, collecting the postcards and stuffing them in her bag. After all, didn't they have all the time in the world? At least for today.

The hotel Le Nègre-Coste was in one of the eighteenth-century houses on the Cours Mirabeau. It was simply furnished in the old-fashioned French style and the old cage elevator creaked upward to their room under the eaves. Enchanted, they peered out the window over the tops of the plane trees. Then, closing the shutters, they sank into the "matrimonial" bed.

"Forget California king, I never want any other kind of bed." Dan's mouth traveled from her nape to her eyelids, to the tip of her nose, to the softness of her waiting mouth. "I've gotten used to this. Only thing is, though, you have to be part of the deal. One *lit matrimonial*, one Lara Lewis."

She was nibbling at his lips, drinking him in. Their bodies were warm from the heat, their gaze languorous with desire, their hands curving and smoothing, skimming and pausing to caress.

"Tell me about your other women." Lara stared, jealous, into his eyes. "I want to know who you've loved, how they were."

Dan shook his head; she was as insecure as ever. "There's never been anyone like you. I swear it. I've never felt like this about anyone, never wanted anyone this way. It's more than sex, more than passion. . . . I need you. I don't think I can live without you now, Lara Lewis."

Her sigh was soft.

"Love me, Lara." He buried his face in her round breasts. "Tell me you love me."

"I love you," she whispered.

Avoiding the sunburned parts of her, Dan traced his way down her body to the paler, sheltered flesh beneath.

"How different is it for you, being with an older woman?" she demanded, caught between what he was doing to her and jealousy of his life before her.

"There is no one but you, Lara," he murmured, "only you. I think of no one else . . ."

And with their bodies wrapped together as one, she finally believed him.

Much later, they lay together, arms and legs still wound around each other, still dazed by their journey of the flesh and the spirit. Content.

Except, the little voice nudged Lara, *there's only six more days, Girlfriend . . . Only six more days of paradise. Then what? He says he loves you now. Let's see what happens when you get back home.*

With a sigh, Lara wondered if she would ever learn the trick of taking her happiness when and where she could. She was a genuine doubting Thomas, always questioning, always setting time limits. Always afraid of losing what she had.

She called Delia later that night, but this time she didn't hide it from Dan. He stood at the window listening to the laughter drifting up from the cafes, while she dialed the number and waited for Delia to pick up the phone.

It rang and rang and she was just about to put it down when Delia's sleepy voice said, "Hello?"

"It's me, Lara," she said, smiling.

"Hey, Lara, how're you enjoying your Second Honeymoon? How's it going?"

"Great," Lara said, sounding guarded.

Delia's hearty laugh boomed down the phone again. "I guess a guarded *great* is better than a mere *nice*. Are you in love with him, or what?"

Lara looked at Dan leaning out the tall window with its long green shutters. The hair at the back of her neck prickled just looking at him. He was wearing only boxers. His muscular back tapered into a narrow waist and she could see the bump of each little vertebrae in his spine, the smooth matte texture of his bronzed skin.

"Yes," she admitted, "I'm in love with him."

She told Delia they were in Aix and tomorrow would be in the Côte d'Azur. "Oh, and by the way," she added, "I changed our itinerary. We're not staying at the same hotels, so you won't be able to call me."

Delia gave a surprised whistle. "You mean you've abandoned the Second Honeymoon tour?"

"Not entirely." Lara remembered the harrowing search for the field of poppies, her own field of dreams. "We're going to all the same places. But this time it's so different. Some-times . . ." She hesitated, glancing at Dan.

"Sometimes what?"

"Sometimes I wonder about the truth of my life."

"The truth of your life, Lara Lewis, is that you are forty-five years old, attractive, sometimes even beautiful, and sometimes slimmer than others. You're intelligent, you have two great kids who love you, as does Dex, who I want you to know is right here next to me, and who I'm sure sends you a big kiss. And the truth is Bill Lewis is in Beijing or India or somewhere with his lover, and you are in Provence with yours. How's that for an analysis?"

Lara grinned. "Trust you to get right to the nitty-gritty of the subject."

"Don't tell me you still have yearnings for the doctor?" Delia sounded disbelieving.

Lara sighed deeply. "Sometimes . . . It's hard, you know."

"I know, I know—after twenty-five years . . . Listen, Girl-friend, have you bought those stilettos yet, like I told you? Sounds to me as though you need them. Give your self-esteem a boost. You always did have good legs." Delia was laughing now.

"I'll do it as soon as I get to Cannes."

"Okay. So introduce me to the boyfriend."

"What?"

"Put him on the line. I want to say hello."

"If you're going to check him out . . ."

"Nah, I just wanna say, 'Hi, there, lover, I hear you're a great fuck. . . .' "

Lara was laughing now. "Dan?" She held out the phone. "My girlfriend Delia wants to say hello."

He raised his eyebrows, surprised, then took the phone. "Hello, Girlfriend Delia." He listened. "Yeah, yeah. True. I'll remember that." He threw back his head and laughed. "Is that right."

Lara's eyes were fixed anxiously on him. "What's she saying?" She reached for the phone but he swung tantalizingly away.

"Hey, listen, Delia," he said, still smiling, "let's get together when we get back. I've heard a lot about you, and after this conversation I feel I already know you. . . . Okay, okay, great," he said, nodding. "See you then, Girlfriend."

Lara grabbed the phone from him. "What did she tell you?"

"Oh, nothin'," he said smugly. "Just this and that."

"Delia, what are you up to?"

"Just putting in a good word for you, honey. Nothing to worry about."

Lara groaned. "Okay, I get the picture."

"Everybody needs a little boost," Delia said, "and you more than most."

"Thanks, but I'm sure I could have lived without it."

"Maybe you couldn't; you'll never know." Delia was unrepentant. "And don't forget to buy those peep-toe stilettos tomorrow. Black, of course, and some sheer black stockings—not panty hose, those stranglers of eroticism. Perhaps a little lacy garter belt . . ."

"Do they still exist?" Lara asked, amused.

"In France I'm sure they do—think of all those sexy women."

Lara thought about them. "I'll buy them tomorrow," she promised as they said "love you" and good-bye.

Dan swung around from the window. "Sounds nice, the girlfriend. Cute too."

Lara frowned suspiciously at him. "What did she say to you?"

He lifted a shoulder. "Oh, nothing much, this and that, you know, just general chat."

"No, it was not. Just tell me what she said, Dan."

"She made me promise not to."

"Aggghhh." Lara hurled herself back onto the bed. "You drive me crazy. Now I'll be wondering all night exactly what she said."

"Just a few family secrets," he said, grinning. "You know, like you're nothin' to write home about and it's real good of me to take you under my wing . . . stuff like that."

Lara was laughing as he flung himself on top of her, pinning her hands over her head. "No, really, she sounds great," he murmured in between kisses. "I can't wait to meet her."

"All my girlfriends are great." She was kissing him back.

"You hungry?" he asked.

"Mmmmmmnnn . . ."

"Then let's go get something to eat." He pulled her up by her hands.

"I was just going to call Minnie, and then Josh . . ."

He let go of her reluctantly. But then she shook her head; she didn't want to lose the moment. She would call them later.

Chapter Thirty-nine

The next morning they were on the road early. It was barely six-thirty and the streets were dappled with pale sunlight. The sidewalk cafes along the Cours Mirabeau were being hosed down, chairs put out, tables arranged. They grabbed a grand crème and a fresh croissant at the Deux Garçons, where last night they had dined on omelettes because, as Lara said, sometimes after all this fancy food she just had a longing for a boiled egg with toast soldiers, and the omelette was as close as she could get.

The A8-E80 La Provençal autoroute slipped eastward out of Aix, threading between green mountains, bypassing farms and hills of vineyards, onward through the Var all the way to the Riviera. Traffic zoomed contemptuously past their tiny Renault—their tiny *hot* Renault; how Lara wished she had known to ask for an air-conditioned car—blowing in petrol fumes and heat simultaneously. Either they closed the windows and roasted, or they opened them and were asphyxiated. Sweating, they pressed on, lining up patiently at the tollbooths, and stopping every now and again at autoroute cafes for an Orangina to swill away the taste of petrol.

They were approaching Grimaud. "Only ten kilometers to St. Tropez," Lara said, scanning the map, praying she wasn't wrong again. Then she told him to take a right instead of a left and somehow they were en route to Cogolin instead of St. Tropez. Then they revolved around the same roundabout several times before picking up the coast road that led (*pray, pray* Lara said silently) to St. Tropez.

"Stop," she shrieked suddenly and the car skidded to a halt. "Oh, Dan," she gasped, delighted. "Look. Just *look*."

The Mediterranean was like a mirage, an oasis in the desert after the long, sticky, gas-fumed drive on the autoroute, soothing to the soul after battling the crazy drivers. And it was as blue as the holiday brochures always promised it would be, sparkling in the evening sunlight. It was a dream come true.

La Figuière was a small hotel tucked quietly away in the middle of vineyards a few kilometers up the Ramatuelle road, outside St. Tropez. It was exactly what they were looking for, a series of small stucco villas each in a different color—rose, ochre, white, blue, and cream, quietly set in a garden. A flowered terrace led to a turquoise swimming pool surrounded by fragrant lavender bushes abuzz with bees. After inspecting their room with its cool-tiled floors, they threw off their shorts and T-shirts, pulled on their swimsuits, and dived right in.

They surfaced, shrieking. The pool was gaspingly cold, refreshing as an iced lemonade on a hot afternoon. And the good news was, Lara's ankle was feeling better.

Later, showered and cool, they drove the battered, mud-spattered little Renault into St. Tropez.

Lara eyed the gleaming Porches, Ferraris, and Rolls-Royces

parked on the Quai Jean Jaures in front of enormous glistening white yachts. Everything glittered, from the cars on the quay and the brasswear on the yachts, to the gold braid on the caps of the chunky old millionaires checking out the delectable, longhaired, short-skirted young girls in the Café Sénéquier across the way. "Maybe we should have had the car washed," she said, awed.

Hungry, they ended up on the terrace at La Gorille on the Quai Suffren, where they drank ice-cold rosé de St. Tropez, and dined on *moules mariniers* and the best french fries they had ever tasted, watching the beautiful people go by.

Later, they strolled back through town, stumbling through cobblestoned alleys strung with laundry, peering into bead-curtained doorways and lace-hung windows, checking out tiny, happening disco clubs and even tinier boutiques selling minute bikinis and that sexy French lingerie, finally finding a cafe in the Place des Lices where they happily sipped cappuccino.

That night as her eyes closed, the little voice warned Lara, *Only five more days*. But she was already asleep and didn't hear.

Chapter Forty

How delightful it was, Lara thought early the next morning, to throw open your shutters and look out onto rows of leafy young vines hung like Christmas tree decorations with bunches of small green grapes and plump purple figs. And how wonderful to breakfast on a crusty baguette fresh just minutes ago from the baker's oven, with sweet yellow butter that tasted the way only French butter did, heaped high with strawberry preserves that were more berries than jam. And all on a flower-filled terrace with the sound of songbirds and the tang of the sea while sipping a huge bowl of café au lait.

Thinking about Cannes, the next stop on their new itinerary, she remembered that even back then on her honeymoon it had been a busy sex-and-shopping kind of place. But Bill had liked it. Come to think of it, he had been a bit starstruck, hoping for a glimpse of Brigitte Bardot or Catherine Deneuve or Princess Grace. While she, naive fool, had eyes only for him.

Bill had insisted on drinks on the Carlton terrace, the glossiest hotel in town, right on the seafront. During the Cannes Film

Festival it was the gathering place of show-business movers and shakers, but the only movers and shakers they had seen were other tourists like themselves, anxious to be counted in with the smart set, plus a few gorgeous wanna-bes hoping to be discovered.

Of course, she and Bill had not been able to afford to stay at the Carlton. Their hotel had been in a back street a block away from the sea. Cute, Lara had thought, liking its green-awninged windows, the tiny metal-grill balconies and green-painted shutters. It was set back in a small garden and she had thought it very French, but Bill had been discontented and she had sensed he wanted to be at the Carlton along with the rich folk. In fact, now she thought about it, Bill's ambitions had always run to accumulating money; plus, he always made sure he flew first-class on those jaunts to Beijing and Rio and London.

Why, Lara wondered, had it taken her twenty-five years to realize that Bill Lewis was a snob? That he had little time for the lesser people in the world? That he cared more about his own image than he did about being there for his wife and his children?

She touched the little diamond necklace, asking herself if it had been a guilt present after all.

And why is it, she asked herself wearily, that despite my "self-discovery," I still veer between thinking I care about him, and thinking what a bastard he is? And yet I do love Dan. Don't I?

On their way to Cannes, Lara picked up miniskirts and cute little tops and tiny, very French bikinis for her daughter and Dan's younger sister at a little boutique. She also bought a simple pale-green tank suit that she knew made her look better than she had in the red because it was one whole size larger. She struggled into it in the cramped little dressing room and took a look in the mirror. She felt like a Reubens maiden, all breasts and bottom, still pink from the sunburn. She only hoped that in the next few days the new green suit and Lancaster suntan lotion would change her into a bronzed South of France sylph, kind of like those makeovers on television where women began as overlarge and unstylish and emerged a half hour later svelte and groomed, with sexy eye makeup and red lips, wearing a flattering new outfit.

They were driving slowly along the coast to St. Maxime and Lara consulted the map anxiously. "Okay, we turned inland here, on the D24. . . . Oh, no, it's the D25," she corrected herself quickly. Dan heaved a sigh, swung around, and tried the roundabout again until they finally got the road leading back to the Provençal autoroute.

Soon they were following the *circulation,* winding around roundabouts on the outskirts of Cannes, on their way to the famous Croisette.

The long seafront avenue was lined on one side with grand hotels and couture boutiques and cafes, and on the other with a coarse, sandy *plage,* covered from end to end in awninged beach bars, striped chaise longues, and half-naked bodies. White-jacketed waiters patrolled the beach with trays of tall, cool drinks for the pampered guests from the expensive hotels and bowls of water for their little dogs, who sat panting beneath the sun umbrellas.

Dan snagged a tiny parking spot vacated by a turquoise Harley and they squeezed out of the Renault then strolled hand in hand along the Croisette, eyeing the French matrons glistening with gold jewelry and walking spry little apricot poodles that exactly matched the color of their hair. At backpacking young-sters who munched on slabs of pizza as they walked; at old men sitting on benches, wrinkled and brown from decades of sun, wearing striped matelot T-shirts and espadrilles, with berets tilted rakishly to one side; at harassed young mothers chasing after children and dogs; and at pale holiday-makers from sun-starved northern countries heading toward the beach clutching brightly colored towels.

Lara spotted the shoes in the window of a boutique near the Carlton. Towering heels, sling-backs, black suede, expensive. The symbol of her new self. Her liberation from the past.

"I have to have them," she said, remembering Delia. She drew the line at a garter belt, though, and instead bought lacy-topped stockings, the kind that stayed up on their own while cutting off your circulation. Who cares about circulation? she thought, happily pacing the boutique's expensive gray carpet in the stilettos, when *amour* is on your mind.

Getting daring, aren't you? the voice of her conscience re-minded her. *Remember, you are a married woman, forty-five years old, a doctor's wife, mother of two grown-up children. . . .*

No, I'm not, she thought confidently. I'm Lara Lewis and Dan Holland's lover, on vacation in France.

But despite that she still said, "Let's have a drink at the Carl-ton." She told herself she had to do it just to remember being with Bill that last time.

It was eleven-thirty in the morning and the terrace was al-ready crowded. Silver-haired men in immaculate linen jackets and panama hats and large gold nautical-looking watches talked business. Their women, expensive in white, their bronze shoul-ders gleaming, hair sleekly coiffed, dark glasses even larger and darker than Lara's, talked shopping.

Dan ordered Kir royales as they took in the scene.

"It's a long way from Ocean Avenue, Carmel," he said with a smile.

"They say travel broadens the mind."

"I enjoy having my mind broadened. I can't wait to tell Hallie that I was sitting here on the terrace of the Carlton right next to Mel Gibson." Lara craned her neck. "Gotcha." He laughed, then leaned across the table, gazing into her eyes. "Is this our kind of France?"

His face was so close to hers they could have kissed. "Is this the France we have come to know and love?" Lara whispered back.

They shook their heads. "Then where do we find it?" Dan looked at the urbanized hedonists surrounding them. "Where do we find the backwater with the cold rosé and the nightingales and the *lit matrimonial?*"

"Let's go look," Lara said.

Chapter Forty-one

The little Renault seemed to pick its own way to the Cap d'Antibes; Lara certainly wasn't navigating and Dan was just going with the flow. Then, quite suddenly, they had left the traffic behind and were on a quiet road running alongside the bay.

On their right were pink stucco villas half hidden behind shady umbrella pines. To their left, a couple of flimsy skiffs floated on the barely rippled sea, the fishermen lounging idly over their rods. The Plage de la Garoupe, a narrow strip of beach tucked into a curve of the bay, was lined with small cafes and beach chairs, and wooden sunbathing platforms built out into the water were scattered with beautiful suntanned bodies.

They stopped at the very last cafe for a glass of rosé and sat happily curling their bare toes in the warm sand. An umbrella shaded them from the midday heat and the air smelled of the sea and the sun, of the sharp, tangy pine trees, of basil and ripe tomatoes, of wine and lemons and suntan oil.

Charmed, they changed into bathing suits and ran to the sea.

Tiny silvery fish darted around their ankles as they waded in then swam toward the horizon. The shore became a mere shadow and there was nothing above them but the clear blue sky and the cry of seabirds, and nothing beneath them but the depths of crystalline sea. The water felt like cool silk on their skin as they floated on their backs, lifted by the glass-smooth little waves. There was nothing in this world but the two of them. Dan suddenly snatched her to him and kissed her. They submerged like two sexy seals beneath the waves, then popped up again, spluttering and laughing, and swam lazily back to shore.

Later that afternoon, they were strolling along the tiny back-roads of the Cap, past little stores selling groceries and newspapers and batavia lettuces and delicious-smelling rotisserie chickens, and Polar ice cream bars, buckets and spades and beach balls in little nets, when they came across the Auberge du Gardiole, a small, square, purple-wisteria-covered *hôtel de famille* set among the pines with a sign that read *Chambre à Louer*.

Lara said it was exactly what they were looking for, small, homey, and very French.

They were in luck; a room—the last one—was available. It was on the second floor, and it was small and the bathroom was down the hall, but they loved it. It had a big, soft, downy bed with the long pillow the French call a *traversin*, a rock-hard bolster that might break your neck if you tried to sleep on it and didn't know that the secret was to look in the vast mahogany armoire, where, mysteriously, the pillows were stored. The wallpaper was flowered and so was the bedspread, though in a different pattern, and the tile floors were cool under their feet. This time their window overlooked a large, square terrace hidden beneath an arbor of vines, and all they could see was a carpet of greenery with a glimpse of white tables and tubs of hot-pink geraniums.

Lara turned from the window and melted into Dan's arms. "How could I be hungry again?"

"For me, you mean?"

She shook her head. Not this time. "I'm starving. I need fuel, I need cold rosé wine and dancing. . . ."

"Dancing." Dan looked thoughtful. "Let's ask the *patron* where we should go."

Lara showered, pinned up her hair for coolness, then put on a soft white skirt and a sleeveless black top that bared her shoulders and also showed off the diamond necklace.

She eyed the necklace doubtfully. Wasn't it about time to take it off? After all, Bill wasn't coming back. And nor was she. Not now, when she knew she was in love with Dan. Still, she hesitated. She couldn't quite bring herself to do it. Not yet.

On the hotel terrace, the little white tables and chairs were already filled with their fellow guests, all of whom seemed to be French and who murmured a polite *"Bonsior, m'sieur, 'dame"* as they passed. Several had little dogs tucked discreetly under the table, all behaving themselves the way French dogs did. Most French hotels, Lara had found, catered for their guests' dogs, charging a supplement and providing special foods if required, and she thought how Dex would have been wild, yapping and racing around and causing mayhem. All of a sudden, she missed him terribly.

They drove into the old town of Antibes, clustered at the foot of the ramparts overlooking the beautiful Bai des Anges, a dreamy old fishing village with palm trees and plane trees, dusty *boules* courts and steeply sloped cobbled streets and a central *place*. There were sidewalk cafes and laundry strung between second-story windows; there was the cry of seabirds and the smell of the sea and rose-pink shadows on faded-stucco houses as the sun dropped into the Mediterranean.

Lara and Dan absorbed it through their pores so that on cold winter nights far away from here, when the fog rolled in from the Pacific, they could say, Remember when? Remember the softness of the air on our skin, like walking through velvet? Remember the flavor of the special white Bellet wine from the hills above Nice? Remember the little bistro where we ate? Clafoutis, it was called, and we had *tapanade* that was the true taste of Provence, made from olives and anchovies and served with that delicious bread. We ate tiny *rouget* fresh from the sea and grilled to perfection, and a salad dressed with the best olive oil and fresh lemon juice, and a Banon cheese wrapped in its little bundle of chestnut leaves and tied with raffia. And then the *clafoutis,* which gave the bistro its name, a custardy pudding made with juicy black cherries, so good it melted in our mouths. . . .

Later, in contrast, Juan les Pins was jumping. Citroëns and Harleys, Renaults and Kawasakis, Vespas and bicycles were parked cheek by jowl along the seafront. Noisy young people crisscrossed the road, dodging traffic with a laughing wave of the arm, and music throbbed through the warm night from a dozen discos.

Dan pulled Lara into a little beach bar with a wooden dance floor and a palm-thatched ceiling lit by twinkling tree lights. A hundred or so young bodies vibrated to the loud music. They edged to the outer limits near the sea and, pressed together by the throng, they wrapped their arms around each other and they danced.

The music changed to a love song. It was Jane Birkin singing

"Je t'aime" in a sexy French whisper, an old paean to making love written by her then lover Serge Gainsbourg, the man they had watched on TV in rainy Blois. Now Jane Birkin had grown-up daughters and Gainsbourg was dead, but that song lived on, as it would for generations of young holiday-makers seeking romance under the stars of the Cote d'Azur.

Tiring of the heat and the throng of bodies, they finally left to watch the "happening" on the street from a sidewalk cafe, sipping coffee and holding hands.

"This was a wonderful day." Dan squeezed her hand.

"Yes, it was," Lara whispered back, lost in his deep blue eyes, never wanting it to end.

Much later, snuggled in the *lit matrimonial* at the auberge, Dan heard a sound in the dark of the night. He opened his eyes, listening. He looked at Lara, asleep in the crook of his arm. Her long hair covered her face and he brushed it gently back with his finger.

"Lara," he whispered, "do you hear it? It's the nightingale."

She smiled in her sleep, nestling into his shoulder, and he lay back against the pillow listening to the bird's sweet song. Lara was so innocent, he'd had to teach her how to love. Now she was his to love. Forever. He knew that, at last, he had found what he was looking for.

They were up at dawn the next morning, anxious not to miss a moment of their last few days. The drove into Antibes early to catch the market and breakfasted, standing at a stall, on thin sweet crepes filled with tiny fresh raspberries dusted with vanilla sugar.

The market was a treasure trove, not just of beautiful fruits and vegetables and flowers, but of crystal-beaded necklaces in jewel colors; of chic white linen chemise dresses—the same ones that were sold in Paris, the young vendor told Lara; of slinky silk pants and soft shirts in a dozen bright colors. There were T-shirts and shoes, sandals, belts and bags, straw hats and scarves, and Lara had a ball picking out gifts for the Girlfriends, and for her children and Dan's.

She had forgotten for the moment that Hallie and Troy were not Dan's children, they were his brother and sister. And forgotten, for once, that Dan was so much younger than she. Somehow, it didn't seem to matter anymore. In France, they had become just two people in love.

Dan had disappeared, making some mysterious purchase of his own, and filled with new daring, Lara bought a very short white skirt with a slit that she knew would reach up to her butt and that would look great with sunburned legs, as well as a clinging black off-the-shoulder top—very sexy and something she would never have dared to wear in her "other" life as Mrs. Bill Lewis.

Dan returned carrying a small brown paper bag but refused to tell her what he'd bought. On their way back to the car with all the parcels, Lara began worrying about Customs. He laughed, but she was thinking of the things bought in Paris, and of the monogrammed boxes of the Countess's Agen prunes that had sweltered in the back of the car ever since the Dordogne. And of the old print of Gordes and the expensive black stilettos, though maybe if she just wore those the Customs officers wouldn't notice.

Later, they wandered up the dusty lane by the ramparts, pausing to take in the breathtaking view of the sweetly named Bay of Angels and the miles of pine-shaded sandy coves sloping into the blue-green sea, and the coral-tiled roofs of the pastel-hued houses shimmering under the sun.

The tiny castle that had once belonged to the royal Grimaldi family was now a museum devoted to Picasso, and walking into its cool halls was like stepping into another, more serene world. The walls were high and white and the tiny windows let in pale shafts of light. It was empty and they were able to stroll around at their leisure, enjoying the coolness and the Picassos.

Then Lara insisted they drive into Nice, because she said Dan had to see the view Matisse had painted from his windows.

The daily market in the Cours Saleya was just finishing, and they lunched at the crowded Safari cafe on French-style pizza with goat cheese and basil and sweet juicy tomatoes, watching the vendors packing up great bunches of the flowers for which the city was famous: stocks and carnations and roses, whose heady scent they breathed along with the aroma of *socca,* the hot, thin chickpea pancakes sold from the market stalls, and the sweetness of *fraises des bois,* the tiny wild strawberries. Unable to resist they bought a box of the strawberries and devoured them walking along the street. Lara thought eating those *fraise de bois* was like inhaling a musky perfume. It permeated the palate, rose through the nostrils, penetrated that portion of the brain directly between the eyes and stopped at the top of the head. It was lift-off time for berries. Her eyes were round with pleasure.

The seafront Promenade des Anglaises, named for the English, who were the first foreigners to come to the then-tiny fishing port to escape the cold, foggy northern winter, was studded with palm trees and ornate hotels. Below, tiny waves crashed onto a harsh, shingle beach. The Matisse exhibit was housed in a villa on the hill of Cimiez beside the Roman arena, and they climbed up there only to find it closed. So, bored with urban pleasures, they drove back to their pastoral refuge and the beach.

Lara thought, satisfied, it was another wonderful day. Dan was happy, she was happy. They were in love and it was all that mattered.

The calm before the storm, the little voice interrupted nastily.

And though she did not know it yet, this time, it was right.

Chapter Forty-two

The next day at the Plage de la Garoupe, Lara stretched out on a pink towel spread over a cushioned lounger beneath a green umbrella.

There was a fashion show at the cafe and pretty models paraded down the beach, stopping in front of them to tell them the name of the designer and that the suits were all from a local boutique, while cute young French girls, topless and tanned to an even golden glow, ran up to ask questions. One pretty girl stumbled over Dan's feet, then apologized charmingly. Lara's eyes swung Dan's way. There was an amused look on his face.

A pang of jealousy hit Lara like a fist in the stomach. Wrapped in her pink towel, she lay back and closed her eyes again, shutting herself off from the little scene going on around her.

Only one more day left, the voice reminded her. *Only one more day for the rest of your life. . . .*

. . .

Through her half-closed lids, Lara could see the young French girls smiling at the handsome young American, flirting with him under their lashes. Their bare brown breasts were firm as fist-sized Cavaillon melons, their pert bronze rumps taut as beach balls, and they wore sinuous gold chains threaded around their narrow waists. They tossed long sun-blond hair, exclaimed in high, pretty French voices about the fashions, begged the American m'sieur to excuse them for stepping on his toes. And Dan laughed, flirting back.

Lara suddenly felt her age. She was plump, out of synch, a being from another world. Wrapping the pink towel around her pale-green bathing suit that she had thought made her look more slender and more French, she stalked onto the cafe terrace. She turned to look back. Dan hadn't even noticed she was gone. A couple of pretty young things crouched at his feet, running their hands through their long hair, laughing flirtatiously. Even from here Lara could tell they were coming on to him.

God had surely given all the good flirt genes to French women, she thought despairingly as she sank into a chair. She had never known how to do that.

Hey, wait a minute, the voice reminded her, *you never had a chance to play that game. You were with Bill from the age of seventeen, the age of those girls now. You were serious, committed; you lost out on all those fun times, flirting with boys, experimenting, learning. You've been a novice all your life because of it.*

She was sipping iced Coke through a straw, and the fashion show was over when Dan finally came to find her. He ran his hand along her arm, dusting off the fine layer of sand that clung to it. "You okay?"

"I'm fine," she said coldly.

"Come on, Lar, what's wrong?"

She shrugged, her nose held aloofly in the air. "Nothing's wrong. I just felt like a cold drink."

"So why didn't you ask me to come with you?"

"You were busy."

He caught her aloof profile, the icy edge to her voice as she stared past him out to sea. A smile curled the corners of his mouth. "You were jealous," he said, unbelieving.

"Jealous. Hah—of what?"

You're hanging yourself, Girlfriend, the voice warned her. *Give him a break this time, why don't you? You're looking for trouble. . . .*

"The beautiful young things on the beach?" He was laughing at her.

"The ones half my age?"

Dan sat back in his chair. "So that's it." He wasn't smiling anymore. "You've got to get over this thing, Lara."

"Oh? And how do you propose I do that? Turn back the clock?"

He put his head in his hands, sighing. "Believe me, it means nothing to me, *they* meant nothing to me."

Dan recognized a pout when he saw one. Heaven knows he had seen it often enough in Britt, and in his own sister. It was just something women did, something they were born with. Just when you thought things were going to be okay, they threw you a curve.

"Sun's setting." He tried changing the subject.

Lara's eyes flickered toward the sea but he could tell she was not seeing the pink-tinted water and the ocher shadows creeping along the beach.

She stared up at him from under the thick fringe of dark lashes, suspicious, angry. The sun had disappeared and she shivered. "I'm going back to the hotel," she said coldly and she stalked back to the beach to get her things.

"Don't wait for me," Dan called angrily after her. "I'll get a ride back."

Fool, the voice told her as she packed her things into the beach bag, *fool, fool, fool. Pride is no comfort in an empty bed.*

Chapter Forty-three

Lara was in the shower when she heard the phone ring. She knew it would be Minnie, because she had called earlier and left her number. She wrapped a towel around her and ran to answer it but Dan was back and he'd already picked up the phone.

"Hi, Mom," Minnie's voice said chirpily. "How's the Second Honeymoon going without Dad? Hope it was as good as you remembered it the first time around."

Dan stared for a long moment at Lara standing by the door clutching the towel. "Just a minute, I'll put your mother on the line," he said quietly. There was ice in his eyes as he handed her the phone.

"Hi, Minnie," Lara said softly.

"Hey, Mom, who was the man on the phone? I thought you were there alone."

"No, I'm not alone." She looked worriedly at Dan, staring out the window, hands thrust in his pockets. "How are you, Minnie? I just needed to hear your voice."

"Well, you're hearing it, Mom. I got your message, and

thanks in advance for all the treats. Hope you get through Customs okay, though." She was laughing, untroubled, young . . . like the girls on the beach.

She would tell Minnie about Dan later, Lara thought as she said good-bye and "love you" and "see you soon."

"Dan?" she said.

He turned and looked at her. Lara put a hand to her heart, shocked by his grim face. He stood, arms folded across his chest, legs apart. "What about that 'Second Honeymoon'?"

Oh, God, she thought, Minnie had let the cat out of the bag. But she hadn't meant to deceive him, she just thought it was better if he didn't know.

"It's true, of course," he said coldly.

"Yes, it's true." Her wet hair swung over her face as she nodded and she put up a hand to push it back.

"All the places we've been, the hotels where we stayed, the cafes, the sight-seeing. You did all this with Bill the first time around."

"It wasn't the way you think."

"And when Bill told you he wasn't going on his 'Second Honeymoon,' you thought you might as well take me instead. Well, you fooled me, Lara. You really fooled me. I thought this was *our* journey of discovery, not a trip to revive your memory bank of your husband. Now I understand all the mood swings, the searching—"

"It wasn't . . . I didn't do that. . . . I mean, it *was* our discovery, Dan, really it was. . . ."

How could she admit that he was right, and every step of the way she had remembered Bill and their time together as honeymooners? But that every step of the way, Bill's memory had failed the test.

Except for that field of poppies, the voice reminded her.

"What did you take me for?" Dan said. "Was I just a change for you? The rough, uneducated guy? The stereotype in the hard hat in the Village People, just there to amuse you?" Lara would have laughed if he were not so deadly serious. "Why couldn't you tell me? At least give me the choice?"

"But it was so wonderful, it all worked out so well. . . ."

Dan stared at her, unbelieving. "I'm going out," he said icily. "I don't know when I'll be back."

He closed the door quietly behind him and Lara heard his footsteps receding down the hall.

She sank down onto the bed, staring into space. For once the little voice offered no comment and no advice. Her conscience was on strike, ashamed of her, and her alter ego had disappeared—like Dan.

Chapter Forty-four

She must be crazy. What was she doing just sitting there? She leapt to her feet; she had to go after him, find him, tell him how sorry she was, beg him to forgive her. Flinging on some clothes, she ran out into the hall. She flew down the stairs, passing other guests on their way up, shouting, *"Je m'excuse, madame, monsieur,"* as they flattened themselves against the wall to allow her to pass. *"Je m'excuse....* I'm sorry...."

She scanned the terrace, wild-eyed. Her wet hair trailed over her shoulders, leaving damp patches on her T-shirt. A dozen or so guests sat at the tables, coolly dressed for the evening, sipping aperitifs before heading out for dinner. Dan was not among them.

She darted back through the front hall, skidding on the tiles, apologizing to people again as she ran out the door and looked up and down the street. There was no sign of Dan. The baby-blue Renault was in its usual place. She felt in her pocket for the keys but of course they were in the room.

She fled back upstairs, grabbed the keys, dashed back down again. The Renault coughed as she slammed her foot onto the accelerator, flooding the engine. She smacked a hand to her forehead in frustration, waiting precious seconds before trying again. The engine spluttered, then caught.

"Dammit, why can't the French have automatic," she muttered, shifting too rapidly through the gearbox and bouncing down the street in a series of kangaroo jumps that rattled her teeth. Was she driving on the proper side of the road? She hoped so, but she couldn't remember . . . she was so scared, *terrified* she had lost him.

At the cafes on the beach, candles were lit and dinner was being served. It was a peaceful, romantic scene, one that she might have been a part of if she were not such a selfish fool. She got out, searched among the tables. She looked in every cafe. Of course, he was not there.

She prowled the back streets in the little Renault. It was dark now and she drove slowly, inspecting every person walking in the shadows, everyone in the sidewalk cafes, in every store.

He must have gone back to the auberge. He would think she had gone away, left him, didn't care. The tires shrieked as she rounded the corner, and, with a final jolt, threw the car into park. She was out and running. There was a thud and the sound of breaking glass. She turned, stared back at the Renault. It had slipped out of park and into the rough stone wall, smashing the headlights. *Oh, shit.* She took off again. What did it matter now. . . ?

She raced back through the garden, through the deserted hall, cast a desperate eye over the now almost empty terrace. Taking the stairs two at a time, she ran down the hallway, flung open the door.

The room was empty.

She slumped onto the bed. "Oh, God," she prayed, "where is he? I was wrong not to tell him, and I was wrong this afternoon, I admit it. Just tell me where he is so I can apologize."

The phone rang, that high, penetrating French shrill. For a second, she couldn't take it in. Then, *"It's him, oh, thank you, God, it's him. . . ."* She snatched it up.

"Lara?"

Her knees buckled and she sank onto the bed.

"Lara? Are you there?" he said again, sounding impatient.

"I'm here, Bill." Disappointment stuck in her throat.

"How are you, Lara?" He was, as usual, calm and collected, knowing exactly what he wanted to say and why he had called. "Minnie gave me your number."

"Oh, did she?"

"She said you were having a good time?"

Lara tried to make her voice sound cheerful. She said loudly, "I'm having a great time, fantastic. Paris, the beach, the sunshine, the clothes."

"And your companion?"

Lara was stunned into silence.

"I found out you didn't travel alone, Lara."

"I guess that makes us even, then," she snapped. "And by the way, how was Beijing?"

"Fine. I did some good work there, made some valuable connections."

"You would," she said acidly, knowing that was the true reason he had gone there.

"I came home early." All of a sudden he sounded hesitant. "I was thinking about you, Lara. Thinking about what had happened between us."

"What you had done, you mean," she retorted. "With Melissa."

"Okay, what I had done. I admit it, Lara. And I'm sorry. Truly sorry about it. That's what I was calling to tell you. That I miss you. The house is so strange without you. . . . You were always there whenever I came home. . . ."

The truth dawned on her. "Melissa dumped you, didn't she?"

"No . . . well, shall we say we had a disagreement."

"Oh, come on, Bill, admit it."

"Well, Melissa did find someone else," he agreed, "an oil tycoon from Texas. My God, the man is old enough to be her father."

"And you are not?"

There was silence on the other end of the phone.

"What do you want me to do, Bill?" she finally asked.

"I want you back, Lara. I need you. I'm ready to forgive your indiscretions. We've been together so long, and remember, there are the children to think of."

She gave a disbelieving snort. "Bill, don't you know your children are grown up? It's too late to play their father. And I don't need your forgiveness. I had a great time."

He ignored that. "I'll fly to Paris to meet you. I can get a flight tonight. I thought we would stay at the Ritz, the way we did on our honeymoon, remember?"

Lara shook her head, disbelieving. "Oh, Bill, I remember. . . ."

"I can be there tomorrow afternoon. I'll call the hotel, get the honeymoon suite—"

"Bill," she interrupted him. "It's too late. It's been too late for years."

"What do you mean?" He sounded incredulous; she had never said no to him.

"It's over, Bill. But thanks for the try," Lara said. And she put down the phone.

She sat for a long while on the edge of the bed, staring into space, rerunning the conversation in her head. She had just told her husband of twenty-five years that she was not coming back.

She looked in the mirror at the little diamond lover's-knot necklace gleaming at her throat. Reaching up, she unclasped it, held it in her hand. She no longer needed the talisman. She no longer needed Bill.

The room was very still. Warm, scented air drifted in from the window, bringing memories of the day. But something about it was different. It was too neat in here, too bare. . . .

Dan's things were gone. His clothes, his hairbrush, the travel alarm clock Hallie had bought him, the paperback mystery he was reading . . .

With a moan, she dropped her head into her hands.

He's left you, the little voice said triumphantly. *Didn't I tell you he would?*

After a little while, she went back downstairs and spoke with the *patron*. Monsieur had paid the bill, he told her, smiling. He had apologized for having to leave so abruptly but had told them that madame would be staying on for another day.

Lara stared blankly into her empty future. It was over. She had lost him after all.

Chapter Forty-five

Very early the next morning Lara carried her bags downstairs and said good-bye to the *patron* and madame.

The dusty, battered baby-blue Renault that had carried the two of them on their stumbling journey through France started on the first try, humming slowly through the cool morning streets. The sun glittered off the sea, the sky was a pure, clear blue. It was just another day on the Côte d'Azur.

She circled onto the Autoroute du Soleil, heading for Paris, only this time there would be no detours of discovery, no lingering in romantic inns, no lovemaking in fields of poppies. Putting her foot on the gas pedal, she headed through the blue morning haze, determined not to get lost.

She stopped only a couple of times at cafes on the autoroute for coffee — with caffeine because she needed a jump-start — and a croissant, or a ham sandwich, much like the one she and Dan had eaten together at the Bar Jurassic in that rain-sodden village in the Loire, so long ago, it seemed now. The past few weeks were like a dream, her old life a harsh reality, the future uncertain.

Determinedly, she pushed the future to the back of her mind, turning up the radio and concentrating on her driving. God, though, how she missed him sitting beside her, how she missed catching his eyes when she glanced sideways at him, at those blue, blue eyes that laughed at her, admired her, loved her. He *had* loved her, hadn't he?

Many hours later, she was battling her way through the fierce Paris traffic. She leaned angrily on the horn, eyes blazing, then she smiled, suddenly realizing it was a when-in-Rome situation. She had become more French than the French.

Paris glimmered in the twilight as she drove around the roundabout where they had had the accident; past the Café Flore, where, after the disastrous dinner at Lucas Carton, they had eaten a *croque monsieur* and drunk brandy and watched the street performers; down the rue Jacob, where Dan had whirled her in his arms; and past the Hôtel d'Angleterre, where they had made passionate love and she had never dreamed of leaving him.

When she finally pulled up in front of the Ritz, the smart doorman opened the door of the battle-scarred baby Renault as though it were a Rolls.

Now that's class, Lara thought, scrambling out and stretching her long, cramped legs. She knew she must look awful, hot and dusty and shabby, but the desk clerk did not bat an eyelash and this time she had the right day and a room.

It wasn't the same room she had shared with Bill. She didn't know if she could have stood the truth those memories might have brought back. She opened the gold silk curtains and gazed out at the beautiful Place Vendôme, wishing Dan was with her, and wondering where he could be. Finally, she took a shower and fell into the big brass bed, too tired even to eat. She was asleep in minutes and that night she dreamed of no one. Nothing.

Of course she woke too early. A soft, pearly light filtered through the luxurious silk curtains and she half turned, as if expecting to find Dan beside her. The reality that she would never again wake in his warm, loving arms felt like a wound that would never heal. She lay for a moment remembering their nights together in the funky hotel near the station, wondering how Dan would have liked the Ritz. She had called it so wrong on Lucas Carton, she thought he might have hated this too.

Later, alone and lonely, she visited the Rodin museum, lingering over the massive marble sculptures, thinking of Dan. She wandered through the museum's gardens, not seeing the glittering, golden day and the beauty all around her, cursing herself for being a fool, such a stupid fool.

A ragged little brown dog tagged along behind her. "Scrounging a walk?" she said with a half-smile. She sat on a bench and the dog sat in front of her, waiting. "Do I know you?" she asked, and it gave a delighted little *wuff*. "That's a French *wuff*, of course," she said, bending to stroke its wiry fur. Then she smiled and said, "Oh, excuse me, I meant a *Parisian* wuff."

The terrier's eyes were a dark reddish brown. Intelligent eyes, Lara thought. He was a streetwise little guy, still young, but she guessed he had seen it all. She laughed at herself. Was this what loneliness did to you? Had you analyzing a street-dog's psyche?

"You know what, mutt?" she said softly. "I'm the greatest

fool there ever was. This was supposed to be my voyage of self-discovery. So what have I discovered—other than the fact that I'm a fool?"

She frowned, thinking about Bill, and the mutt cocked his head, waiting. He gave an encouraging little whine.

"I see now how hard Bill worked to impress me on our honeymoon with his man-of-the-world act." Lara smiled as she remembered how they had fought, bickered, bitched. "Only trouble is, he never quit that act. Oh, I loved him then, there's no doubt about it; he was the only man I ever really wanted. And in his fashion, I suppose he loved me." She thought for a minute, then her eyes met the mutt's again. "But y'know what?" she asked him solemnly. "Were we ever really friends? Companions? Sharing things together? The small pleasures, the high points as well as the lows? Oh, no. Never." She shook her head, wondering how many other women had found out that bitter truth.

"Don't think I'm going to cry." Determinedly, she sniffed back a tear. "Because I'm not. No, sir. No more tears." But they were already trickling down her cheeks. "Oh, hell, what am I, Superwoman or something? Why shouldn't I cry when the guy I love ditches me because I wounded him? Hurt his feelings. His pride. Of course, I'm going to cry."

The mutt whined anxiously as the tears streamed down her face, trickling into her ears and down her neck, soaking her shirt.

"You want to know what else I've found on my journey of discovery?" she sniffed. "That life is a matter of give-and-take. I have to give up my old life and look for the new. I have to give up what I was—and take what is. And if I'd been honest with myself and not filled with false pride, I might have been looking forward to a future with Dan. For better, for worse. And for as long as it might have lasted."

The dog cocked his head inquiringly to the other side.

"And you know what else I know? That age would not have mattered. Time would not have mattered. I would not have spent my life worrying about the future. Today would have been enough." The little mutt barked approvingly and Lara laughed at it through her tears.

She went to a cafe, bought a chicken sandwich, and left the terrier hungrily wolfing it down on the sidewalk. He didn't look at her as she walked away and she smiled. Yesterday's Lara would have said food was all the dog had wanted from her, anyway. But not today's Lara. This one was ready to take what she could get.

As she swung through the doors back at the Ritz she heard her name called and she spun around.

The light left her eyes as she stared at Bill. Her husband, the famous surgeon, the distinguished man of the world, immaculate as always in a dark suit. He was looking at her with that superior little smile, confident that she would not say no to him. After all, no one ever did.

Her eyes glittered angrily. "What are you doing here? I told you it was over."

He took her arm, moving her out of earshot of the interested bellhops. "Now come on, Lara. I said I was coming to get you and I'm a man of my word. And remember, you *are* my wife."

She jerked her arm away. "Hah! Since when did that make a difference?"

He rolled his eyes, sighing. "I can understand you felt a little neglected; things were a bit rough there for a while, I admit it.

But now it's over. I'm prepared to forgive you—and I can't say fairer than that. I promised you the honeymoon suite and that's what I've got. I've already asked them to move your things in."

She flung away from him, stalking down the long aisle with its sparkling windows of expensive baubles. He hurried after her, took her arm again.

"I have reservations at my favorite restaurant. And let me tell you, they were not easy to come by. It's lucky they knew who I—"

"Bill!" She turned to look at him, chest heaving, anger flashing. "For God's sakes, don't you ever *listen* to me? Don't you hear what I'm *saying*?"

He stared back at her, really looking at her, seeing the new Lara. His eyebrows lifted in surprise. "I must say you're looking terrific, Lara. A great improvement. I always told you, you should take better care of yourself."

"Jesus Christ!" People turned to stare but she didn't care. Her hands curled into fists, she wanted to punch him.

"Really, Lara, people are looking." He took her arm again, walking back down the red-carpeted aisle. "By the way, Minnie sends her love. Y'know she misses us, Lara. Really misses us. She and Josh both. They want us home, they want us back together."

He glanced at her out of the corner of his eye, saw her hesitate, knew he was getting her where she was really vulnerable. "We are their reality, sweetheart. You and I. Mom and Dad. We've always been there for them and they expect us to be there for them now. After all, isn't that their right?"

Lara looked doubtfully at him. "Minnie said that?"

"Let's talk about it over dinner," Bill said triumphantly. "You'll feel better after something to eat."

Chapter Forty-six

Of course they went to Lucas Carton. As the maître d' swept them to an excellent table, Lara figured wearily she might have known. It suited Bill perfectly; he was in his element being shown to a good table, being fawned over.

"If this is all you need to keep you happy, Bill, then you're a lucky man," she said. Ignoring the sharp glance he threw her, she looked for the table where she had sat with Dan, where he had spilled the champagne, been shocked by the prices, hating it. Hating *her*. She shrugged, sighing. Well, now she had two guys hating her, because despite what Bill was saying, she didn't believe him.

Bill studied the menu, consulted with the headwaiter, ordered for both of them. He chose the wine with the sommelier as though it were a life-and-death decision, just the way he had twenty-five years ago at the Tour d'Argent on their disastrous honeymoon. Lara sat back, disinterested. She had deliberately not worn the Paris dress because that was part of her life, brief though it was, with Dan. Now she guessed she would never wear it again. Like a Mafia widow, basic black would be her style.

The sommelier poured the Krug and Bill lifted his glass to her. "Come on, Lara, perk up, we're here to enjoy ourselves. We're in Paris together again. This is our Second Honeymoon."

She refused the champagne. "I've already had my Second Honeymoon," she said, "and I'll remind you it was not with you."

He raised exasperated eyes to heaven again. "Why are you being so difficult? I'm just trying to express my love for you."

He had a pained look, as though he were the one who had been wronged, and Lara could feel the pendulum already swinging back to his side, where the only viewpoint was Bill's.

"You know, Lara, you really didn't have to go this far," he added.

"What do you mean?" She didn't know what he was talking about.

Bill took a sip of the excellent champagne. "Oh, come on, I know you said you were with another man, but do you really expect me to believe that's true? You're just not the type. Look at yourself, Lara. You're a middle-aged housewife, and—though I love you—you've never exactly been the type to turn men's heads . . . though I must say you do look very well tonight."

"Are you saying I *invented* a lover just to make you jealous?"

He lifted a shoulder, smiling. "Don't worry. I understand completely. What I did was wrong and you felt the need to retaliate."

"You pompous, self-satisfied prick!" The words came out in a furious hiss. "How *dare* you say that to me." Lara struggled to her feet and a waiter hurried to help her. She grabbed her purse and, with a final furious glare, swept off to the powder room.

Bill glanced after her, astonished, then he signaled to the waiter to refill his glass. Lara was having a little tantrum, that was all. No woman really cared to know the truth about herself, not even Melissa—and certainly not Lara, whom he had sheltered from reality all her life. He had taken good care of her, provided for her; she'd had a good life. She would get over this and come back to him. Another five minutes and she would be back, apologizing. And so would he, of course. It was only fair, though he had little to apologize for. Melissa was only a passing fancy, even if he had taken her a tad too seriously in the beginning. But that's the way it was with men. Sex came first. Then the letdown. He glanced around the room to see who was there. This place was always filled with famous people; there might be someone he knew.

His eyes lit on the young man talking to the maître d'. Surprised, he saw that he was coming his way. Bill looked up at him, then at the bunch of rapidly wilting poppies he was clutching. He must be a vendor.

"Well, really, I didn't know you were allowed to sell flowers in a restaurant like this," he said, dismissing him.

Dan had known Lara would be at the Ritz, had found that Bill was there, found where they were dining. "I'm looking for Lara," he said. "I knew she would be here with you."

It suddenly dawned on Bill that Lara hadn't been pretending after all, and he inspected his rival carefully, up and down, pegging his station in life exactly. "Well, let me tell you, young fella," he said in a vicious whisper, "you had better get out of here before I have you thrown out."

"I'm waiting for Lara," Dan said, determined.

Bill half rose from his seat. "Oh, no, you're not, fella. And you want to know why? Just look around—ask yourself whether you belong with a woman who's used to places like this. And let me tell you something else you should know. Lara asked me to come to Paris to get her; she wants to reconcile."

"I don't believe it," Dan said, but despair lurked behind his eyes.

"Lara is *my* wife, buddy," Bill said, still in that vicious whisper. "She's the mother of my children and I'm damned if I'm gonna let you near her again."

Heads were turning toward them and waiters hovered anxiously, sensing trouble. The maître d' hurried over and took Dan's arm, urging him away. Dan shook his head, unwilling to believe Bill. Then knowing it must be true, he dropped the fading poppies and walked out of the restaurant.

And out of their lives, Bill thought, satisfied. He summoned the maître d', tipped him lavishly, and thanked him for "taking care of things." He had sorted that little matter out to his satisfaction. Lara was his again. He glanced idly at his gold Rolex. What on earth could she be doing in that powder room?

Lara was standing in front of the mirror attempting to powder her nose, but every time she got the powder on, her tears washed it off again. She was wondering how to sort out her life; how to deal with Bill; what to do about Dan; wondering how she'd ever got herself into this mess in the first place.

She glanced at the woman standing next to her, also powdering her nose. She was older, smart, glamorous in that chic Parisian way, red hair swept back from a smooth brow and dark eyes that knew enough to understand Lara's trouble.

The Frenchwoman raised her eyebrows. She smiled. "Don't cry," she said. "Just ask yourself is he worth your tears." She put a comforting hand on Lara's shoulder as their eyes met in the mirror. *"Courage, chéri.* Men can be so . . . *unsympathetic.* Take it from one who knows." And with a final smile, she was gone.

Lara slumped into a chair. She put her chin in her hands and stared at her own face in the mirror. The woman was right. Why should she shed tears for Bill Lewis? Hadn't she cried enough over him? Damn it, if she was going to cry then it should be for losing Dan, for being a fool, for ruining something beautiful.

What she had told that little dog in the museum gardens was right. Now she told it to the mirror. "I've lost Bill, but I lost him a long time ago, I just refused to acknowledge it. And now I've lost Dan. All that's left is *me.*" She heaved a wobbly sigh. "But now at least I know who I am."

Determinedly, she powdered her nose, put on fresh lipstick, combed her long hair back like the redheaded Frenchwoman's. She pirouetted slowly in front of the mirror. The clinging black dress looked pretty darn good—and so what if it showed off the extra couple of pounds?—and the black stilettos showed off her legs. Besides, Delia was right; she had always had good legs. She was a pretty woman and age didn't have a thing to do with it.

Taking a deep breath, she straightened her shoulders, lifted her chin, and strode confidently from the powder room, ready to take on Bill. He got politely to his feet when he saw her coming, but he still had that "what took you so long" look on his face. She knew it only too well. Bill didn't like to be kept waiting. Well, tough.

She stopped short when she spied the poppies lying on the

floor. She bent and picked them up, laying each one carefully on the table as though it were a precious jewel. "I see Dan was here," she said when at last she could speak.

"You'll be pleased to know I got rid of your toyboy." Bill ignored Lara's lethal look, ignored the danger signals that she was coming to the boiling point. That she had finally had it with him. "It's for the best and you know it. Just think of your children," he lectured. "And besides, it's time you stopped being silly and acted your age. Now sit down and for God's sakes let's have a civilized dinner."

She picked up the poppies, clutched them to her breast. "How *dare* you lecture me about having an affair," she said icily, "when you're the one whose been fucking your assistant. And *I* was the last to know." Then, with a single ferocious blow, she swiped the champagne glasses off the table.

Life at the grand restaurant suddenly stopped. Lara leaned closer to Bill and said loudly, so he was sure to hear, "I want a divorce. *Now.* Understand?"

Not even the clink of silverware and crystal broke the silence. Everyone stared, hanging on to every word. Even the haughty waiters were frozen in their tracks.

Remembering where she was, Lara glanced around. She picked up her purse, put her chin in the air and, still clutching the poppies, strode regally to the door, acknowledging with a little nod en route the admiring glances of the other women in the restaurant.

Bill stared after her, unable to believe the scene she had just created. How *dare* she do that to him? How *dare* she, when he was trying to save her from herself? How *dare* she embarrass him? He would never be able to come here again. He sank back into the booth, smoothed back his hair, straightened his immaculate cuffs, checked his gold Rolex.

"Women," he said loudly to the room, trying to shrug it off. Every woman in the place fixed him with an icy stare.

Chapter Forty-seven

Back at the Ritz, Lara asked that her bags be brought down, she was checking out. Then she got into the car and drove aimlessly around until she realized she had passed the Café Flore half a dozen times already, that she had been hoping to find Dan there. But he wasn't and she ended up at the Hôtel d'Angleterre, begging the dragon lady for a room, where she lay wide awake all night, alone in the *lit matrimonial*. When dawn came, she was up and dressed, downing a cup of coffee, then back in the little Renault en route to the airport.

It was good-bye to Paris, she thought sadly as she drove through the quiet, early morning streets. Would she ever return? Somehow, she didn't think so. Her love affair with the city would be forever unconsummated.

At the airport, she tried to explain to the rental company official—in French—about the damage to the bumper and the broken headlights and that of course she would pay for it—or at least her insurance would. After much throwing of hands in the air and *Mon Dieu* and *quelle horreur* and *les américains,* she was relieved of the key and presented with a sheaf of documents to sign, none of which she understood and which, she guessed, would someday come back to haunt her.

By the time she had finished doing battle with the car rental people it was after eleven. Exhausted, her nerves shattered, she decided she was beyond coffee and needed a drink.

For the second time in her life, she took a seat at a bar alone. She stared at the flashing neon sign over the bar. *PARIS IS FOR LOVERS,* it announced triumphantly.

She ordered a Ricard. The white-coated barman slid the glass across the counter and she smiled, thinking, Yeah, this is really me, the new Lara Lewis, woman of the world, in a bar alone.

She checked the clock on the wall. Ten after eleven. Her flight did not board until twelve-thirty. She wondered what to do until then; she couldn't just sit here and watch that sign reminding her of what she had lost. Morosely, she took a sip of the Ricard, pulling a face at the sharp anise flavor.

Dan stood, arms folded across his chest, looking at her. He had seen her walk into the bar, straight-backed, chin up, hair in a sleek knot at her neck. She was wearing the short St. Tropez white skirt and the sexy black heels and her legs were a suntanned gold. She looked cool, beautiful, self-assured. He hesitated, wondering where Bill Lewis was, then, telling himself this was his last chance, he decided to go for it.

"Lara?"

Her heart did a triple somersault. She could not move, couldn't even turn to look at him.

"I guessed you would be here for the flight." He was standing close to her, hands thrust in the pockets of his jeans. "I was worried about you."

Numb, she stared straight ahead at the neon sign. *PARIS IS FOR LOVERS*—it flickered on and off, endlessly, infinitely. . . . *Okay, so now say you're sorry.* She could almost hear the voices of the Girlfriends urging her on. *Or are you going to blow it all again just because of your stupid pride? Give yourself a chance, just say you're sorry, ask him to forgive you. . . .*

And if he doesn't want to?

Then at least you tried. This is your life you're talking about, Girlfriend. . . .

She turned and met his eyes—those blue, blue eyes that knew her too well. Knew who she was, what she was. "I'm sorry," she whispered.

"I'm sorry too." He said it so quietly only she could hear. They might have been the only people in the bar, the only ones at the whole airport. "I hurt you and I never wanted to do that."

"No, no." She shook her head. "It was my fault. I was the one who hurt you."

"Only my pride." His voice was a murmur; it seemed to caress her like the soft waves of the Mediterranean.

"I never meant to hide the Second Honeymoon from you. I . . . I guess I thought it would spoil things. I just wanted to be with you." Her voice trembled. "Believe me, it had nothing to do with Bill."

"I believe you."

He was so near, all she had to do was reach out and take his hand. But she knew it was hopeless. He was going to say, It's been nice knowing you, thank you, and good-bye.

"I love you, Lara," he was saying. "I want to be with you for the rest of my life. I want to take care of you. I want you to be my wife." He took her hand in his hard, warm one. "Will you marry me, Lara?"

She stared at him, all big topaz eyes. "For better or for worse?" she whispered.

He pulled a crumpled brown paper bag from his pocket and took out a golden ring set with a tiny blue stone, the exact color of the Mediterranean. "I bought it in the Antibes market when you weren't looking," he told her. "It's nothing, but if you said yes, I thought it would do until I could get you a proper diamond."

Her eyes brimming, Lara held out her hand and he slipped the little ring onto her finger. It was a bit big but that was okay. She turned her hand this way and that, admiring it. It was perfect. She leaned toward him and their lips met in a kiss, sealing their pledge.

There was a spatter of applause and they swung around, smiling as cries of *felicitations* and *bon chance* came from the crowd at the bar. And behind them the prophetic sign flashed the truth—*PARIS IS FOR LOVERS*.

Lara's heart was still turning somersaults. "I thought I would die without you."

"And I was in hell. I couldn't believe I'd left you, that I'd been such a selfish fool. Never again, Lara. I promise." She hesitated and Dan wondered what was coming next.

"About Bill," Lara said, because she knew she finally had to get things straight between them. "About the honeymoon. I know now that it was France I was in love with, not Bill. France gilded my memories with sunlight and happiness." She clutched his hand hopefully. "Don't you see, Dan, I've always had a love affair with France."

He understood. He picked up her hand and kissed the ring on her finger, making her laugh. "We'll come back," he promised. "And next time we'll bring the kids."

"*Excuse me?*" Lara's eyes popped. "Did you say *kids?*"

He grinned cockily. "Oh, I thought a boy and a girl would be nice."

And they fell into each other's arms, helpless with laughter.

So there you are, you're young after all. The inner voice was having the last word. *Soon you'll be a mother again. Only this time with a man who loves you.*

Sounds good to me, Lara thought, still laughing as she kissed him.

They were so enthralled they didn't hear their flight called and were still sitting at the bar, arms around each other, planning their new lives when the announcement came over the speakers: "Will Madame Lara Lewis and Monsieur Daniel Holland please hurry to gate number seven, where the flight to San Francisco has already boarded and is ready to depart? This is the final call for Madame Lewis and Monsieur Holland."

Holding hands, they ran through the long hallways. They were out of breath when they finally got to the gate and were shepherded onto the plane by an irate attendant. She slammed the aircraft door behind them and they slunk guiltily to their seats, the late ones, the focus of all eyes.

They were already taxiing down the runway. In seconds they were over Paris, sparkling in the sunlight. Then the plane was in the clouds and it was gone.

Their eyes met. "Do you remember the ending of *Casablanca?*" Dan asked.

Lara looked at him, puzzled, "You mean at the airport when Ingrid Bergman is about to leave and she says to Bogart, 'But what about us?' "

Dan was smiling at her now. "And Bogart replies, 'I guess we'll always have Paris.' "

"They can write that in our epitaphs," Lara said, laughing.

Because she knew, no matter how far away they were, they would always have Paris.